D1519543

DISAVOWED

HOSTAGE RESCUE TEAM SERIES

KAYLEA CROSS

DISAVOWED

Copyright © 2015
by Kaylea Cross

* * * * *

Cover Art & Formatting by
<u>Sweet 'N Spicy Designs</u>

* * * * *

ISBN: 978-1505998863

Dedication

I'm dedicating this one to my long-suffering hubby, who not only has to put up with me and my vivid imagination, he often gets pressed into plotting sessions against his will too. Thanks, babe!

Author's Note

Matt DeLuca is about to meet his match in this intense romantic thriller. Giving characters second chances at love is one of my most favorite things to write about. Both DeLuca and B have been through a lot so it was my honor to give them both a shot at a happy ending together. Hope you enjoy it.

Happy reading!

Kaylea Cross

Prologue

Four Years Ago

Special Agent Matt DeLuca adjusted the brim of his San Diego Chargers hat as he scrubbed down the grill on the back patio of his home just outside Quantico. *This* was why he'd served his country for so many years and why he continued to serve. To protect the American way of life and make days like this possible.

Water splashed in the pool in front of him, his young nieces' shrieks of delight mixing with his wife's and sister-in-law's laughter as they played. A familiar summer soundtrack.

It was the perfect Fourth of July, not a cloud in the sky and a steady breeze helped stave off what would have been the sweltering heat of the Virginia afternoon. For once he technically had the day off, though as commanding officer of the Hostage Rescue Team he could be called in at any time if a situation arose, so with any luck he'd be able to stay and enjoy the planned festivities.

Lisa's voice floated across the patio. "Cassie, what sort of dive should I do?" she called out.

"Cannonball!" the four-year-old shouted excitedly.

Matt smiled to himself. There was nothing his wife loved more than being with her family, and this holiday they had something even more special to share with her sister than time spent together. In a little while they'd feast on the spread he and Lisa had prepared. Later on once the sun went down they'd watch an outdoor movie projected onto the large white bed sheet his wife had already set up on the side of the detached garage, lounging on the patio furniture with a drink until the fireworks display at their neighbor's place around ten.

He glanced up from the grill in time to see Lisa walk to the end of the diving board. Her long brown hair was slicked back from her face, her generous curves highlighted by the red pin-up-style suit she wore. She looked over, met his gaze and shared a secret smile as she poised there at the end of the board, her eyes sparkling with excitement. One he shared. They'd been trying for three years and finally, having hit the safety of the three-month mark, had a much-awaited announcement to make after dinner.

Lisa grinned and said something to their two-year-old niece Annika, who was splashing around in the shallow end with her new pink water wings. From the happiness on her face there was no sign of the debilitating headaches Lisa had been getting lately and he was relieved. The doctors had assured them that headaches could be a common symptom early on, had to do with elevated hormone levels, and not to worry. All Matt cared was that she was feeling well enough to enjoy this special day with her family.

"Hey, you need a hand with anything?"

Matt turned to find his brother-in-law, Jordan, standing in the open kitchen doorway with a couple of

2

beers. "Just about to put the burgers on. You can get all the rest of the stuff set up while I grill if you want. Everything's ready to go in the fridge."

"I love your fridge. Here." Jordan twisted off the tops and handed him a cold one with a smile. "Cheers, man. Thanks for having us over. Again," he added with a smile.

"Anytime. You know we love having you guys here." They tapped the necks of their bottles together and took a pull, just as an excited shriek from the pool sounded behind them.

He reached for the first hamburger patty, placing it in the center of the grill just as a loud splash signaled that his wife had performed her famous cannonball for the girls. A moment later he heard the patio chair fall over, then a startled, "Lisa?"

He glanced over his shoulder in time to see his sister-in-law on her feet, staring at the pool, her face full of concern.

"Lisa!" Heather took a hasty step forward, her face full of alarm.

Matt whirled around to follow her gaze. Lisa emerged slowly from the depths of the pool, floating face down in the water.

The beer bottle fell from his hand and smashed on the tile at his feet as he leaped forward. Jordan's curse sounded in his ears as he set one hand on the railing and vaulted it.

His bare feet hit the hot deck tiles, his eyes locked on his wife's inert form as he ran headlong for the edge of the pool. He launched himself into the water in a shallow dive, his heart in his throat.

He reached her in three strokes. Immediately he grabbed her around the chest and turned her over, forcing her head out of the water and back against his shoulder. Her eyes were closed. "*Lisa.*"

She didn't respond.

"Lisa!" Nothing.

Terror like he'd never known slammed through him. He started toward the edge of the pool. She was an expert swimmer. There was no way she could have hit her head on anything. He dragged her to the edge with sure strokes, every muscle in his body taut. Jordan was there waiting. He grabbed Lisa under the arms and pulled her out, laying her on her side on the hot deck.

Matt sprang out and knelt at her side, dripping water everywhere. "Call 911," he barked to Heather, who was standing with her hands cupped over her mouth and nose, an expression of horror on her face as the two girls huddled behind her fearfully.

He swept Lisa's wet hair back from her face, trying to keep the panic at bay. The only way to help her was to stay calm. "Lisa, open your eyes. Come on, baby." His voice was a pleading rasp as he checked her airway and felt for a pulse. There was nothing blocking her nose or throat and a faint beat throbbed beneath the angle of her jaw against his searching fingertips. But she wasn't breathing.

"Baby, no, don't do this," he begged raggedly, turning her onto her back to begin CPR. He stacked his hands on her chest, put the heel of his hands over her sternum. Started compressions. She still wasn't breathing. He tipped her head back and thrust her jaw forward to open her airway and gave her a breath, the whole time praying. *Please don't leave me, please don't leave me...*

"Ambulance is on its way," Heather called out shakily from the sliding doors leading into the house. Matt didn't bother replying, all his attention focused on keeping Lisa's heart beating.

After another set of compressions he quickly put his ear to her chest.

Silence.

Fuck! Sweat beaded his body as he did another set of

compressions, gave a breath. *Come on, come on…*

Her color began to change. From pink to purple, then a telltale bluish tinge. "Godammit, *no!*" he shouted, the muscles in his arms cording with every compression, choking back a roar of agony and denial. He wouldn't let her die. Refused to let her go. They had so much to live for. She was everything to him.

He didn't know how long he stayed like that, continuing with CPR until the paramedics finally arrived. One of them was asking Jordan something. The other tried to take over from Matt. "Defibrillator," he snarled at the man and kept going, pressing and pressing and pressing on Lisa's chest, sweat pouring down his face and back, refusing to let up.

I can't lose her. I can't.

The helplessness was terrible. Someone placed an oxygen mask on her face while another readied the paddles. His own heart slammed against his ribs as he awaited the high-pitched sound that would signal they were ready.

Finally it came. "Clear!" a medic ordered.

Matt lifted his hands and eased back, panting as they applied the paddles to his wife's chest. The shock jolted her whole body, arching her ribcage upward.

Matt's eyes shot to the device's screen as he grabbed her hand and squeezed, waiting for a heartbeat to show up.

The faintest blip appeared. A torrent of tears rushed to his eyes.

Please, baby. Please.

"Again."

Matt resumed compressions while they readied the paddles once more. *I won't let you go. I won't.*

"Clear."

He pulled away and watched the next shock travel through Lisa's inert body.

This time the screen showed only a flat line.

"No," he cried, huge, painful sobs wracking his chest as he placed his hands back on her breastbone.

One of the medics grabbed his wrist. Matt snarled at him and broke the hold, all his attention on his wife. It wasn't too late. They could still save her. They had to.

He pumped out more compressions, numb all over, the buzz of voices receding around him. He could barely see Lisa's blue-tinged features through the tears. This wasn't real. This wasn't fucking happening.

Another hand wrapped around his wrist. Didn't let go. "Matt. Matt, stop."

He jerked his head up, ready to scream at Jordan to get the fuck away from him. The quiet grief in the other man's eyes stopped him cold.

Matt's stomach pitched, twisting into a hard knot.

Tears glistened in those warm brown eyes. "She's gone." Then softer. "She's gone."

Matt heard the words but they wouldn't register. She couldn't be gone. His entire body felt frozen, his pulse still hammering away in his ears. He was shaking. Shaking all over, so bad he couldn't stop it.

Jordan released his wrist but didn't look away. "I'm so fucking sorry," he rasped out, his voice breaking. Then he pushed to his feet and took a step back. Matt finally looked up, slowly became aware of the others watching. Heather and the girls were all crying too.

He blinked, looked back down at his wife and wiped away his tears that had fallen on Lisa's face.

Gone.

Was she really gone? Except for the blue tinge to her skin she looked so peaceful, her dark lashes curved against her cheeks, her expression calm, like she was sleeping.

A strangled sound escaped his tight throat.

He curved a hand around the back of her neck,

wishing with everything in him that she'd open her pale blue eyes and smile up at him. On instinct her grabbed her hand, laced their fingers together and placed them atop her softly curved abdomen where their child lay tucked inside her.

Gone. They were both gone now.

Forever.

It broke him.

"Oh, Jesus," he choked out, hauling her limp body up to pull her into his lap and lock his arms around her. He buried his face in her hair and just held on, as tight as he could, rocking her back and forth. Holding her close while the warmth slowly faded from her.

"Jesus, *why*?" How was he supposed to bear this? How the hell could he accept it?

I can't. I can't...

Uncaring of the audience he had, Matt cradled her cooling body against his, pressed his face into the curve of her neck and sobbed as his heart shattered into a thousand pieces.

Chapter One

Present Day

It was never a good sign when his work cell rang in the middle of an op. Barely anyone had this number and those who did knew he was on a job, so the sight of the number on the call display had Matt's heart rate kicking up as he answered.

"We've got a problem," Assistant Director Harrison of the FBI's Counterterrorism Division said without preamble.

Matt's entire body tensed at his tone. "What kind of problem?"

"Someone infiltrated the target area before you arrived on scene."

What the hell? Matt went dead still. He didn't ask if Harrison was sure. He wouldn't have called if the intel hadn't been verified. "When was this?" And how was it possible that no one had noticed before now?

"Still trying to figure out exactly when the infiltration occurred, but likely an hour or so ago. We're watching the recorded satellite feed now, trying to locate and track whoever it was. But someone's been there and is likely still in the area."

Matt's jaw tensed. *Dammit.* "Civilian?" How incredibly ironic would that be, to have some random person stumble upon this remote site just as a critical and exhaustively planned op was going down?

"We don't think so. Analysts are working on this as fast as possible. You'll be updated when we have more."

Shitload of good that did him now, when the team was minutes from their target. "Yessir." How the hell had this breach been missed in the first place when they'd had eyes in the sky watching the target for the past two days? Someone was gonna be in deep shit for this lapse. "Excuse me a second, sir."

"Sure."

Lowering his cell, Matt cursed and tapped his earpiece. "Tuck, hold up," he told his team leader, poised at the head of the seven-man HRT assault team halfway up the slope leading to the isolated cabin. The one no one else should have been anywhere near.

On the laptop screen in front of him he watched the team halt as Tuck spoke in a whisper. The snow helped deaden sound, but none of his guys could risk speaking at normal volume in their position. "Roger, maintaining position. What's up?"

"Op's been compromised. Stand by and maintain your secure perimeter," he responded, anger building in his gut. Somebody was going to lose his or her job over this lapse. Hell, the entire Critical Incident Response Group taskforce had flown to Denver four days ago in preparation for this op, after months of investigative work and specific training for it. They'd had to wait for a break between storms and act during a tight weather window to execute it, all the while praying the target would stay put long enough for them to move in.

No op ever went completely according to plan. But this wrinkle was a concern until they figured out who had been skulking around because they could be an additional threat to his guys. Matt shook his head.

They'd come up here to the mountains this morning and spent the past five hours getting everything and everyone into position for the op so the team could move under cover of darkness. A shitload of taxpayer money was funding this—the entire investigation—and he was not happy to learn that someone else might have received classified intel and beaten them to the target as well.

An incredibly high value target the HRT had been tasked with capturing. Hassan Ramadi, an Egyptian-born chemical engineer, responsible for training militant operatives in chemical weapons use and planning attacks here on American soil.

Matt didn't like the unknowns here. There was no way any of this intel had been leaked to the outside world, so it had to be someone with training.

His gut said someone else was after Ramadi. There was no other plausible explanation, not in these conditions.

He put his phone back to his ear. "My team's waiting in position." He listened to what Harrison was saying about the person who'd infiltrated the perimeter earlier. He could just imagine what his guys were thinking right now, huddled down in the snow in the darkness, freezing their balls off because of the biting wind chill, despite their cold weather gear. Until a few years ago, he'd have participated in the op as a sniper.

Now that he was overseeing everything he wasn't sending his guys anywhere near that cabin unless he knew it wasn't a trap. Because it was beginning to smell like one to him.

"...no other security breaches, from what we can tell," Harrison was saying.

An icy gust of wind roared down the mountainside, biting through Matt's Gore-Tex jacket. He angled his body, putting his back to the worst of the wind. "Understood. What does the video show?"

"A single individual, approaching the cabin location on foot. From the way he used the trees as a screen to avoid satellite detection we think he has training and so far we can't get a good image of him. I've already called around and nobody else within the intelligence community authorized anyone to be here except us."

Well, shit. "So what's the thinking? Is he here for Ramadi, or is he one of his foot soldiers?" Depending on the answer, his guys could be in a whole lot more danger than they'd anticipated.

"Unclear. The individual never approached the cabin beyond the far tree line. He waited there for about twenty minutes, then left. Tracks seem to be leading northwest up the mountain but he's gone to ground someplace because there's no trace of him on satellite now and the wind's already covering his tracks. We're sending you the footage now."

"Have there been any phone transmissions?"

"We're digging deeper into that, but initial investigation shows none."

So it was possible Ramadi was still unaware that they were coming for him.

Matt ended the call with the promise that he'd send his team in to investigate and carry out the intended op— capturing Ramadi—if he determined the area was secure enough to do so. While he wanted to nail the terrorist's slippery ass, he wanted all his guys to go home safely even more. If repercussions came his way later because he made the call to abort the op, so be it.

He accessed the satellite footage and stood around the laptop to view the footage with other FBI agents assigned to the op. On screen he watched the feed showing a shadowy figure, visible only because of the man's heat signature, ease into position among the tall pines thirty yards northwest of the target. With the trees blocking the satellite's view it was impossible to tell what the guy was doing, or whether he was standing or kneeling.

Matt frowned as he watched the man, wondering what he was doing there. Scouting the cabin? Watching Ramadi through a high-powered scope, hoping for a shot? He fast-forwarded through the video. The man didn't move from his position until the twenty-two minute mark. Then, as stealthily as he'd approached, he melted back into the trees and headed northwest away from the cabin.

One of the other agents looked at him. "They're sure this guy's no longer in the area?" she asked.

"That they know of." Not exactly an answer that made him feel warm and fuzzy inside, but this entire op was time sensitive and if he was going to pull the trigger on this one he had to do it soon. They had backup in the form of several SWAT teams, and helo crews waiting at a nearby airfield to transport them. If all went well, Matt wouldn't need them. The fewer assets involved, the better. Less chance of a screw-up that way.

On the laptop he accessed the feed from the drone currently circling the vicinity, checked to make sure their unwanted guest wasn't around, and tapped his earpiece again. "Tuck, the area's clear. We need eyes and ears on site to verify the target's inside." Tuck was former Delta, and one of the best operators Matt had ever worked with. Every guy on the team was former military, most of them from tier-one units. They were the best in the business for a reason.

Tuck's voice came back, calm and confident. "Copy that. Moving into position now."

Matt watched their progress on screen, remotely zooming in the drone's camera. While they began creeping up the hill he contacted his sniper teams and received confirmation that they were both able to cover the assault team, one from either side of the target. Neither sniper team had seen anyone leaving the area.

So we're dealing with a fucking ghost? Matt almost snorted at the thought. He didn't believe in ghosts, unless he counted the ones living inside him. Those were very real. But whoever this guy was, he was still out there, and likely close by.

He turned part way around at the sound of a vehicle's tires crunching over the snow on the road behind him. A big SUV pulled to a sudden stop. The back doors opened and agents Greg Travers and Celida Morales approached at a brisk walk, dressed in their winter gear. Both were assigned to this case, and top agents within the agency's domestic terrorism division.

"You heard?" he called out to them.

Travers nodded, headed straight for him. "Just. Your guys see anyone when they moved in?"

He shook his head. "Assault team's about to get eyes and ears on the target." He glanced at Celida. From beneath her hood the end of her dark ponytail whipped in the wind as she studied the screen before them. Watching her fiancé lead his team forward in the darkness. "Washington says the area's secure," he said to reassure her. And with all those trees between the cabin and their trespasser, the chances of a sniper shot on one of his guys was miniscule.

Celida flicked him a glance and nodded, her gaze going right back to Tuck at the head of the line of men moving up the snowy slope. "Think we'll get lucky and Ramadi will really be in there right now?" she asked.

"He's gotta be," Travers muttered, crossing his arms over his chest.

There was no smoke coming from the chimney and there hadn't been since two nights ago, but the property housed three generators so whoever was inside had plenty of juice to stay warm and cozy in spite of the frigid temps if they wanted to. Up here Ramadi was hopefully lulled into a false sense of security in the little hideaway he thought nobody knew about.

In reality one of his inner circle had revealed his location for a nice payday.

Everyone got quiet as the team moved close enough to get a good look at the one-story, log-constructed building. They were nearly an hour away from the closest town, and the nearest neighbor was just shy of two miles south. On arrival they'd set up a secure perimeter to keep any civilians out of the area. Nobody would interfere from here on out.

Another twenty-one minutes passed before Tuck came back on comms. "Location's secure. No eyes inside, all windows and doors covered except for a few inches of the upper window in the north gable. But we can hear a radio going. What do you want to do?"

Green light. "Execute."

The team's breacher kicked in the door and a flashbang exploded. The seven-man team rushed single file into the cabin, disappearing from view for a moment until one of the techs pulled up a live feed streaming from the camera attached to Tuck's helmet-mounted NVGs.

Matt didn't move, his gaze locked on the screen. He knew every inch of the cabin by heart, as did his guys, from the floor plan they'd memorized. He watched as they swept the kitchen, the living room, the tiny bathroom on the first floor.

"Clear," he heard Bauer report.

He has to be in there, Matt thought, his heart thudding harder as the seconds ticked past.

"Heading up to loft area," Tuck said quietly.

The tension was palpable as Matt and the other agents gathered closer around the laptop to watch as Tuck ascended a short set of wooden stairs, weapon raised to eye-level. Evers and Vance were right behind him, the others providing security below. Tuck's camera swept around the room and paused on something. The feed was grainy and dark, so Matt couldn't tell what Tuck was looking at, but from the way he was pausing, it was something important.

No shouts. No shots.

"Clear," Evers said from the far side of the room.

In the silence that followed Matt heard Tuck lower his weapon. The camera dipped and slowly focused on something lying on the floor near the window.

A body.

"Target's down. Single shot to the head, and there's a hole in the gable window," Tuck said quietly. "Guess we really were late to the party."

Ah, shit.

Matt removed his Chargers cap and scrubbed a hand over his head before replacing it. "Roger that." He turned to Celida and Travers, who were both watching the screen, grim-faced. "What do you want to do?"

Travers met his gaze, his expression livid. "Find the shooter."

****

Concealed by a large rock outcropping that would hide her from any overhead satellites or drones, Briar Jones watched the happenings at the cabin through her high-powered, night vision binoculars. The black balaclava covering her face provided some warmth, but more importantly, it also helped conceal her identity.

A cold blast of wind whistled through the rocks and cut through her special winter gear, but she didn't move, barely noticed the discomfort. Because the current surge of anger flowing through her veins was keeping her plenty warm at the moment.

Her back teeth clenched together as she stared at the team assembled below. Dammit, that had been way too close. And what the *hell*? She'd been told no one else had Ramadi's location.

At least, not yet. They were supposed to leak it later tonight, once she had time to clear out of the area and confirm her kill. Her handler had verified the intel personally. Janaia had never lied to her before, and she was one of the only people on earth Briar trusted. Briar knew this screw-up wasn't on her.

Clearly the CIA didn't know everything though, because that team was currently moving up the hillside toward the cabin she'd just moved away from forty minutes ago. Seven men moving in a line, their movements careful and choreographed. Military precise.

Could be SEALs or Delta, but she didn't think so, even though Ramadi was as dangerous and valuable as they came. More likely FBI's HRT.

Dammit.

She thought she'd felt something earlier—a tingle at the back of her neck that warned her someone else was out here on the mountain. Must have been this team or their support team, wherever they were. She'd bet not far away.

Even though logic told her to run, escape while she had a lead, years of training and discipline held her in place. Although she knew she had to move, she had to be patient. Wait until they left. If the CIA or FBI were here, they definitely had either a drone or satellites on station right now. Someone would have seen her coming and going earlier, no matter how careful she'd been to stay invisible.

They'd hunt her.

Even though she'd tried to conceal her tracks and the wind was helping shift the snow around, someone with training would be able to find them unless they were completely covered over. If they were still visible, it was only a matter of time before someone came after her, maybe even caught up to her if they used a drone to guide a helo in.

Not happening.

Briar stared through the binos at the scene unfolding down the mountain as the wind whistled through the rocks around her. The men disappeared behind the screen of trees blocking her view of the cabin and she lost sight of them.

She still didn't move, kept her breathing slow and her heart rate calm. Patience had never come easily to her but her trainers had demanded it and she'd learned to master her restlessness in a situation like this. Concealment offered the best protection for now. Because as soon as those men searched the cabin, they'd come looking for her.

Inwardly, she smiled.

I'll see you, but you won't see me.

The moment Briar considered it safe to move, she'd pull a phantom and disappear.

Chapter Two

S omeone was following her, and it wasn't the team down the mountain. Not with how fast she'd been moving on her snowshoes.

Briar felt that all too familiar prickling at her nape again as she paused in her ascent and swept her gaze across the snowy ground behind her. Nothing but swaying branches and swirling snow filled her vision. She knew better than most that just because she couldn't see her enemy didn't mean they didn't have eyes on her.

It had been a little over thirty minutes since she'd left her hiding spot and headed up the mountain. The NVGs fitted to her ski goggles allowed her to see in the darkness. Here tall pines and Aspens grew in thick stands, their branches stretching up toward the swirling storm clouds. The wind blew through them with a loud moan that rose to a wail, shifting the drifts of snow around and scattering the icy snowflakes in every direction. The next storm system had moved in much faster than predicted.

Briar stood motionless as she surveyed her surroundings. Nothing else moved, there were no other sounds to alarm her but she knew someone was out there, dogging her steps.

Nobody there. Get moving.

She hitched her pack up higher on her shoulders and adjusted the sling on her rifle before starting forward once more. She'd left the snowmobile hidden below the ridge about a half mile from here, a safe enough distance from the cabin that even if someone heard the sound of the engine, they'd never catch up to her.

It was too miserable out here for a random civilian to be out and about. No, it had to be someone else, and to track her in these conditions despite her considerable skill at avoiding detection, it had to be someone with motivation *and* training.

This development upped the urgency of her escape because getting caught wasn't acceptable. She'd never had her cover blown, not in all the ops she'd performed over the course of her seven year career. And she wasn't going to wind up being dumped by The Company after busting her ass to build an impeccable service record as a clandestine operative.

When they needed a dangerous target eliminated, they sent her, off the record. They'd trained her to be invisible, and expected her to remain so. If she got caught they'd deny any knowledge of her or the op. Risks she knew well and accepted because she was just that good.

Her snowshoes bit into the icy crust on top of the dense snow as she quickly made her way through the trees. There was only so much she could do now to conceal her tracks and she couldn't afford to slow down to do a better job. All she could hope for now was that the wind and snowfall from the intensifying storm continued to obscure her movements and that the forest protected her from any eyes in the sky searching for her. Forecasts had called for another ten to fifteen inches of snow by morning, with another storm moving in hours after that.

By then she'd be long gone, safe and warm, on her way back to her place in New York, talking to Janaia and figuring out just what the hell had gone wrong with the intel for this op.

At least Ramadi was dead. Another confirmed kill to add to her tally.

Her body warmed quickly as she rushed up the slope. The altitude here made the air thinner than in the mountains back home. Already her cardiovascular system was working harder than normal to allow her to maintain her pace. She could feel the sweat gathering beneath all the layers, was glad for the moisture-wicking material that would take any wetness away from her skin and prevent her from developing hypothermia when she stopped.

The wind and snow slowed her progress a little but at least the weather was nasty enough that no helo could fly in here. As the forest began to thin near the top of the tree line, she again felt that internal warning signal and paused behind the trunk of a tall pine. Her breath puffed in and out in icy clouds, whipped away from her mouth and nose by the swirling winds.

Whoever was out here was getting closer.

Briar scanned her surroundings. Couldn't see anyone.

Dammit.

She cast a glance up the slope, where she'd left her snowmobile. It was maybe an eighty-yard dash but she'd be mostly out in the open and have nothing to screen her movements.

Briar regulated her breathing, took one last look around and darted from her hiding spot. She wasn't nearly as fast as she would be on pavement in running shoes but the snowshoes helped her get a solid footing and prevented her from sinking in the snow as she ran. Her pack bumped against her back with each step, hands steady around her rifle, her eyes locked on the abandoned mineshaft entrance ahead. In just over a minute she was there.

Her footsteps echoed slightly in the cavernous space as she rushed inside. Dropping her pack, she disassembled her rifle and packed it, stored her snowshoes and hefted the pack over her shoulders once more.

Straddling the snowmobile's seat, she turned the engine over and hit the throttle. The sleek vehicle tore out of the mineshaft and shot through the drifts of snow. With the wind beating against her body Briar gunned it and headed due west toward an access road that would take her to where a truck waited to get her out of the area. From there it was less than an hour's drive to the highway where she'd left yet another vehicle to take her to the airport.

Icy snowflakes pelted her, the snowmobile's tracks kicking up a slight spray behind her. Couldn't be helped. She rose to the balls of her feet as she took it over the crest of a small rise, sailing through the air for a second or two before landing with a thud. Easing back on the throttle she quickly regained control and sped onward, racing across the open ground between her and the start of the tree line ahead.

She entered the trees at full speed, only cutting back when the increasing density of trunks forced her to slow. The whine of the engine lowered in pitch as she twisted left then right, then right again to dodge the trees. The GPS on her wristwatch showed the access road less than a mile away.

The treads tore through the snow, the vehicle steady beneath her. *Almost there—*

She gasped and jerked in her seat as a sudden hot, searing pain tore across the top of her right hipbone, the impact of the bullet throwing her off balance. She released the handlebars, her right hand automatically flying down to press against the wound. The snowmobile came to a sudden stop, pitching her forward. Briar flew off it and fell heavily to her knees in the snow. Automatically she rolled to her uninjured side then scrambled behind a tree trunk and reached for the pistol in the holster strapped to her thigh.

Pain burned through the right side of her waist and even though she couldn't feel the blood because of her gloves, she could smell it. Her breathing increased as she raised her sidearm and swung it in an arc, searching for a target. Nothing moved except the tree branches.

She pushed to one knee, gritting her teeth against the pain, fighting back the shock that would make her numb if she let it. Numb would slow her reflexes and get her killed. She preferred the pain, used it to center herself and keep her senses alert.

As she started to push to her feet a round slammed into the snowmobile, just yards away. Briar leaned around the tree the other way, only enough to steal a glance and saw the giant hole through the engine block. Her heart sunk.

Shit. She was pinned down and the only way out was on foot.

****

Hidden in a natural sniper hide made of fallen pine boughs, George paused, gloved finger on the trigger of the customized M40-A1 rifle. The first shot had hit the target in the right side. She'd fallen, then kept moving. No telling if the wound was fatal or not. The second round had punched through the engine block.

Stranded, and with blood loss slowing her down, the target would be easy enough to smoke out now. Almost unfair, really, to kill a fellow assassin when she was weak and helpless.

Then movement from down the mountain caught George's attention. A look through the rifle's high-powered scope showed a team of men moving up the slope. The same ones from earlier at the cabin.

Now they were after the same quarry. Except they were no doubt hoping to capture the female operative.

No way. She's mine. They could carry her body down the mountain when they found it.

Swinging the barrel of the rifle around toward the target once more, George tightened the scope's focus, a gloved finger resting on the curved edge of the trigger. No further visual of the target or movement among the trees now and it was too dark to see a blood trail at this distance. The men moving toward them made it impossible to risk taking another shot. Only remaining option now was to retreat and double back around, maybe take the target from behind.

Assuming she was even still alive.

Moving fast, George rose, slung the rifle, shrugged on the pack and slipped on the cross-country skis before melting away into the darkness.

****

Hidden by the trees, Matt lay on his belly in the snow and waited. Those gunshots had been faint over the sound of the snowmobile and wind, but he'd heard them. And he didn't think it had been their trespasser.

"Motor's stopped." Matt paused next to Tuck and Bauer, speaking louder than normal to be heard over the increasing wind.

Tuck nodded, scanning the slope before them. "No movement."

Matt was wary of approaching farther. They had no eyes overhead now, the weather system making it impossible for any drone or satellite to see through the murk. Command had said they'd spotted two heat signatures earlier, one moving to the northwest and the other approaching from the west but had quickly lost visual. With no helos able to access the remote location and no time to call in more help, it was up to Matt's team to find the mystery assassin.

"Whoever that was, they're not shooting at us," Matt muttered, straining to see much of anything through the NVGs and binos he was looking through. "Direction's wrong." Previously they'd wondered if the two signatures the drone had spotted were working together.

Matt now guessed not so much. And now it looked like they were hunting *two* armed suspects, although there might be more hidden beyond the area the FBI had searched earlier.

"So who the hell *is* shooting?" Vance muttered from a few yards down the slope.

Matt had no idea, but he didn't like lying out here in the snow like a static target, screen of trees or not. With hand signals he ordered them to split into two teams, him leading one and Tuck leading the other.

The snowshoes they'd brought as part of their gear allowed them to maintain good traction as they rushed up the hill, crouching behind trunks as cover to regroup, check the surrounding area and move forward once more in a series of leap-frogging movements. A few minutes later Cruz's voice came through his earpiece.

"See some blood up ahead. Trails toward us, north to southwest."

The trespasser?

"Copy that. Hold your position." Using the forest to conceal their movement, the rest of the team reached Cruz and gathered to assess the situation.

"See anything else?" Matt whispered.

Cruz shook his head. "Nope. From the amount of blood, I'm guessing the wound is more than superficial." He shifted aside for Matt to take a look. In the darkness it was hard to spot initially but through his night vision binos he saw what appeared to be black stains in the snow. The thin, spotty trail snaked up and around, disappearing from view behind a cluster of fallen logs.

Gotcha.

"Tuck, keep your boys here to cover us while my team moves in for a closer look," he said.

"Roger that."

Pulling his 9 mm, Matt edged around the tree trunk and glided forward, staying in a crouch. The trees acted as a kind of buffer, filtering out the worst of the wind. Sound now seemed amplified, each footstep louder than it probably was. Bauer, Vance and Schroder followed him up the rise toward the cluster of logs. In a concealed position he paused once again to search the area. Still no movement from the logs and no further sign of a blood trail.

Whoever had been wounded, they were still there.

Matt gave more hand signals to indicate he wanted an encircling movement to converge on the target. When he gave the sign, everyone moved.

Matt ran as silently as he could, dodging trees and rocks as he raced toward the logs. His heart thudded in his ears, mixing with the sound of his elevated breathing. Weapon aimed, he burst from the cover of trees and approached the fallen logs.

He saw the discarded helmet and what looked like it might be a balaclava lying on the ground beside the logs. The target came into view and he had only a split second to take it all in. A body lay on its side in the snow. Slender. Bare-headed, jaw-length hair, smooth face and delicate features.

A female?

Confusion set in for an instant but then she moved. Matt drew up short and planted his feet in a shooting stance, adjusting his aim as the woman rolled, her arm flashing up to aim her pistol dead center at his chest.

Chapter Three

Briar's hand shook slightly with a combination of shock and adrenaline as she held the weapon leveled at the man's chest. Something kept her from pulling the trigger as they faced off. It was too dark to see his features and the wind made it impossible to keep her eyes open above a squint for more than a second as a time. She wished she'd managed to keep her damn goggles on.

Before she could move, other men began appearing around him, rifles aimed at her. Others approached from behind.

Trapping her.

She blinked away the snowflakes tangling on her lashes, trying to see more of the man before her. The leader, she could tell by the way the others stayed back slightly. He was around six feet tall and wide through the shoulders. She didn't think any of these guys had taken that shot at her, otherwise they'd have killed her already. They appeared to want to take her alive.

But if she was wrong and they'd come to finish the job, she wasn't going down without a fight. Her index finger tightened around the trigger.

"Drop it," the leader commanded, his voice low and menacing over the wind.

Nope. No way in hell. She maintained her aim, ready to fire if necessary. She vowed to kill at least two of them before they took her down.

The man didn't move, the barrel of his pistol never wavering from her center mass. "Drop it, *now*."

Her mind raced. She was trained for this. She'd made contingency plans long before coming here tonight. These guys might not be here to kill her, but they weren't going to let her go, either. There was no way she could take the leader down and get past him before the others shot her. She kept her free hand pressed against her wound, aware of the warmth of her blood as it leaked down her right side and leg. There was only one choice.

Slowly, hating to do it even though it was her only viable option, Briar complied with his order, lowering her weapon.

The man took a gliding step forward, his aim steady, his movements precise, practiced. "Toss it aside and show me your hands."

Pushing out a breath, ignoring the way her mind screamed in protest at being unarmed in this situation, she tossed the H&K aside in the snow and raised both gloved hands so he could see she wasn't holding a weapon. She was shocked and disheartened at how weak her arms felt.

Immediately two men approached, one from either side. They grabbed her roughly by the shoulders and flipped her over onto her stomach. Briar bit back a growl as a hot flare of pain speared her side and more blood flowed over her skin.

One secured her hands behind her back with a zip tie while the other patted her down for more weapons. He removed her backup pistol strapped to her left ankle and the KA-BAR knife sheathed to her right calf. Her rifle was with her pack, ditched behind some rocks about ten yards back.

Briar maintained awareness of all of the men as the leader walked over and got down on one knee next to her. She tensed at his sharply indrawn breath.

"*B*?"

The startled recognition in his voice made Briar lift her head to peer up at him. He pushed back his goggles and put a hand on her shoulder. She stiffened and squinted up at him, then stared in shock. Supervisory Special Agent Matteo DeLuca, commander of the HRT.

Shit. Briar internally groaned as humiliation and anger churned in her gut, mixing with the pain, burning away the awful shakiness. She resisted the urge to look away.

He scowled down at her. "What the hell are you— You took out Ramadi?"

Clenching her jaw, Briar lowered her gaze and rested her cheek against the snow, uncaring of the freezing cold against her skin. If word of her capture got out, her career— hell, life as she knew it—would be over.

The hand on her shoulder tightened. "Who shot you?" he demanded, clearly out of patience with her silent routine.

She didn't know, so she didn't answer. She was acutely aware of the seven other men standing around watching and listening while she tried to come up with a way out of this mess. Being caught burned a hell of a lot worse than the bullet wound, and it hurt plenty.

DeLuca hunkered down more, shielding her from the worst of the wind with his body. "I don't know who sent you but we're on the same side and I want to help you. So talk to me."

There was nothing to say. She didn't answer to him or anyone else waiting down this mountain. Ramadi was dead, and that was all he needed to know until she cleared things with Janaia.

DeLuca pushed out a frustrated sigh and waved one of his men forward. "Schroder, come take a look at her. The rest of you maintain the perimeter. Other shooter's likely still in the area." He stood and pulled out what she assumed was a satellite phone. The screen gave off a faint illumination in the darkness.

Good luck getting a call out in these conditions, she thought with a mental snort.

Another man, she assumed Schroder, the team's medic, came over and squatted beside her. "Your name's B?"

She flashed him a cold look that only made him grin, his teeth a startling white against the camouflage paint on his skin.

"I'll take that as a yes." He started pulling things out of his ruck and she heard the snap of latex gloves going on.

Briar closed her eyes against the wind for a moment and braced herself for more pain. She could hear DeLuca moving around close by as the medic began searching her for injuries. She involuntarily hissed through her teeth when Schroder's hand swept over the wound.

"Anywhere else besides this?" he asked, continuing his assessment.

Gritting her teeth, she gave a terse shake of her head. She'd been lucky. The wound hurt like a bitch but it wasn't life-threatening or anything. Just enough to slow her down, piss her off and make her miserable. It felt like someone had taken a blowtorch to her skin as Schroder cut through her clothing and exposed the wound.

The low beam of a pen light lit up the darkness as he took a closer look. "That's a pretty good gash." He turned to DeLuca, who'd put his phone away. Likely because he couldn't get reception in this storm, let alone with all the trees around to block the signal. "She'll need stitches."

"Put a dressing on it for now. You can do the honors when we get her down to the command center."

And there it was. They were taking her in.

"Let me go," she said, surprised at how rough her voice was.

DeLuca looked down at her sharply and shook his head. "Not a chance."

Briar fought back her impatience at the clipped answer, not about to argue her case or try and explain who she was. No one could know that. They were going to take her down the mountain where all kinds of other agents and officers would see her. There'd be more questioning. Phone calls.

If she could convince him to let her call Janaia or someone higher up the chain of command first, before this situation was leaked to anyone else aside from DeLuca and his team, she could still maintain her cover. Maybe even keep her career and reputation intact.

As for any possible repercussions about her being tied to Ramadi's death, it depended on whether anyone leaked her presence here before she could get away. Not that she'd be with DeLuca and his crew long.

She'd escape the first chance she got, go to ground and contact Janaia. Worst case scenario, she always had the option of changing her identity, leaving the country and starting over elsewhere. But only as a last resort. She'd spent most of her adult life learning to be invisible and planned to get her life back to the way it had been half an hour ago, before that goddamn bullet had jeopardized everything she'd worked for.

As Schroder continued working on her, her mind backtracked to the op, reviewing every move and wondering what she could have done differently. Who had leaked Ramadi's location to the Feds, when she was supposed to be out here alone? And who the hell had shot her if it hadn't been one of these guys?

With a practiced touch Schroder put on a dressing and helped her to her knees, then her feet. The onset of shock and sudden change in hydrostatic pressure made her woozy. She swayed momentarily on her feet, fighting the urge to rip her arm from Schroder's supporting grasp.

DeLuca spoke to someone in a low voice, and she realized he was talking via an earpiece. "Prisoner in custody. Single gunshot wound to her side." He paused a moment. "Yes, *her*. Have an ambulance brought in."

"I don't need an ambulance," Briar called out.

His head turned toward her. It was still too dark to make out his features but she remembered them and not because of her almost photographic memory. Matt DeLuca wasn't the sort of man a woman ever forgot. "Can you walk?"

"Yes," she muttered, yanking against Schroder's hold but he didn't release her.

The wind picked up, howling through the tops of the trees with a mournful sound. Briar mentally listed possible escape options. Escaping here on the mountain would be best, but with her hands bound and eight armed, highly trained men surrounding her, that wasn't going to happen. Her best bet would be once they reached wherever they were taking her. She could slip away there. Even escape from an ambulance if they tried to transport her to a hospital, or from another vehicle if they planned to take her somewhere else.

Another two men approached out of the darkness, carrying the supplies she'd ditched on her crawl from the snowmobile. "M40 and her ruck," one of them said. "Nothing else up here but the snowmobile, single round through the engine. We ID'd a few possible sniper hides to the west but didn't see tracks leading to or from any of them."

DeLuca looked away from her and spoke to his men. "Let's go."

Without the aid of her snowshoes and her hands bound behind her, walking in the snow was difficult. Her boots plunged deep into the drifts, making her body exert far more energy than on the climb up here. The team moved along with her, each member's rifle up and ready in case they met with any threats. That telltale tingle at the back of her neck was gone, however, so she knew the sniper who'd shot her was long gone.

After ten minutes descending the hillside, Briar was already panting for breath. Her legs were showing signs of weakness and were starting to shake, her heart and lungs laboring to supply her muscles with oxygen.

Freaking bullet wound.

Whenever they emerged into a gap between the thick stands of trees the wind slapped at her like angry hands, kicking up snow in every direction. Schroder stayed right next to her, his firm hold on her upper arm never easing, and another man remained glued to her left side. Even if she were foolhardy enough to risk an escape attempt now, she wouldn't get two feet before they caught her and used a much less gentle method of transporting her the rest of the way.

At the head of the team, DeLuca paused on a low ridge and looked back. She knew she was lagging and slowing them all down, her strength reserves dwindling. When she stumbled and almost fell to her knees in the snow, Schroder grabbed her and unceremoniously hoisted her over his broad shoulder.

Briar resisted at first, hissing through her teeth as his shoulder dug into her wound, then gave in and braced herself against his back.

"I know, but the pressure of my shoulder will help slow the bleeding," Schroder told her as he trudged after his teammates.

The whole time he walked, still managing to keep his footing in the snow even with her additional weight, she tested and discarded various plans for when they got to the bottom of the mountain. She needed to talk to Janaia ASAP, maintain her anonymity and later, once she was on her own again, find out what the hell had happened out here tonight.

Now that her adrenaline had officially crashed, the blood loss and cold began to affect her. She shivered, her muscles shuddering in hard bursts in an effort to warm her. Her teeth began to chatter.

"Just another half mile or so," Schroder said to her, maintaining pace with the others. She'd rather be moving under her own power but this way she could recharge and save her strength for when she really needed it. When she made her escape, she'd only have one chance.

Finally, when the cold had turned her hands, feet and nose numb and she was shaking all over, they finally reached the access road where the support team had set up. Schroder carried her directly to a large truck that must serve as the mobile command center and took her inside. Briar blinked against the sudden brightness as the door shut behind them. Immediately she felt the warmth compared to the frigid air outside.

Several agents stopped what they were doing, staring as they backed out of the way to give them room. Schroder set her down on a bench seat against one side and paused to look into her face, his hazel eyes assessing, dark auburn hair mussed from the knit cap he'd been wearing. "If I kneel down in front of you, you're not gonna try and kick me in the nuts or anything, right?" His tone told her he was only half-teasing.

Still shivering violently, Briar shook her head. With her hands bound her options for attack were limited. She knew how to incapacitate and even kill with strikes to the right places, but he wasn't in danger from her unless he threatened her in some way. Based on what she knew of him, he wasn't that kind of guy so she wasn't worried.

Right now she was going to use her gender to her advantage, make it seem like she was too weak to fight when in reality she was just saving her strength and biding her time for when she made a break for it.

"Good." He knelt at her feet and peeled away her torn jacket and bodysuit to check the injury site, his hands gentle. "Stretch out on your left side for me." She did, her movements clumsy because of her inability to use her hands. He turned to one of the agents. "Get me a blanket."

Someone brought one over and Schroder tucked it around her, pulling one edge aside to access her wound. Briar propped up on one elbow and craned her neck to get a better look at it. Although she'd known it wasn't serious, she was surprised to see a five inch gash above her right hip bone. The round had torn across her skin and probably through some muscle, splitting her flesh wide open. It was still bleeding freely despite the pressure and bandages Schroder had put on it.

The door swung open and DeLuca appeared in the opening, bareheaded, framed against the blackness behind him. Briar's heart sped up. He had short, medium brown hair, thinning slightly at one spot near the crown of his head. He was dressed in woodland camouflage tactical gear like the others. Unlike his men, his face wasn't cammied up, which made her think his going after her had been an afterthought. A few days' worth of dark stubble marked the lower half of his face, making him appear even more rugged and masculine than the last time she'd seen him.

His green eyes locked on her face for a moment, and Briar felt a jolt of awareness deep inside before he looked at her wound. "Got what you need?" he asked Schroder, motioning for the others to leave the command vehicle with a wave of his hand.

"I'm good," Schroder, a former Air Force Pararescueman replied as the others filed out into the cold.

Briar had read files on every member of this HRT team back in September, including Commander DeLuca. Because she made it a point to research people before she met them.

He walked over to stand behind Schroder, arms folded across his chest. A wide, well-muscled chest, she couldn't help but notice. Last time she'd seen him he'd been wearing business attire, black slacks and a dark blue dress shirt. In his utilities he looked every inch the lethal warrior he'd once been, until the promotion to commander had taken him out of the direct action. He was a good-looking man, forty-one years old, with an impeccable service record. And the laser-like focus in his gaze as he stared at her would have made a lesser woman squirm.

Lucky for her, Briar wasn't like most women.

"So, you gonna tell me who you really are?" he asked with a slight tilt of his head. Assessing her. Gauging her expression, body language and response.

He could examine her all he wanted, he wouldn't get anything she didn't want him to. And for right now, that included her name. "I need to make a phone call."

He snorted. "I don't think so. Tell me who you are and who sent you to take out Ramadi."

Briar lifted her chin, looking down the length of her nose at him even though he was towering over her. She hid a wince as Schroder pinched the edges of the wound together.

"Can you hand me a suturing kit?" he asked DeLuca, frowning in concentration.

DeLuca reached over to search in a med bag and handed him one before meeting Briar's eyes again. "Not gonna tell me?"

She gazed back at him calmly, determined to hold her ground.

His jaw tightened. "Fine." Pulling a phone out of his

jacket pocket, he dialed a number and held it up to his ear, his expression closed and unreadable. "Rycroft, it's DeLuca. I've got a situation."

Briar bit back a gasp and half sat up, barely stemming the urge to snatch the phone from his hand. NSA agent Alex Rycroft wouldn't give her away, at least she didn't think so, but with one phone call he could alert people within the intelligence community she didn't want knowing about any of this.

He listened to whatever Rycroft said, those hard green eyes never leaving hers. "Know anything about a sanctioned hit on Hassan Ramadi in Colorado tonight? Because he was already dead when my team went in and we just captured your friend B less than two miles from the target location."

****

Matt generally had a long fuse, but given that his team had been put in direct jeopardy *twice* tonight—once by the leaked intel on Ramadi and the other while finding and capturing B, or whatever the fuck her name was—he wanted some goddamn answers.

"Is she injured?" Rycroft asked him, sounding concerned.

Matt studied the woman in question. He'd thought about her several times over the past few months, wondering who she truly was and what she was doing. Her bronzed skin looked a bit grayish and there was a blue tinge around her mouth from the cold. Her nearly black eyes stared back at him with quiet defiance, her coffee brown hair now cropped to chin length instead of falling halfway down her back like it had when he'd met her in New Orleans in September.

"Flesh wound. Someone else was hunting her too but we didn't find them. If the round had hit her a few inches to the left, we would've brought her body back down the mountain with us."

Rycroft was silent a moment. "Let me make a call. I'll get back to you."

"Yeah," Matt said and disconnected.

Slipping the phone back into his pocket, he folded his arms across his chest and sized up the female operative before him. She was pretty, even now when she was pale and wounded and in shock, and young, mid to upper twenties if he had to guess.

When he'd first met her through Rycroft at the major security conference in New Orleans, he'd immediately noticed something mysterious about her that just didn't add up. She'd been a knockout in that business suit, the snug skirt hugging her hips and her high heels showing off the sleek muscles in her bare, bronzed calves. Though he'd suspected from her watchful gaze and the way she moved that she was a trained agent, finding out she was a full-on assassin had come as one hell of a shock.

It had happened after an op in Baton Rouge just as the security conference was wrapping up. They'd received perishable intel on another major player in the domestic terror game the same night his team had gone in to rescue two female hostages from a dirty undercover DEA agent. One of whom had been Clay Bauer's girlfriend, Zoe.

"Thanks for the tip in Baton Rouge, by the way," he said to B now, unable to keep the sardonic edge from his tone. He'd received an anonymous text with the target's name, along with an address and a cryptic *From one of the good guys*. At the time he'd mistakenly assumed Rycroft had sent it.

Her eyes flashed up to his a moment, then she nodded in acknowledgement and looked away.

All these weeks later, Matt still didn't know what to make of her or her actions that night. Al-Tunisi had been a critical, high value target. When Tuck's team had finally gone in to get him that night, they'd found him dead on his bathroom floor with his pants around his ankles, a double tap to the chest and one to the forehead. Later, when they'd done satellite analysis of someone seen climbing the outside of Al-Tunisi's house, he'd been stunned to identify her features on screen.

So he didn't find the idea of her taking out Ramadi that surprising.

"I'm gonna give you some lidocaine to freeze this before I stitch you," Schroder told her, already prepping a syringe. B said nothing but finally broke eye contact with Matt when his medic began injecting the topical analgesic into the wound.

He watched her features go flat as Schroder stuck her with the needle and began stitching her up, clearly not wanting to betray any hint of pain. She'd have been trained to hide that or any other weakness.

Matt resisted the urge to drag a hand through his hair. This entire situation was frustrating as hell. She knew as well as he did that they were on the same team. She also had to know that her cover was blown, at least for this op. He was going to find out who she was and who she worked for, whether from her or someone else. It'd been a long day and there was a small mountain of paperwork ahead of him so he'd just as soon skip the bureaucratic bullshit and find the truth out now before he turned her over to Celida and Travers for more questioning.

Schroder was inserting the fourth stitch—and she was gonna need at least ten more to close the worst of that wound, by the looks of it—when Matt's phone rang. He pulled it out, saw the "unknown number" message and answered. "DeLuca."

"I need to speak to the woman you're holding," a clipped female voice said, her tone urgent.

He almost snorted at her nerve. *Like hell.* "Who is

this?"

"Alex Rycroft informed me of what happened. This is time-critical. I need to speak to B right now."

"Again, who are you?"

"Call me Lily."

He'd bet his left nut that wasn't her real name.

"Put her on. It's urgent."

Matt fought for patience. "Schroder. Give us a minute, will you?"

The medic looked up at him, clearly surprised at the order to leave in the middle of stitching her up. "Uh, sure." He took B's hand and pressed it to a sterile bandage he placed over the wound. "Keep pressure on it 'til I get back." With a questioning glance at Matt he got up and left the command unit.

"I'm putting you on speaker," Matt told Lily and hit the button. "Okay, she can hear you."

"B, it's Lily."

Something flashed in B's eyes, the only change in her expression as she pushed up farther on her elbow. "Hey." Her voice sounded slightly husky. Relief?

"What's your favorite ice cream?"

B glanced up at Matt for a moment and he clearly read the indecision in her eyes. Then she looked away and answered. "Maple walnut."

"Good." Lily sounded relieved too. "Okay, tell me what's going on. Rycroft said you were shot."

"It's nothing," she said, her pallor and the blood seeping through the bandage belying her casual tone.

"Who shot you?"

Again, those dark, fathomless eyes met Matt's. "I don't know. Never saw them, but the intel I got said no one was supposed to be anywhere near here tonight, *including* the Feds."

Matt stared right back at her, finding that tidbit very interesting.

"What the hell's going on, Lily?"

A pause. "I don't know. Who else knows about this?"

B raised an eyebrow at him in silent question so Matt answered. "Nobody outside of my team, you and Rycroft."

Lily grunted. "I don't like this, not at all. Only a handful of others had the intel I sent you, B. So you're going to enact emergency plan Charlie immediately. Got it?"

B's face tightened at the news. "Okay."

What was emergency plan Char—

"Agent DeLuca."

He blinked at the woman's commanding tone. "Yes?"

"I need you to take B out of there immediately while I assess the threat and do some digging. She'll direct you to a safe house—"

"What? You want *him* to take me?" B's eyes were wide with alarm and incredulity as she stared first at the phone, then Matt. "You can't be serious," she protested, a scowl on her face. "I'll be out of here as soon as they patch me up and contact you from the safe house. I can handle myself, I don't need anyone to—"

"Rycroft vouched for him and that's good enough for me. Until I know who was after you, you're going to ground. And with you wounded and the shooter still likely in the area, I'm not taking any chances so you'll accept the protection. Agent DeLuca, I'll get this cleared with your superiors and have them confirm it with you. B will handle the rest. And B, I know you don't like this but this one time you need to trust someone else, at least temporarily. DeLuca has Top Security clearance, he was a Corps Scout Sniper, and—"

"I know," she muttered, glaring up at him as if this fuckup was somehow *his* fault.

Matt had heard enough and wasn't about to be ordered around by whoever the hell this *Lily* person was. "I don't know who you are, but I've got a dead tango inside the cabin that B so thoughtfully took care of for us and I don't take orders from you."

B's eyes flashed and her mouth thinned. "I can take care of myself."

He looked pointedly at her wound then back at her face and raised an eyebrow. *Not at the moment, sweetheart.*

Lily let out an aggravated sigh. "Agent DeLuca, off the record, I think we could be dealing with a matter of national security here. I've already contacted your superiors—"

As if on cue, his second line rang. This time it was the Deputy Director of Counterterrorism. *Shit.* "Got another call," Matt said.

"I'll wait," Lily answered. "Tell Keith I said hello," she added.

She was on a first-name basis with the Deputy Director of Counterterrorism? Who the hell was this woman? *Goddammit...* Matt switched lines and answered. "You heard the news?" he said dryly.

"Yes. Did Lily call you?"

He'd bet every penny of his small but hard-earned pension that Lily wasn't even close to her real name. Fuck, if he'd wanted to play this cloak-and-dagger shit, he would've joined the CIA. "I've got her on the other line."

Harrison grunted. "We need you and your team to guard B. Only she and Lily know the location of the safe house. Disable all your electronics before you leave, and you're solely responsible for her. Brief your team and get her out of there. I'll handle everything else. You're both going dark, I'm talking Stone Age, until we get to the bottom of all this. If anyone shows up at the safe house, shoot first and ask questions later."

Matt frowned. "What the hell's going on, Keith?"

A pause. "We're getting word from another agency that they might have a leak that needs plugging."

Matt watched B's gaze sharpen at the words. He was ninety-nine percent certain they were talking about the CIA. A leak that involved taking out a fellow agent to cover it? Serious shit. He pushed out a breath. "That all you're gonna tell me?" You know, since they expected him to put himself in harm's way to protect her and all.

"It's all I can tell you, for now, except that there could be some big players involved so right now it's a matter of damage control and limiting the number of people in contact with her. I'm assigning you for a reason. As of this moment you're officially on paid leave. Have Jack take over the investigation before you leave and don't tell anyone what's going on."

When the Deputy Director of Counterterrorism gave you an order like that, you didn't argue. But Christ, this was already a fucking nightmare. Matt glanced at B. From the look on her face she was every bit as unhappy about this as he was. There was a small measure of satisfaction in that, he supposed. "There's a bad storm coming in. Roads are going to be impassible in a couple hours."

"So you'll need to get moving."

"Yes, sir," he said grudgingly, then ended the call and got back on the line with Lily. "You still there?"

"Yes. What did Keith say?"

"*Keith* told me I've been demoted to babysitter for the foreseeable future and to keep my mouth shut about it." Hooray.

"Perfect. B, you contact me through secure channels when you're squared away."

B met his gaze, the resentment he saw mirrored there matching what he felt perfectly. "All right," she muttered.

Once he hung up, Matt tucked his phone away and

walked over to open the command vehicle's door. "Schroder. Finish patching her up." He turned his head to look back at her. Celida and Travers's questioning session with her would have to wait. "Looks like I'm driving her into town."

Chapter Four

S pecial Agent Nate Schroder waited until the SUV he was riding in pulled out behind the second vehicle in line before asking the question that had been burning a hole through his brain for the past twenty minutes.

"Is anyone else not loving the fact that our CO is alone with that female sniper right now?" He looked around as the rest of the guys raised their hands. Evers and Cruz in the back with him, and Vance riding shotgun. The others were in the vehicle in front of them, following behind DeLuca to wherever the hell they were going.

At the wheel, Bauer was the only one who responded with a grunt. "He'll be fine."

"Oh, okay," Nate said, all sarcasm. He respected the hell out of the former SEAL, but in this case didn't agree with him.

What if DeLuca *wasn't* okay alone with her? What if she attacked him while he was driving or something? That chick had just taken out their HVT with a single, spectacular head shot through a tiny gable window in the middle of a snowstorm, without anyone detecting her presence until it was too late. He'd been serious when he'd asked if she planned to knee him in the balls, because her gaze had been flat out hostile when he'd started tending to her in the mobile command center. He was glad he hadn't been able to see her expression while he carried her down the damn mountain.

They knew nothing about her, except that she was deadly, and Nate was willing to bet not just with a rifle. He knew DeLuca could hold his own if a dangerous situation arose, but he didn't trust the woman one bit. He'd have felt way better if at least one of them had been able to accompany them on the drive, but for whatever reason, DeLuca had refused.

"Wonder what the deal is," Cruz murmured beside him, staring out the window as the snow swirled outside, then glanced his way. "You said he was talking to someone on the phone when you were outside the command trailer."

"Yeah, but I don't know who and I didn't hear most of the conversation." He wished he had. He was curious as hell about what was going on, because this whole thing was *way* outside normal protocol.

"Must have been talking to someone high up there in the intel world," Vance said. "He sure moved in a hell of a hurry after that."

"I don't like it," Nate announced, folding his arms. Who the hell was that woman, anyway?

"You don't have to like it," Bauer muttered, steering the big vehicle down the steep, winding road.

Nate refrained from replying, reminding himself that Bauer was missing an emotion chip and had ice water in his veins instead of warm, red blood. He was remote and a total hardass, but one of the best operators on the team, aside from Tuck.

Well, okay, he wasn't completely immune to

emotion because everyone knew how bananas he was over his girl, Zoe. Not that anyone could blame him. Zoe was hot in an edgy, I-don't-take-shit-from-anyone way. Nate liked her and she'd done wonders for Bauer's usually grim personality. If she could make the grimmest guy on the team happy enough that he actually smiled in public these days, then that said it all.

"As long as he stays in radio contact with Tuck, we'll know she hasn't killed him yet," Blackwell said dryly from Nate's right.

"Great," he muttered. As the newest and youngest man on the team Nate had vowed to learn as much as he could from these guys.

Ever since getting out of the Air Force he'd wanted to make the HRT and on his second try he'd made that dream come true. He paid attention and did what he was told, made sure he wasn't a weak link and they all treated him well in return, albeit with a shitload of ribbing, since he was the FNG—fucking new guy. He didn't mind. Hell, even the worst of their verbal and physical abuse barely registered on his measuring scale compared to what he'd endured until he'd left home at eighteen. Besides, the guys meant well, and he'd learned something valuable from all of them.

These guys were like brothers to him, a family that meant more to him than the people he was embarrassed to be related to. Nate had every one of his teammate's backs, no questions asked, same as they had his. It was the biggest reason why he loved this job so much.

And so yeah, he *really* didn't like the idea of his CO alone and unguarded with that woman.

With a snort of laughter Cruz reached up and scrubbed his knuckles against the top of Nate's head. "Don't worry, Doc, he'll be okay."

Nate grunted and batted his hand away, his narrow-eyed gaze pinned on the glowing taillights two vehicles ahead. With the seven of them following close behind, DeLuca had plenty of backup should he need it. If that woman tried anything funny, she wouldn't make it down the mountain alive this time.

****

Only ten minutes into the drive and the tense silence was already beginning to grate on her nerves. Briar was used to working alone and often went a week or more without human contact, which was fine by her. Being trapped in this SUV with DeLuca, the lack of control over the entire situation, was making her crazy.

She shifted gingerly in the seat and pulled on the strap of the seatbelt where it kept digging into the bandage above her hip. At least her hands were free and she had a weapon again. Her 9mm SIG was strapped to her thigh in its custom-made holster. Her sniper rifle was stowed in the back with the rest of her gear. She didn't have much— the rest she'd left in a stash she'd hidden on the mountain that she obviously wouldn't be getting to any time soon. Still, the cold weather gear, weapons and ammo were good enough to get her to the safe house.

"So," he said as he steered down the icy gravel road that wound its way down the mountain. His team was following them in two other SUVs. The others would accompany them for a few miles up the highway past Golden, just in case anyone tried to follow them, then head back toward Denver while she and DeLuca continued on. "Where are we headed?" She didn't miss the underlying sarcastic edge to his seemingly pleasant tone.

Her eyes darted about the cab of the truck. She'd already watched him turn off his phone and take the battery out of it, but… "How do I know there are no bugs in here?"

He shot her an incredulous look and raised one dark eyebrow before looking back at the road. "Seriously?"

She shrugged, not caring if he thought she was overly paranoid. He hadn't been shot by an unknown sniper and his life wasn't on the line here. She wasn't going to apologize for being suspicious and even his team couldn't know their final destination. Her so-called paranoia had kept her alive so far.

He sighed. "There aren't any hidden microphones anywhere, unless you count the Bluetooth system and since I already disabled my phone, I won't be using that. So again, where to? Denver? Boulder?"

"Glenwood Springs."

"Where's that?" he asked, frowning.

She looked out her window, fighting the urge to fidget. They were just outside of Golden now. She'd left her getaway vehicle a few miles west of this very road, tucked away off an access road in the woods. She'd been careful not to leave prints behind but she'd intended to give it a thorough wipe down tonight after the op. The chances of anyone finding her DNA or prints in it were minimal but she still felt uneasy leaving it there.

"About two-and-a-half hours west. In this weather, could be double that," she said. It was already almost one in the morning. They should be able to get to the safe house before the sun came up.

"Have you been there before?"

"Yes."

When she didn't say anything else he gave a humorless laugh. "Can I at least get your real name now? You know, since we're about to be stuck together for a few days at least?"

With his security clearance and background she decided it wouldn't hurt to tell him that much about herself. "Briar. Jones."

He flashed her another dubious look. "Is Jones really

your last name?"

"Yes." Not the one she'd been born with, but he didn't need to know that or anything else about her past. As far as she was concerned, once he got her to the safe house and Janaia—he'd been told her name was Lily—arrived, his obligation would be fulfilled, then he could leave and they'd never see each other again.

"Who do you think's after you?"

"I already told you, I don't know." Coupled with what Deputy Assistant Harrison and Janaia had said on the phone, that unknown was enough to make her stomach churn with worry. Other little pieces of the puzzle were bothering her too. Someone had intentionally leaked Ramadi's location to the Feds, knowing she'd already be up here hunting him.

Maybe the same person who'd sent the sniper after her. It was too much of a coincidence for it to be anything but a setup. But why? Why would someone from her own agency want her dead?

The SUV's front tires hit a bump. She braced herself against the seat, trying and failing to hide a wince as the seatbelt bit into her wound.

DeLuca saw it. "Sorry. Road's pretty rough. I'll be more careful."

The conditions weren't helping, no matter how careful he was. "It's fine." He didn't need to coddle her. She looked young, younger than she actually was, but she was tough. A dozen or so stitches was only an inconvenience.

The wipers swished back and forth across the windshield in a steady rhythm, the fluffy flakes falling so fast and thick now that it looked like some kind of Star Trek warp speed special effect against the beams from the headlights. The old logging road continued twisting back and forth in a series of steep switchbacks down the mountainside, its origins probably dating back a hundred years or more to the timber boom in this part of the state. With each hairpin turn she braced herself against her door to keep from banging her wound.

The snow fell harder and soon they were forced to slow to what seemed like a crawl. "So much for the flurries they forecasted for the next few hours. It's a damn whiteout," he muttered, straining to see the road in front of him.

The silver lining in all this was that Briar's would-be assassin, whoever they were, was trapped in this too. With any luck the storm would give her enough time to get out of the area and give them some breathing room, if not an outright clear path to Glenwood Springs with no one tailing them.

After he rounded yet another tight turn, the back wheels sliding despite the chains and four wheel drive transmission, up ahead in the distance Briar could see the faint red glow of tail lights. As they drew nearer she saw that it was actually a lineup of about a half dozen or so vehicles.

DeLuca got on the radio to the drivers of the two SUVs behind them. "Tuck, you pull ahead and check it out. Bauer and I'll hang back."

"Roger that," the other man replied. Brad Tucker, former Delta operator and now assault team leader. Engaged to FBI Special Agent Celida Morales, who worked in the domestic terrorism division. Briar had seen her when they'd gotten into the SUV. She knew the woman and her boss, Travers, had wanted to question her and was glad they hadn't gotten the opportunity.

Briar kept checking their surroundings as Tuck's SUV passed them on the narrow road and pulled ahead. The chances of the sniper finding them in this storm were small but she wasn't letting her guard down and DeLuca was being vigilant as well.

A few minutes later Tuck came back over the radio.

"Two vehicle accident up ahead where this road meets the highway. Only one alternating lane's getting through at the site and they've closed the highway down completely about a quarter mile from the highway entrance due to the weather. Everyone's being diverted into town until morning."

Great, Briar thought sourly.

"All right," DeLuca said. "I'm gonna hang back from you until we clear this snarl. Evers'll stay behind me. We'll find a motel in town, stay there for the night and move out as soon as the road reopens. Hopefully before sunup."

Briar agreed. She'd prefer moving in the darkness as well.

"Roger that," Tuck answered.

Briar blew out a breath and fought back her impatience at being stranded all night in Golden. She was an expert navigator. Maybe once the storm let up a little she could head out on foot then find another vehicle to take her the rest of the way to Glenwood Springs. Staying put all night in a motel wasn't a good idea, not even with an entire HRT there to protect her. She needed to keep moving, put distance between herself and her would-be killer, bodyguard detail or not.

Neither of them spoke again until they reached Golden. Tuck had called ahead and managed to get them some rooms. The motel was booked solid for the night and the parking lot was packed. DeLuca divvied up the room assignments and told her he was staying with her. She'd expected it, though it was going to make slipping out unnoticed harder. If DeLuca insisted on waiting for the roads to clear even after sunup, she was moving out on her own, orders to accept his protection or not.

They stayed in the idling vehicle on the road across from the motel while two of the team members, Vance and Blackwell, went inside to get the room keys. They checked the room she'd be staying in with DeLuca and a few minutes later one of them appeared at the top of the stairs leading to the second floor, waving them up. DeLuca pulled up as close as he could get to the stairs and three guys escorted her upstairs to the room. Total overkill but she didn't say anything.

Inside she found the curtains already drawn over the windows. She closed and locked the door behind her and glanced around the room. It smelled slightly musty and the carpet and bedspreads on the two double beds looked worn. Not that she minded. What she minded was being stuck in here with a near stranger for the night, forced to deal with awkward silences and making small talk to alleviate the tension.

Social niceties weren't her strong suit. She'd flexed her social muscles to the max back at the security conference in New Orleans, the whole time wishing she could crawl out of her own skin just to escape all the people. She'd done enough forced socializing there to last her a year at least.

She was sitting on the bed when footsteps sounded outside on the concrete stairs. A fist rapped on the door twice. "It's Matt," he announced, then put the key in the lock and opened the door.

A gust of wind came through with him. He was carrying a duffel and her pack. He shut and locked the door, then set the bags down on the floor and glanced around before settling his gaze on her.

Just like that, the room seemed to shrink in half. She was acutely aware of his size, the sound of his steady breaths in the sudden quiet, the scent of the wind he brought with him. He was an attractive, intensely masculine man and all those things were impossible to ignore.

Realizing she was staring, Briar jerked her gaze away and folded her hands in her lap. She wasn't good with people, hated being made to feel awkward because of it.

"How are those stitches doing?"

She glanced up at the question, surprised that he'd care, let alone ask. "Fine."

He studied her for a moment. "Better go take a look, just to make sure. Schroder's the best but I rushed him with the stitching. You should check to see if the bleeding's stopped."

She'd planned on that, but hadn't wanted to leave the door unguarded until he came back. Rising, she headed for the bathroom.

"Want this?" he asked, picking up her pack.

She went back for it, took it with a murmur of thanks then hurried to the bathroom. With the door locked she set her pack on the linoleum floor and lifted the cut edge of her bodysuit to peel off the bandage. The tape came away from her skin easily enough and the row of stitches seemed solid. Her skin was puckered and red around the edges but it looked like the bleeding had stopped except for some seepage, probably from when she'd been jostled around on the drive down the mountain.

DeLuca knocked on the door. "Got you some clothes to change into if you want."

Briar eyed herself in the mirror. The custom-made bodysuit was ruined and crusted with blood. Her pack held an extra pair of gloves, another knit cap and some socks. Great for helping her retain warmth in the field but not a lot of help in the wardrobe department. She opened the door, saw he was holding a T-shirt and sweat pants.

"They'll be way too big, but they're better than nothing and they'll help keep you warm."

"Thanks." She took them, noticed the way his gaze dipped to her side and felt a strange stirring at the hint of concern she saw there.

"Still holding together?"

"Yeah, it looks good."

"I'll help you get a fresh bandage on there and seal it up so you can shower. If you want," he added.

She debated that for about two seconds before giving in. She wasn't going anywhere for at least the next few hours and as she was grimy and had dried blood all over her right side and hip, a shower sounded like heaven. "Okay."

Briar peeled away the cut and torn edges of the white bodysuit while he went to grab some supplies. He set a small kit on the counter and ripped open a package of gauze bandages. This close she could smell the faint scent of soap on his skin and see the way the muscles in his thick forearms flexed with each movement. His hands were strong, the fingers long and lean, nails clean and cut short.

His fingertips brushed her bare skin as he put the bandage in place and she was unprepared for the jolt of sensation that shot through her. She froze, looked into his face as butterflies took flight in her stomach, hoping he hadn't noticed her reaction. He stared back at her with those bright green eyes that she now realized had a band of caramel around the pupils, his face only inches from hers. And even though she was inexperienced with men, she clearly read the answering flare of male awareness there.

Pulse kicking erratically, she forced her gaze to the floor and held the ripped edges of cloth out of the way so he could put the pad in place and secure it with medical tape. The tiny bathroom suddenly seemed charged with a different sort of tension, one unfamiliar to her yet not altogether unwelcome. Which made no sense whatsoever, because she didn't want to be attracted to him or anyone else. Shit, how long until she could be on her own again?

DeLuca surprised her by pulling out a roll of duct tape and pulling a strip off. "Stuff has a million uses," he said when he saw the startled look on her face, the corners of his eyes crinkling slightly in a hidden smile. He measured off a short section, ripped it with his even, white teeth and laid it crosswise over the bandage. The light pressure of his fingertips as he pressed the tape in place set off a wave of goose bumps. Briar swallowed and fought the urge to squirm as tingles scattered across her skin, her nipples tightening.

He tore another strip and overlapped the previous piece with it. Then another, and another, until he'd completely covered the bandage. "There," he said, tossing the tape back into the kit and zipping it shut. "That'll keep it dry for the shower. Take it off when you come out though, so it can breathe. Schroder said he gave you a shot of antibiotics but you should still take precautions to make sure it doesn't get infected."

"I know." It came out way grumpier than she meant it to.

His expression shuttered and he stepped back. "Take your time. I'll grab us some food when you're done."

Briar turned the shower on as hot as she could stand it and scrubbed herself clean. It was bliss, even if her side was throbbing like hell and she felt bruised all over. Simple pleasures like hot showers and clean beds were things most people took for granted but they were luxuries she looked forward to most when she returned home from an op.

When she was done she toweled off and used the motel hair dryer to dry her hair. She put her bra back on but tossed her blood-stained panties and put on the clean clothes. They smelled like fabric softener and the same soap she'd detected on DeLuca. The black T-shirt hung to mid-thigh and she had to roll the waistband of the pants over four times to keep them from falling off her hips, then roll up the cuffs twice. When she emerged from the bathroom she found DeLuca looking through a phone book.

"There's not much in the way of restaurants here. I'll send one of the guys to pick us all up something. You okay with soup and sandwiches?"

"Sure." Her stomach rumbled.

He set the phone book down and she was struck again by how attractive he was. "Any preferences?"

"As long as I don't have to eat organ meat, I'm good."

His lips twitched. "No organs. Roger."

She noticed the edge of what looked like a laptop sitting in his open duffel. "Is that thing secure?"

He followed her gaze. "Secure enough." He looked back at her. "We're supposed to go Stone Age, remember?"

"I need to check something. Lily needs to know we've been delayed and I can reach her through someone else." And she needed to reach out to her old friend to see if she'd heard any chatter about the Ramadi op yet.

He raised an eyebrow. "Someone you're willing to trust with your life?"

"Yes."

The blunt answer seemed to surprise him. After a second he got up and brought the laptop to her. He booted it up, seemed to be teasing her when he turned the screen away and tapped in his password, his gaze on her. "There," he said, turning it back to her. "You're not going to hack anything, are you?"

"No, I just want to see if anything's shown up in the press or not." Hacking wasn't her specialty anyway. That was one of Trinity's many talents.

He pushed it toward her. "Be my guest."

He stayed on the edge of the bed while she checked some news sites, and dammit, when he was this close she found it hard to concentrate. Pretending her body wasn't buzzing with awareness, she clicked from one site to the next, relieved when nothing about Ramadi showed up. "Nothing's been leaked. Yet," she added before accessing one of her e-mail accounts. It was encrypted and registered to an alias, and only two other people knew about it.

Her heart thudded when she saw that Trinity had left a flagged message for her.

Saw this and had to check with you. Did you hear about it?

The time stamp was dated nine hours ago. Briar had gone dark two days ago and hadn't been able to access any media since. She clicked on the link.

Suspect Linked to Ibrahim Ramadi Dies

Surprise flashed through her, followed by dread when she saw the picture below the headline. Instant recognition flooded her. Jerry. A company asset and Iraqi-immigrant informant she'd been in contact with prior to the op. He'd been the one to give her Ramadi's location and tell her when he'd be at the cabin.

She quickly read the story, her alarm growing by the second. Jerry had been driving home on the highway from his job as an IT tech outside of Boulder when his vehicle had slammed straight into the concrete supports of an overpass, killing him instantly. Police blamed high speed and believed he'd been drunk, as his blood alcohol levels were three times the legal limit. Preliminary reports suggested his brakes might have malfunctioned, exacerbated by the reduced reaction time from the alcohol.

Except Jerry was a devout Muslim who would never touch a drop of alcohol, and he'd just picked up his car that afternoon from a tune-up at the shop.

Cold settled in her gut. Had someone drugged him and cut his brake lines?

The timing was too coincidental, and he wasn't the first company asset to die in mysterious circumstances in the past few months. An asset from the Al-Tunisi investigation had died of an apparent fall from his third floor Baton Rouge apartment the night after Briar had eliminated Al-Tunisi. The asset hadn't been a careless sort of man, so Briar had trouble imagining him falling over his balcony railing in the middle of the night.

She closed the program and typed a short response back to Trinity.

Thanks for the tip. Won't be in contact for a bit. Busy at work. Her oldest friend would know exactly what that meant. *Tell Lily I've been delayed. Will get in touch when I can. Hugs.*

Aware that DeLuca was watching and reading everything, she shut the laptop down and closed the lid.

"What's wrong?" he asked.

Feeling his gaze on her, she turned her head and looked over her shoulder at him. He was watching her closely, a slight frown creasing his eyebrows. "Nothing," she lied. "Just…an acquaintance was killed in a car accident tonight."

Hours after meeting with her in Boulder, she realized with growing trepidation. Where she'd stayed for the two nights prior to leaving for Golden.

Chapter Five

When the phone rang early the next morning Matt rolled over in bed and grabbed it from the nightstand before the first ring ended. Tuck calling. "Yeah."

"Just got word the highway's open again."

He rubbed his fingers over his eyes as he finished waking up. "'Kay. Thanks." It was just after four in the morning. He'd stayed up watching a national news station with Briar until almost two before he'd finally convinced her to get some sleep. Thankfully there'd been no mention of the Ramadi hit, or the man dying in Boulder.

With Briar just coming off an op and needing to recover from the gunshot wound, sleep was the most important thing for her right now. Yet it was clear she still didn't trust him because she hadn't let herself go into a deep sleep, merely stealing little snatches of it before opening her eyes to check her surroundings. And she was wide awake now, and from the looks of it, had been for some time.

"Want us to grab you guys some coffee?" Tuck asked. "Stuff in the lobby is shit but there's a place across the street Blackwell hit last night that he said was pretty good."

"I'll ask. Hang on." He put the receiver to his chest and looked at Briar, who was seated on the floor cleaning her rifle and pistols for the second time since checking in last night. He knew she still hadn't slept enough, and understood why. She was antsy as hell about the delay and anxious to get moving. "The road's open."

A look of sheer relief flashed across her face. "Thank God."

"You want some coffee? Something to eat for the road? One of my guys can grab us something."

"Sure, coffee would be great. Nothing too heavy to eat though. Just some fruit or a muffin. Thanks," she added as an afterthought, glancing up at him through her lashes.

The effort at politeness was a nice change from her icy detachment. He'd never met such a self-contained woman. Her aloof manner just made him want to uncover all her secrets. "Cream? Sugar?"

"Both. Please." This time she didn't look up at him.

"Two coffees with cream and sugar, some fruit, muffins and sandwiches to go," he told Tuck. Because she needed something more than just fruit and a muffin to get her through the day if they couldn't stop for more supplies.

"You got it. Be over in a few minutes."

Matt placed the receiver back into its cradle and pushed into a sitting position. Briar had already packed her weapons into her ruck, he saw, save for the one pistol she was tucking into the back of her waistband. He watched as she pushed to her feet, her face pulling tight for a moment at the motion. "How're you feeling?"

"Little stiff," she admitted. She glanced toward the bathroom, then at him. "Mind if I...?"

"Go ahead. You need me to cover your bandage

again first?"

Briar paused. "Um, sure." She closed the small distance between them, averting her eyes when she got close and turned so he could see her side as she lifted the hem of the shirt up her ribs.

She'd taken the duct tape off her bandage last night after her shower to let it breathe. Blue and purple bruising spread out from beneath the edges of the gauze, and those were just the ones he could see. She had to be damn sore. "I'm gonna check first to make sure it's not getting infected."

She nodded and didn't say anything, still looking away from him.

Matt carefully grasped one corner of a piece of medical tape he'd used to adhere it to her skin. The moment he touched her, goose bumps broke out across her ribs. The thermostat on the wall was set at seventy-two degrees and his hands were warm, so it wasn't because she was cold. For some reason he liked knowing she wasn't as unaffected by him as she'd like him to think.

He peeled the tape back to take a look. The wound was red and a little swollen but there was no drainage or red streaks around it. "Looks okay. I'll cover it up now."

As he tore pieces of duct tape and laid them across the bandage, he let his fingertips linger against her skin. He liked the feel of it, all warm and silky beneath his fingers. She was lean and toned with the body of a competitive athlete, and lethal despite her deceptively non-threatening appearance. A very deadly weapon, wrapped in a gorgeous package.

When he continued to take his time covering the bandage, fingertips resting gently on her skin, she tensed ever so slightly and at last turned her head to look at him over her shoulder. There was something he'd been wondering about and now seemed like as good a time as any to ask. "Why'd you send me that text in Baton

Rouge?"

She looked away again. "I knew you were in the area with Morales and Travers," she said with a shrug, as though it was no big deal. "Al-Tunisi was a high priority target, and since I'd already met you in person and Rycroft trusts you I figured I'd give you the heads up. How'd you know it was me?"

"I recognized you during analysis of the satellite feed after the op."

At that she swung her gaze back to him and frowned. "You saw my face?"

"Not well, not even when they zoomed in and tightened the focus, but yeah. Based on the text, proximity to New Orleans and having met you—" *And remembering every little detail about the way you look, because what man wouldn't.* "—I knew it was you."

"Who else knew?" She didn't sound alarmed, merely curious. Probably because by the time he and the others had analyzed the footage, she'd no doubt been long gone from the area. From what he'd seen so far, she was damn good at her job.

"Nobody in my circle. I'm sure Rycroft and your people were alerted soon after though."

Briar nodded. "I contacted Lily to confirm Al-Tunisi's death before I caught my flight out that night."

He was insanely curious about her, and what made a woman like her tick. He'd met one Russian and several female Israeli assassins in his day, but never an American. He wanted to know about her background, who had trained her, and how. Why she'd chosen that line of work and how she balanced her personal life with her work. Not that he'd probably ever find those things out. "Flight to where?"

"Home."

"Where's that?"

"New York State."

He nodded, somewhat surprised that she'd told him, but he wondered if it was the truth. "I'm from California."

"San Diego."

His gaze cut to hers, his fingers paused on her skin below a strip of tape. "How do you know that?" he asked. Touching her like this was no hardship. Her skin was velvety and smooth, so soft. Actually, everything about her looked soft, except for her eyes. Those were a dead giveaway that she'd been in combat and seen people die, some of them by her hand. It always took a toll, no matter how well a sniper compartmentalized everything.

Eventually it caught up with you. He wondered if she ever battled with her inner demons.

"I read your file."

Well, hell. Matt frowned. He didn't like being at that kind of disadvantage.

"Don't worry, I'd never divulge anything in there to anyone. Your record's impressive. You must be proud."

He was, but it still rankled him that she'd read up on him and he knew next to nothing about her. Matt put the last piece of tape in place, suddenly wanting to know everything about her. "There. You're good to go."

She let the hem of the shirt drop. "Thanks. I'll be quick."

She disappeared into the bathroom and a moment later he heard the shower running. Less than ten minutes later she came back out, her dark hair still a bit damp as it fell against her cheeks and jaw. His shirt and sweats swallowed her slender frame, yet somehow she still managed to look sexy.

And he had to stop thinking about her that way. She was his principle. A job.

Matt got up, walked over to his duffel at the foot of the bed and took out a bottle of ibuprofen. His right shoulder that he'd dislocated in training years ago bothered him sometimes, especially in the cold and damp, so he always kept some with him. "Here," he said, holding the bottle out to her.

"Thanks." She took three tablets and took out a bottle of water.

He was just heading to the bathroom for his own shower when a knock sounded on the door and a familiar voice called out. "It's Tuck. Breakfast delivery."

Matt let him in and took the tray of to-go cups and brown paper bag from him. "Here," he said, handing Tuck a twenty. "Tell Blackwell thanks."

"Will do." Tuck put his hands in his pockets and glanced between him and Briar. "So what's the plan? Still want us to follow you for a bit then turn back for Denver?"

Matt nodded. "Yeah, that works. Just need to make sure no one's following us out here. I'll be off the grid for a few days at least."

Tuck nodded and focused on Briar. "You need anything before you head out? Want Schroder to come take a look at you?"

"No, I'm good. He did a good job." She flashed a little smile at the team leader, the hint of a dimple appearing in her right cheek.

A twinge of something like jealousy flared inside Matt, taking him off guard. He didn't like her being more comfortable around Tuck than she was with him. Especially when he was the one sticking his neck out for her and they were going to be alone for at least the next day or two. Moreover, he didn't like being attracted to a woman who preferred to ignore him.

Since Lisa's death he'd slept with just three women, two of them hookups and one he'd dated for a few months. The hookups had left him feeling guilty and lonelier than he'd felt since losing his wife, and the dating thing hadn't worked out because of his job. His work schedule was insane at the best of times and though she'd been a nice woman, she hadn't been able to handle it.

Though to be honest, his heart hadn't been involved the way it should have been. Sometimes he thought that part of him had died along with Lisa.

Briar was the first woman who'd interested him in almost a year, and he had about as much chance of getting together with her as he did of getting Lisa back. He told himself that was a good thing. She was way younger than him, she was now under his protection and she was the most closed-off woman he'd ever met.

In addition to all her other secrets, he knew Briar was keeping something big from him and it had to do with that article he'd skimmed over her shoulder a few hours ago. He wasn't sure who she'd contacted after reading it but it was clear Briar didn't trust easily so whoever it was, they were important to her. He'd bet she let very few people get that close to her.

That made it doubly disconcerting for him to want to be one of them.

Time to go. "Okay, I'll grab a quick shower and then we'll get moving," he told her and Tuck.

The sooner he could get her to the safe house, the sooner he could go back to his own life and forget all about her.

****

Will Balducci was a man with a mission.

This morning he'd risen at four to hit the gym, run his daily standard of five miles then oversaw the final arrangements he'd put in place. A simple matter of signing and filing some paperwork. Some of the pieces he'd needed to set this in motion had been complicated but he'd managed to pull it off and within a few hours he'd be able to move forward without ever looking back. He had far more important things on his mind now.

The country had gone to shit under the previous and

current administrations and he was looking forward to helping reinstate it to its former glory. The United States had once been the glowing example of democracy and prosperity in the world, its armed forces feared by its enemies and respected around the world. He and his like-minded patriots were going to elevate it to that standard again.

Will straightened his bowtie and tugged at the cuffs of his black tux jacket before checking his reflection in the full-length mirror in his upscale hotel suite. At forty-nine he was still in good shape and had a full head of hair, albeit graying slightly around his temples. The Navy was responsible for his confident posture and bearing.

It had also given him the tools to embark on this next phase of his life.

He studied the view revealed in the mirror, liking what he saw. This suite was the best money could buy in New York City. It cost triple what a regular one did at this swanky hotel but the added privacy, security and level of discretion practiced by the staff made it worth the exorbitant price. The woman he'd brought back with him for the evening—an infrequent indulgence he'd begun two years ago—had been quietly ushered from the room by his bodyguard at just after midnight, and the security footage of her presence erased. Besides, money was no object right now, and shouldn't be for the rest of his life as long as his carefully planned investments gave even a paltry return.

The man reflected in the mirror looked rich and powerful, imposing, and Will had been meticulous in honing that very image. Money and power talked in every culture on earth, but especially in the world of Washington politics. One thing he'd learned early on was that if he wanted people to take him seriously when he announced his intention to run for Senate, then he had to look as well as act the part.

Tucking his hand-written notes into the breast pocket of his jacket, he picked up his phone from the marble counter of the vanity and checked the many messages and e-mails he'd received overnight after he'd silenced his phone. Officers had contacted him from the NSA, DHS, FBI and CIA. One or two of whom he'd worked with in contract and paramilitary work before taking an office job with The Company.

Some congratulated him and wished him well on his early retirement; other messages were work related.

It didn't surprise him that a large portion of the remaining e-mails had to do with the new situation with Briar Jones that had happened in the past hour. He'd timed it that way.

He was even less surprised with the angry response and demand for a retraction from her handler.

Not likely.

But one text stood out from all the others and made him pause, a frown pulling at his forehead. From an unknown number, the only message a minus sign bracketed by asterisks.

Jones was still alive.

Shit.

This was the fucking last thing he needed to deal with this morning. He typed back a brusque reply to the operative and hit send.

Deal with it. Now.

He didn't need to elaborate on what would happen if Jones wasn't eliminated in the next few hours.

Already his mind was thinking three steps ahead. Will had been so careful but he couldn't leave this new development to chance. He'd have to use an outside contract agent to take out the assassin he'd sent after Jones. Otherwise there were too many unknowns happening all at once and he couldn't risk someone exposing him.

Unfortunately Jones was smart and so was her damn handler. They were all capable of ruining his plans so they'd all have to go.

Will took out a burner phone from his briefcase that couldn't be traced to him and made two calls. Within ten minutes he had what he needed and wired the deposit from his offshore account to the new man he'd hired. Next he deleted all his messages and e-mails, immediately putting them out of his mind. He couldn't dwell on what was happening with Jones, he had the most important speech of his life to prepare for.

D.C.'s wealthy and political elite were attending this brunch in New York to celebrate his upcoming retirement next weekend. His wife would be in attendance also. Currently Barbara was being pampered in the city's most expensive and exclusive spa, where he'd booked her last minute for the past two days with one call to a contact.

Being connected in his power circle had its advantages for almost anything and as an intelligence officer of some repute he'd long ago perfected the art of knowing how to manipulate people to get what he wanted. His marriage, while not perfect for either of them in many aspects, was necessary to his political career. He'd made sure Barb understood that early on, and that she knew how to play her part. In return she'd live the life of a socialite, attending various social events with the country's most powerful people. Something she'd always wanted. Her loyalty to him had never wavered, and he was thankful for that.

Voters expected their candidates to be settled, responsible, trustworthy. Staying married was necessary to project that image, and it was in his personality to never quit anyway. He had a reputation for being uncompromising on his positions and he was proud of that.

Will fastened the buttons on his jacket and smoothed

a hand down the front of it. His wife might not be in love with him anymore the way she had been when they'd first married, nor he with her, but she sure as hell was in love with the money they had now. Easily ten times what he'd made in his best years with The Company. All of it earned in side ops that were off the books and decidedly on the dark side of the gray scale that made up the American legal system.

Manipulating the system wasn't that hard, if you knew how to play the game. After all this time running clandestine ops all over the world from both sides of the desk, he was an expert. Barb knew that damaging his image would have severe repercussions for them both and that if she ever tried to divorce him, their prenup would leave her back where she'd started. As long as he was discreet about his affairs and didn't embarrass her with a public scandal, she would stay with him. Their marriage might not be perfect but it was a hell of a lot better than most in Washington.

He'd just tucked his phone into his pants pocket when it vibrated with another incoming message. Pulling it out, he was annoyed to see yet another e-mail from Jones's handler. This one was the angriest yet, the accusation clear.

This is wrong and you know it.

Will almost snorted. Did she seriously think he was afraid of her, or that anyone would believe her if she tried something so stupid as to accuse him of hanging Jones out to dry? He had solid proof about Jones's actions and the handler had nothing. His fingers tightened around the phone as a jolt of anger surged through him. She would never find anything to prove he was linked to all this, least of all directly responsible for setting up this situation with Jones.

No one would ever trace this back to him, least of all a female Clandestine Services officer who somehow still didn't understand shit about the way things really worked in the intelligence world. Maybe what he'd done over the past fourteen months was on the wrong side of the law, technically speaking, and about to get uglier, but it was all in the interest of the greater good. The funds from his side ops would allow him to take charge and turn the country around. No one was going to get in his way now.

Will didn't reply to the message. He deleted it and used a custom-made encryption program in his phone to make it disappear forever, then blocked both her e-mail and phone accounts. He wasn't too worried about her.

She wouldn't be a concern much longer anyway.

Slipping his wallet and room key into his other pants pocket, Will whistled the first few bars of his favorite tune as he walked to the door, excitement bubbling in his veins. He'd been looking forward to this for so long and was finally about to live his dream, free and clear of all the sins of his past.

Chapter Six

Twenty minutes into the drive, Briar was kicking herself for not getting more sleep last night. The rhythmic motion of the tires on the snowy road and the steady swish of the wipers were already making her drowsy.

Maybe she shouldn't have insisted she drive, but she was flying her control freak flag high and proud and refused to apologize for it. She was surprised that DeLuca hadn't argued though. Most men in his position would have flat out refused or at least put up a fight before relinquishing their spot in the driver's seat. Or at least they did in her experience. She had a feeling he was just picking his battles with her.

She tightened her grip on the steering wheel and kept glancing in the side and rearview mirror every so often but as far as she could tell the only vehicles behind them were the two carrying DeLuca's team. They'd checked all the vehicles for tracking beacons before leaving the motel as a precaution. "I think we're clear."

"Yep." Seated beside her in the passenger seat, DeLuca reached up and tapped his earpiece. The gold wedding band on his left hand caught the dashboard lights. She had to admit she was curious about that. She knew he'd lost his wife four years ago and nothing in his file had said anything about him remarrying, so the ring must be from his first marriage. If he still wore it, he must have loved his wife very much. Maybe he still did.

"Okay, Tuck, I think we're good. You guys can turn back any time now. I'll call you when I get to Quantico, probably in a few days." After ending communication with his team he took the earpiece out and slipped it into his jacket pocket.

Briar watched in the mirrors as the tailing vehicles turned off at the next junction. She couldn't see any headlights behind them.

They were on their own and totally dark, as ordered.

Breathing a little easier now that they didn't have an entourage to announce her presence, she shifted her grip on the wheel and settled back against the seat. It felt strange to be making this trip with DeLuca, knowing they'd be staying alone at the house together. The pre-dawn sky was still dark and heavy with clouds unleashing the predicted flurries but the eastern horizon behind them was getting brighter by the minute. No matter how good she was, she didn't like moving out in the open in broad daylight in an area she'd just operated in. It made her feel too exposed.

"Roads aren't too bad," DeLuca commented, holding his coffee cup in one hand. She'd finished hers half an hour ago and the jolt of caffeine was already waning. "At this pace we should be there within a couple hours."

"Yeah," she answered, mostly to avoid being rude, but also hoping the one word response was a clear indicator that she wasn't interested in having a conversation. Problem was, she couldn't shut off her awareness of him and it irritated her.

Considering the kinds of jobs she usually performed, a few hours' drive with him should be easy, but it wasn't. They had at least two more hours alone in the vehicle together with nothing but the radio to break the subtle tension simmering between them. Briar found his calm, decisive and confident manner hot as hell. Knowing he was a good guy on top of all that and adding in his looks, just being in the same room with him pinged her internal radar.

He didn't seem to be bothered by her unwillingness to talk, but he unnerved her and that wasn't normal for her. She didn't know how to handle her growing attraction to him, except to ignore it.

She knew he must have questions, and that she'd have to give him *some* answers sooner or later. It'd been so long since she'd trusted an outsider she wasn't even sure if she was capable of it anymore, even though she'd read his file and he had both Lily's and Alex's approval. Some lessons learned the hard way were impossible to forget, however, and after her ex's betrayal she didn't know if she could ever open up to another man again.

"When we get there, you need to sleep."

She raised an eyebrow at the order, even though she knew he was right. And that deep voice of his was freaking sexy.

He glanced over at her, his expression completely unapologetic, all that dark stubble on his face turning up her long-forgotten libido. "I could see why you didn't want to crash last night, but once we're squared away at the house there's no reason for you to be on guard anymore. Besides, there's another storm front moving in and it's supposed to dump double the amount of snow we got last night. Wherever Lily's coming from, it'll probably delay her arrival. Staying up any longer than you have to is just going to set back your recovery, and there's no reason for it if I'm there to take over."

He was right, but she didn't like being told what to do by a near stranger, let alone depending on one, no matter how capable he was. "Once I'm sure everything's locked down tight, I probably will." Maybe. She knew how to handle sleep deprivation. She could probably go another twelve hours or so if necessary.

He sipped his coffee and was quiet a few minutes before speaking again. "So how do you want this to go? You want to talk only when necessary? Or would you rather things be a little friendlier than that? We're gonna be together for a few days. It'd be easier if we can get along well enough to be in each other's space without things being awkward. You good with that?"

Her stomach muscles tensed at his blunt assessment. "I guess."

He didn't seem to take offense at her less than enthusiastic reply. "Okay, so let's break the ice a bit. I'll go first. I love the San Diego Chargers and classic rock. You?"

His choice of topic took her off guard. She'd been certain he would want something bigger from her, far more personal, though he was likely working his way up to that and hoping to get her talking. He kept staring at her, apparently expecting a reply. *Fine.*

"I'm not a sports fan. I like a lot of different kinds of music, and I only use a bolt action rifle because they're the best."

His lips curved upward at the last part and the grin set off a weird fluttering sensation in her belly. Damn butterflies. "So we do have something in common after all."

She snorted. Of course they did, or Janaia would never have set this up. "Lily didn't want you to come with me just because of your service record and current position."

"No?" He sounded curious and vaguely amused.

She shot him a sidelong glance. "Lily thought I'd be more comfortable with you since we'd already met and everything. She figured you being a former sniper would make it easier for us to relate to each other." Or something like that, anyway. Because no way Janaia had just chosen him at random.

"Yeah, 'cuz we're so tight we're practically finishing each other's sentences already," he said dryly.

Briar couldn't help but grin in response. "Well, I know that's why she requested you." She darted another glance at him. He was a powerful, commanding man, and had a disconcerting ability of distracting her by simply being near. She shouldn't care what he thought of her, but somehow she did. "I just…I'm used to working alone. I'm not good with people." It was why they'd tapped her to be a sniper when she entered the program.

He nodded once. "Fair enough. So, where are you from?"

"All over." The vague and defensive answer was automatic. Normally she just gave people her standard cover story but for some reason she didn't feel comfortable outright lying to him.

"Okay, then where were you born?"

That was pretty harmless too. "L.A."

His eyebrows rose. "Really? I lived there for a while before joining the Corps."

"I know."

Another smile, this one with the hint of a deep, ironic chuckle that seemed to vibrate inside her. The man was both sexy and charming, making it difficult to ignore him and the effect he had on her. "Right. My file."

He took another sip of coffee, seeming totally calm. Patient. As though nothing could ruffle him. She'd bet very few things ever did. He'd never realize it, but Briar had studied him carefully back in New Orleans. A few times up close when she'd had the occasion to actually speak to him in person, but other times from afar. Something about the way he moved, the way he carried himself with that calm self-assurance, drew her. Having observed him that intently, she could see why he'd been such an effective sniper and why he'd wound up in command of the HRT.

"You said you live in New York State. Whereabouts?" he asked, digging subtly enough that it didn't feel like he was interrogating her.

She hesitated a moment, then surprised herself by answering, deciding to trust him that much. "Small place in the country."

His lips twitched at her evasive answer. "Been living there long?"

She shook her head, for some reason not annoyed by his fishing. "Few years." Almost two and that meant it was time to move again soon. Staying in one place too long was dangerous for someone in her line of work, as were personal attachments. Another reason why she didn't mind telling him, since she wouldn't be with him for more than a couple days and she wasn't staying in New York much longer.

He reached out to adjust a heat vent in the dashboard, his long fingers pushing the button upward. He'd touched her so gently when he'd changed her bandage and covered it. She couldn't help but wonder what those fingers would feel like all over her naked skin. "You have family there?" he asked.

"No. No family at all." He turned his head to look at her but thankfully didn't press for more. To deflect the question and show basic manners, she lobbed it back to him. "What about you?" As soon as she said it she inwardly cringed. The man had lost his *wife*. She shouldn't have brought up his family.

"My parents and an older sister. A whole bunch of aunts, uncles, cousins and my in-laws. Pretty tight-knit family, on both sides. My job doesn't let me see everyone as much as I'd like, but we all keep in touch."

Briar found it telling that he still had such close ties to his in-laws.

He was silent for a long moment, swallowing a sip of his coffee as he stole another glance at her. "How old are you?"

"How old do you think?"

Rather than dodge the question like it was some sort of landmine, he studied her for a few heartbeats. The feel of that intense green gaze on her sent a wave of warmth over her skin, pooling deep in her abdomen. It was disconcerting as hell. "Twenty-five."

"Nope. Twenty-nine. People always think I'm younger than I am." She eyed him. "How old are you?"

He raised his eyebrows at her in silent challenge. "You read my file but didn't bother with that part?"

She shrugged, wanting to see if he'd tell her.

"Forty-one." He lifted his ball cap off and ran a hand over his chocolate-brown hair, revealing the slight graying at the temples. "So what branch did you serve with when you first started out, anyway?"

She shifted in her seat, covering a wince as her stitches pulled. Maybe she should have taken the no-talking option. Except then she wouldn't have gotten to learn more about him and enjoy his deep voice as he revealed more of himself to her. *So worth it.* "It's...complicated."

DeLuca never looked away. "I'm sure it is, and I'll bet it's one hell of an interesting story. Maybe you'll tell me about it sometime."

Briar didn't dare look at him. The man affected her more than any other had in years. She had the feeling he could uncover all her secrets—that he could make her *want* to divulge all her secrets if she wasn't careful. "Maybe."

When silence spread between them this time it was devoid of the lingering tension that had been there initially. She smiled to herself. He was much more personable than she'd realized. He had a way of making her at ease, to feel less awkward than she usually did around people. Hell, now he had her *wanting* to keep talking. No easy feat. "Bet you're good at interrogation."

"I'm not bad," he said with a shrug and looked her way again. "But with you I'd rather find out what I want to know without having to resort to coercion."

Something about the way he said *coercion* held a sexual undertone even she couldn't miss. Subtle, and far more intriguing than if he'd been more heavy-handed or obvious about it. She had no trouble imagining that when he used his brand of *coercion* on a woman, she'd be putty in his hands. Even she wasn't immune to his quiet, confident charm.

Briar had to be careful not to let her guard slip too much around him. She didn't fear him as a threat to her safety, but she was starting to think that he would prove a hell of a lot of trouble for her heart if she let him in.

Nope. Never again. She'd learned her lesson the first time.

The rest of the drive passed more quickly than she'd believed possible under the circumstances, and by the time they reached Glenwood Springs she felt far more comfortable with the idea of letting DeLuca into her inner sanctum. He was always alert but she could tell he was cataloguing every turn as she wound her way into the hills above the town Doc Holiday had once lived in.

Dawn had just arrived, the leaden sky overhead unleashing flurries of large snowflakes. The big SUV's tires gripped the fresh snow easily, propelling them up the winding road. At the turnoff half a mile up the access road, her heart was already beating faster. The log home appeared in the distance as she cleared the grove of trees blocking the view from the road. No one outside of Briar, Janaia and her immediate family had ever been here. Janaia's husband had built this place for them the year after they'd been married. Not even The Company knew she owned it, since it was registered to a fake identity outside the U.S.

"Nice place," DeLuca commented.

It was breathtaking. The home was tucked away from the world up in the mountains, the nearest neighbor a quarter mile back down the road they'd just driven up. A wide lawn sloped down toward the two-lane gravel road, and from the deck there was a one-eighty view of the mountains, with the town nestled into the valley at the bottom. On clear nights during previous visits here she'd sat out on the front deck and watched the lights twinkle below.

There were no tire tracks or footprints in the snow leading up the long, curving driveway. No marks on the lawn or around the garage as she pulled around back. She parked under the covered carport and got out, scanning the house. All the windows were closed and covered by either blinds or curtains. The back door looked secure.

DeLuca followed her up the back steps to the main floor, watchful and vigilant. Briar felt a surprising rush of relief that he was taking her safety so seriously.

At the back door she punched in an access code. A panel in the wood slid open, revealing a biometric scanner. She placed her palm against it, waited a few seconds until a sharp beep sounded and the lock popped free. She could feel DeLuca watching her, knew he must be surprised by the advanced security. "I'll add your prints into the system later." And she'd erase them from the system before they left.

Twisting the knob, she opened the back door and immediately felt a rush of nostalgia as the familiar smells of pine and leather greeted her. "I'll show you around then we can unload the truck."

"Sounds good." He looked around the kitchen, a cozy room with exposed log walls and state-of-the-art stainless steel appliances. She led him through an entryway into the great room, a two-story wonder of gleaming, golden pine logs and a river rock fireplace that stretched from floor to ceiling. Soft leather couches with heirloom quilts draped over the backs framed the area, an oriental rug Briar had sent them from Pakistan covering the polished pine floor in front of the hearth.

"Wow," he said. "I didn't expect all this."

"I'll bet. It's my favorite place in the world and it's also very secure. There's a backup generator in case the power goes out but there's always plenty of firewood to burn and the stove and oven are gas, so we won't starve or freeze if the storm knocks the power out." There were also a whole lot of other bells and whistles here as well that she didn't intend to show him unless it became necessary.

She looked back to find him taking everything in, then his gaze stopped on the hand-carved mantel that displayed a series of framed pictures. Most showed a honey-blond woman and a dark-haired man with two young children, a boy and a girl. A few showed Briar with them. One of the largest was of her standing with the woman, their arms wrapped tight around each other, both of them beaming at the camera. She tensed, hating that her private life was being exposed to an outsider, even though she liked DeLuca.

His gaze slid to hers. "The woman in the pictures with you. This is her place."

Briar nodded. "Yes, her and her family's." He was going to find out anyway once Janaia arrived. She took a deep breath and told him the truth. "That's Janaia. Janaia *Lily* Grande. She's my handler."

He stared at her. "Not *just* your handler."

"No." Janaia was…everything to her. Her and her husband and beautiful kids. They were the closest thing Briar had known to family since she was orphaned at seven.

When he didn't say anything or ask more questions, Briar let out a breath of relief and showed him the rest of the place. A basement with a built-in bar and entertainment system, then upstairs where the master bedroom, both kids' rooms and a guest room took up the entire floor. Each bedroom had its own connecting bath and commanding views of the mountains. The ultimate vacation home.

A smile quirked DeLuca's mouth. "What if I never want to leave?"

She found herself smiling in return. "I wouldn't blame you." She slid her hands into her coat pockets. "So that's it. Once we're all locked in, we're pretty safe. And if anyone sets foot on the property, the system will alert us."

He nodded, still watching her. "I'll go unpack the truck."

"All right."

Down in the great room she lit the kindling beneath the logs waiting in the grate. DeLuca brought in his duffel and her ruck, as well as the few bags of groceries his guys had grabbed for them. Briar locked the door and set the security system, then put the food away. When she walked back into the great room, DeLuca was standing in front of the fireplace, his body silhouetted against the dancing flames. Since he couldn't see her, she allowed her gaze to drink him in, lingering on his broad shoulders and lean hips.

He glanced over his shoulder at her and for a moment she faltered, suddenly nervous at being alone with him here. A slight smile softened his face. "We all secure?"

She nodded and found her voice. "Everything's set

up." She looked away from him, her body humming from his masculine presence. Nerves danced in her belly. *Now what?* "You want some more coffee? I can make us—"

"Go to bed, Briar."

Her gaze snapped back to his. God, the way he said her name, all deep and sexy like that, made it feel like he'd trailed his fingers across her bare skin. "I'm okay for another few hours."

He shook his head. "Go crawl into one of those comfortable beds upstairs and get some sleep. You *need* it."

She knew she did. But…

Faint amusement glittered in his eyes, the corners crinkling slightly. "I've got this. And if anything happens, I'll come get you."

Briar hesitated. The need to stay vigilant and take care of herself was ingrained in her on the deepest level. It felt entirely wrong and bizarre to entrust her safety to someone else, and yet she knew DeLuca was more than capable of keeping her safe. Sparks danced in her stomach as she held his gaze, mixing with the flutters. She mentally shook herself. The sooner Janaia got here, the better.

"Okay, but only for a little while." Annoyed at herself and her instinctive reaction to him, she turned and headed up the stairs, feeling his gaze on her the whole way.

****

In the crude kitchen of the hunting cabin about a mile from the motel where the target had stayed the night, George booted up the laptop and used the special program to activate the tracking beacon. It was a new technology and practically undetectable since it was made up mostly of plastic components. Few metal detectors could find it, and it was so small it was easy to plant on a person or vehicle without any risk of someone seeing it.

The storm had shut the roads down but the target had been wounded and wouldn't have gone far anyhow. After searching the surrounding area and calling all the local motels and hotels, one front desk clerk had confirmed a group of big men escorting a woman into a room. All it had taken was that tip and a bit of recon and voila, George had the license plates of all three vehicles registered to the HRT.

Following such highly trained agents by vehicle would have been too dangerous, not to mention stupid. The orders were clear, to kill this rogue agent by any means necessary. A terse response had come in reply to the message George had sent, relaying that the target was still alive. The man behind this op was not happy about the turn of events and wanted everything taken care of within the next few hours.

All three of the possible target vehicles had left the motel just before four-thirty a.m. Two had turned off the highway about forty miles west of Golden and carried on to Denver. The remaining vehicle had continued west. It had to be the target's vehicle.

A few keystrokes and the beacon blinked in green on the screen from the satellite feed. The target was now in Glenwood Springs. Or rather, just outside of it.

George zoomed in with the satellite, the image on the ground obscured because of the heavy cloud cover. But it was enough. A single house on a big property in the hills outside of town. The lone vehicle, a dark SUV, was parked beneath what looked like a covered carport.

After memorizing the address and directions, George shut down the laptop, grabbed the gear by the back door and headed out in the snow to the pickup truck waiting in the driveway. It didn't matter how many HRT members were at the safe house acting as guards.

By nightfall the target would be dead and this job would be over.

Chapter Seven

Janaia checked for e-mails on her phone as she waited for the rental company to bring her vehicle around front. The sounds of traffic flowed around her, mixing with the murmur of voices in the office and the roar of jets landing and taking off at Denver International Airport.

There was nothing from that sanctimonious prick Balducci, and nothing from Briar. Not surprising, since the man was arrogant enough to think nothing could touch him, and Briar had gone dark with DeLuca last night. She *knew* Balducci was behind this, even if she couldn't prove it.

Yet.

But she would. No matter how long it took, she'd find what she needed and get justice for Briar.

Briar still had no idea what had happened over the past few hours, or that teams would have been dispatched to find and arrest her by now.

Janaia had to get to her before anyone else and figure out a way to fix this mess. No one seemed to want to help considering the evidence the CIA had against her friend, so Janaia would take care of this herself.

She tucked the phone back into her pocket when the woman behind the desk called her name.

"Someone's bringing your vehicle around for you now, ma'am. It's a black Ford Explorer."

"Thanks." Janaia wrapped her scarf tighter around her neck and slipped the strap of her backpack across her shoulder before stepping outside. The cold, brisk air seemed to sear her lungs for a moment. She'd been fighting a bug the past few days and her asthma always got worse in the cold. Winters in Colorado were not her friend.

Reaching into her pocket, she pulled out her inhaler and took a hit. Almost immediately her bronchioles dilated, allowing her to breathe easier, her chest already feeling looser.

The Explorer appeared around the corner and slowed at the curb closest to her. The driver's door opened and a man stepped out. Before he could say anything Janaia spoke. "I don't need a run through of everything, I'm good," she said, in a hurry to get to the house in Glenwood Springs. He stepped back without a word and walked toward the office, already tugging off his gloves.

Janaia slid behind the wheel, tossed her bag onto the passenger seat and shut the door. The interior was all toasty warm and she sighed at the feel of the seat heater warming her rear. It had a heated steering wheel too, she saw, so she took off her gloves and put them atop her bag. A few quick adjustments to the seat and steering wheel, and she was good to go.

She put the SUV into gear and turned out of the lot onto the airport access road. When she stopped at a light a minute later she noticed her chest had begun to feel inexplicably tight. Maybe the inhaler dosage hadn't been enough. She tugged her scarf away from her neck, but it didn't help ease the sensation that she was slowly being suffocated. She pulled out her inhaler, took another puff.

It didn't help.

Her heart started to pound as her airway closed off. Janaia gasped, struggling to draw in air. Her hands shook so hard she couldn't grip the steering wheel. The gasps turned to wheezes.

Panic set in.

She tore away her scarf and ripped the neckline of her sweater, her mouth opening and closing in an effort to breathe. Her vision began to blur. Horns blared in warning as the Explorer careened across the lanes of traffic. She jerked forward against the seatbelt when the vehicle slammed into a concrete support pillar. The airbag punched into her but she barely noticed, too busy clawing at her throat.

Help. I need help.

Blindly she undid her seatbelt buckle and groped for the door handle, managed to get it open. She fell out onto the road on her hands and knees as cars screeched to a halt around her.

No air.

Terror washed over her. She dropped onto her side on the frozen asphalt. Could feel the blood trapped in her face, her eyeballs bulging from the pressure, cold sweat coating her skin. Her stricken gaze shot back to the rental car office.

Help!

Then, through the panic, realization hit her.

The man. He'd been taking off his gloves as he walked away.

He'd killed her.

Denial and anguish exploded inside her. The world grayed, narrowed around her as her mouth opened and closed in a useless effort to suck in air.

Someone was crouched beside her, trying to turn her over onto her back. "Ma'am? Ma'am! Are you—she's choking. Help, she's choking!'"

Janaia rolled her eyes toward them, tried to form the words to beg for help. Tell them what had happened.

Poison.

Nothing came out.

The voices around her began to fade along with her vision. The front of her neck was bleeding from where her own fingernails had slashed her skin. Her husband and children's faces swam before her eyes.

No! No, I can't die here like this. My kids need me—

Her body convulsed once and the entire world went black.

****

Matt added more logs to the fire and stirred the embers to get the flames going. The house was slowly warming up but it was still cold away from the fireplace. And quiet. The kind of quiet that seemed to blanket everything, partly from the snow outside but he suspected the soundproofing in this place was solid too. Nothing but the pop and crackle of the flames filled the room.

Briar had been asleep for nearly eight hours now and it was almost dark outside. The expected storm had closed in just before noon and fat, fluffy flakes fell thick and fast from the low cloud deck.

It didn't surprise him that she'd crashed so hard. After everything that had happened and however long she'd been up before starting the op, she'd needed the sleep. He'd checked on her once and found her sound asleep in the king size bed in the master suite. She'd looked small and fragile lying there in the big bed, but he knew better. The woman was a force to be reckoned with.

In all his years in the business, he'd never met anyone like her. She'd hate knowing just how much she fired his protective instincts, but he couldn't control his instinctive need to shield her, watch over her. She'd said she had no family outside of Janaia's. Briar was hurt and exhausted and on the run and he was glad she wasn't alone, that at least he was here to take care of her.

She'd hate that too. Not to mention how much he wanted her.

It was crazy and he didn't pretend to understand it, but there it was. Hell, she was a dozen years younger than him. Except he didn't care. She might be twenty-nine but she seemed much older than that, more mature, no doubt due to everything she'd gone through and experienced. One look in her eyes and anybody could see the world-weariness there. Her life hadn't been easy.

She must trust him at some subconscious level, though, to let herself go under that deep when she slept. And she'd revealed a few things about herself when he'd asked. It was a start, anyway.

Over the past few hours he'd checked all the sightlines from the house, careful to keep hidden in the shadows when he pulled back the curtains or blinds to take a look outside. He crossed to the east side of the house and checked again. No new tracks marred the snow on the front and back lawns and the SUV's tire treads were already half-erased on the driveway.

The time alone and the quiet had given him all kinds of time to think. Too much time. He liked his solitude more than most but no matter how he tried to ignore it, he couldn't stop thinking about the woman sleeping upstairs. Briar was like a force of nature and he couldn't ignore his reaction to her even if he wanted to. And part of him didn't anymore.

She wasn't immune to him either, thankfully.

He'd caught the female awareness in her gaze a few times when she looked at him and he'd seen how his touch affected her even without any sexual intent. It made him wonder how she'd react if he kissed her.

KAYLEA CROSS

It'd been a long time since he'd been involved with a woman. Though he knew it was wrong, he'd imagined Briar naked and willing in that bed upstairs with him, all that bronzed skin laid bare to his hands and mouth. He'd thought about what she'd feel like as she moved beneath him, her hands in his hair as he sucked at her nipples and teased the soft flesh between her thighs with his tongue.

Shaking himself, he shoved the fantasy aside. Except unlike the other times in the past when he'd fantasized about someone other than Lisa, there was no guilt. Only a growing desire to make the fantasy a reality before they parted ways.

But it was never going to happen.

Soft footfalls on the carpeted stairs had him looking up from the hearth. Briar appeared at the foot of them, rubbing a hand over her face as though she was still waking up. She saw him by the fire and paused, her eyes puffy from sleep. Even rumpled she still managed to look sexy, because of her confident, self-assured air. That was fucking hot.

"Hey," he said. "Feeling any better?"

"Groggy as hell," she muttered, starting toward him. "Feel like someone drugged me."

"Not surprising. You were out cold."

She stopped and eyed him. "You checked on me?"

He nodded. "Few hours ago."

She frowned, clearly not liking the idea. "Can't believe I didn't hear you."

"I'm quiet, and you were pretty much unconscious."

"Doesn't matter. I never sleep that hard."

"Well you did, and nothing bad happened."

The frown melted away. "True. I slept the day away though."

"You needed it. How long since you last slept?"

She thought about it a second. "Can't remember. A while."

"How are the stitches?"

"Fine."

They'd still be sore but he knew she'd never admit it. He rose, his knees cracking as he straightened. "You hungry? I put some soup on to warm."

"Um, sure." She followed him into the kitchen where he'd left the range light on and perched on a stool at the granite-topped island in the center of the room. "Can you cook?"

He lifted a shoulder. "I'm not bad. Nothing fancy, though I'm pretty good on the grill." He reached for one of the bowls he'd set on the counter next to the stove. "You?"

"I like cooking, but I don't bother often because it's just me. Seems kinda pointless."

Matt ladled out the canned soup the guys had picked up for them. "Yeah, I hear ya." Most of the time he didn't bother either. Cooking for one got old in a hurry.

He carried the steaming bowls to the island. As he set hers down in front of her he noticed the way her gaze strayed to his wedding band. He sat across from her and dipped his spoon into his soup. It felt intimate somehow, sitting in this cozy kitchen with her, just the two of them while the snow fell outside.

"I'm sorry about your wife."

He looked up at her, surprised she'd mentioned it. "Thanks."

Her gaze dipped to his hand again. "You still wear your ring."

The muscles in his stomach grabbed, his hand tightening around the spoon. "Yeah."

"You must have loved her a lot."

Matt nodded and looked down into his bowl. "Miss her every day. She was a good person." Would have been an amazing mother, too.

Briar was silent a long moment but he could tell she

was still curious. "Can I ask what happened?"

"It wasn't in my file?"

"I didn't read that part."

Now he was curious. "Why not?"

She lifted a shoulder. "Seemed too personal and wasn't relevant to what I needed to know, so I skipped it."

Few people ever came right out and asked him what had happened. He didn't talk about it much because it made others uncomfortable and dredged up memories he was still learning how to deal with. They weren't as painful or sharp as they'd once been, but it would always hurt. Yet somehow he found he didn't mind telling Briar.

"Aneurism. She'd been having lots of headaches but the doctors said it was nothing to be worried about. She wouldn't take anything for them, because…" He stopped and heaved a breath, unprepared for the sharp stab of pain beneath his sternum. It'd been a long time since the memory had affected him this way.

Briar kept watching him, quiet and patient, and that gave him the chance he needed to collect himself before saying the rest. "She was three months pregnant."

"I'm so sorry." She looked straight at him as she said it, didn't wince or look away. It felt honest and like a different kind of intimacy. Because they'd just shared a meaningful part of themselves with each other.

"Thanks." He stirred the spoon through the soup. "We'd been trying a long time. No one knew yet and she was excited to tell her family. We had her sister and family over for the Fourth of July. She jumped into the pool to play with our nieces and somehow the aneurism ruptured. She died a few minutes after I pulled her out."

That image of her, hair slicked back as her face turned blue was something he'd never been able to shake. So often when his mind wasn't occupied with other things, that's the picture he'd see of her. He knew he still blamed himself for what happened.

Matt felt he should have pushed harder with the doctors, should have insisted they investigate further. Logically he knew there was nothing they could have done about her condition, especially while pregnant. Lisa would absolutely have refused surgery or medication that might harm the baby. Still, maybe they could have done something to prevent the rupture if they'd found it early enough.

"That's so awful." Briar shook her head and got quiet, seemed to be lost in her own memories as she stared into her bowl. "I know what that's like. Losing someone you love, right in front of you and you can't stop it."

Now it was his turn to remain quiet as he watched her, waiting for her to elaborate.

She lifted her spoon, let some soup dribble back into the bowl. "My parents died when I was seven. Car accident. I was in the back seat. We got hit head-on and the engine came through the dash. Crushed them both."

Jesus. He winced. "I'm sorry."

She kept playing with her soup. "People say the dumbest things after something like that, don't they? 'They're in a better place', or 'it'll get easier' or something else just as stupid."

They did. "I guess because they don't know what else to say."

A slight frown creased her forehead. "It doesn't really get easier, though, does it? You just kind of learn to…cope with it better as time goes on. It doesn't go away, it only becomes less sharp, that's all." She glanced up at him, her dark eyes haunted.

Matt tightened his hold on the spoon and gripped the edge of the counter-top with his free hand to keep from reaching for hers. Holding her gaze, he nodded. "That's exactly how it is." She understood what he felt far better than he'd imagined.

Briar began eating, taking little mouthfuls of the

soup.

"Where were your parents from?" he asked her, taking a spoonful for himself. He was amazed she'd opened up to him this much, but hoped she kept going. There was so much more he wanted to learn about her.

"Dad was Palestinian and Mom was from Venezuela. Both were refugees from the wars going on in their countries. They met in L.A. of all places, fell insanely in love and got married three weeks later."

He smiled. "That's fast."

"No kidding. They had me two months before their first anniversary."

"I like that story."

She looked up, smiled at him with a kind of wonder, as if she was surprised by his admission. "I would never have pegged you for a romantic."

One side of his mouth turned up. "I try not to let it show. Messes with my image." He had a romantic streak; he just wished he'd shown it more often with Lisa.

Briar took another spoonful of soup, still smiling that mysterious smile. "You're a very interesting man, DeLuca."

"Matt," he corrected. The most primal part of him didn't want her even thinking of him by his last name, it was too impersonal. "Where'd you go after your parents died?"

The humor in her eyes vanished and she focused back on her spoon. "That's a long story I'm gonna save for some other time."

Whatever the answer was, he bet it was fascinating. "Okay, then what about the guy in that article last night? Jerry." He'd been waiting to ask her about it, and now seemed like the perfect time.

For a moment he thought she was going to shut down, but then she sighed and answered. "He was an asset I'd been using to get to Ramadi."

Matt sat up straighter, watching her carefully. If Briar was linked to Jerry personally, it made things more complicated than he'd originally thought. "Had you met with him in person?"

"Yeah, the night before the op. I met him at a bar in Boulder to get Ramadi's location."

Not good. "The same night he died in the accident?"

She looked up at him, her expression grim. "It wasn't an accident."

He blinked, part of him not wanting to believe it. "You took out an asset?"

She made an annoyed sound in the back of her throat, scowling at him as though she was insulted. "No. But I think someone wanted it to look like I did. And," she added, looking down again, "Jerry's the second asset I've been in contact with who's died under suspicious circumstances over the past few months. The first died the night I was in Baton Rouge."

Oh, shit. Now he understood the reason for her alarm. This was a very disturbing pattern to say the least, but he believed her. Based on what he knew of her, he was willing to bet she was innocent. "What did Janaia say about it? The first one?"

"She said she'd keep an eye on the situation. I don't even know if she knew about Jerry until my friend sent her the message last night." She frowned and glanced at the digital clock on the stove. "She should have been here by now."

"Weather's probably delayed her flight." Wherever she was coming from.

Briar shook her head. "Then she would have found another way to get here. Something's wrong."

The words had just left her mouth when a sharp beep came from the back door. Briar dropped her spoon and stood up so fast her stool scraped against the wood floor. She stared at the door, her entire body tense.

95

Matt jumped to his feet and followed her gaze, on full alert. "What's wrong?"

Another beep, ominous in the taut silence.

Briar didn't move, her eyes pinned to the keypad next to the door. "The security system," she said softly. "Someone's breached the perimeter."

Chapter Eight

"Follow me." Without waiting for a response, Briar turned and raced for the great room.

At a bookshelf along one wall she stopped and pulled out the leather-bound copy of *War and Peace*, revealing a hidden keypad. She entered the code and a quiet snick sounded as the bookcase swung open. In the wall behind it, she pressed her palm to the biometric scanner and the inner door popped open. "In here." She ducked inside the room, her breath fogging in colder air as the emergency lighting overhead came on.

"Whoa," DeLuca—Matt, she reminded herself—breathed as he looked around at the computer hardware and weapons lining the walls.

Ignoring his reaction to the insanely high-tech loadout room, glad Janaia was paranoid enough to insist on building it after the house was finished, she hurried to the opposite wall where the security system's main computer showed an overhead map of the property. On screen, a single blip blinked in the far southwest corner.

"Looks like just one person, but I can't tell for sure." She typed in a command on the keyboard to zoom in as

Matt came up behind her.

He peered over her shoulder at the screen, infusing the air with his body heat and clean scent. She shouldn't even have noticed those things right now, which just went to show how easily he affected her. The dark stubble on his face made him look even more rugged this close up. He'd brought her here, stayed with her, to protect her. She had the overwhelming urge to stroke her palm over his cheek, his jaw, then glide her thumb across his lips. They looked soft.

"Could it just be a neighbor, or even an elk or something?"

"Maybe on the neighbor, no on the elk. The system can differentiate between humans and animals, so that," she said, pointing to the blip, "is human. And the chances of a neighbor being out in this weather are slim." She looked over her shoulder at him, secretly caught her breath at the sight of his face so close to hers. Their eyes locked and the sudden leap of heat in his set her heart pounding. Against her will her gaze dropped to his mouth and for one crazy second she allowed herself to imagine what they'd feel like, taste like if she leaned forward and kissed him.

She gave herself a mental shake and jerked her eyes from him, moving a step away from the desk. "Grab whatever you want, then we'll go get a better look at whoever's out there." Because she wasn't taking any chances.

He straightened, quickly perused the selection of weapons and wound up taking only some ammo. "I'll use my own."

Fine. She grabbed a few spare magazines for her pistol, and the M40 bracketed to the wall. With one last check on the monitor to make sure the trespasser hadn't moved, she led the way out of the secret loadout room, locking everything up tight before rushing to the kitchen where they'd left their bags by the door.

Briar quickly suited up in her knit cap, jacket, gloves and boots. By the time she was done, Matt was ready as well, his own rifle slung muzzle-down across his chest. There was no time to cammy up their faces and she wasn't going to stay inside and risk a possible attack on the house. Better to be proactive and apprehend the trespasser now.

"I'll take the west side and you take the east," she said, handing him a pair of night vision binos. "If whoever's out there decides to come at the house, cover me while I take them."

He shook his head, frowning. "If that happens, *I'll* take them. You've been wounded and—"

"No," she argued, adamant. "I know the property and surrounding area better than you do, and I'll feel safer moving around if I know you've got my back." It had been so long since she'd had a teammate, it was a revelation to know he had her six, and to trust him with that responsibility.

The frown disappeared. Reaching out, he set a hand on her shoulder. Strong. Capable. He squeezed and nodded once. "Definitely got your back."

At another time, his touch might have given her more flutters in her belly. Right now they set off a flutter in her heart instead. "Okay then." And damn, it was a pretty incredible feeling, to know she had someone with his experience and skill to back her up. He definitely knew what he was doing. If anything went wrong, she didn't doubt for a second that Matt would do what he could to protect her and take the tango out.

He lowered his hand and she stepped back. "We'll go out the side entrance." She opened a door that led down a set of concrete stairs. The temperature dropped with each step they took. By the time they reached the bottom, it was below freezing. The wind chill outside would make it even worse but she'd worked in the cold enough to know how to handle it. If she reached the end of her endurance before they got the trespasser, she'd worry about it then.

A gust of wind buffeted the house as Briar adjusted her goggles. She unlocked the door and set her hand on the knob. Matt was right behind her, locked and loaded. So freaking badass and sexy, and risking his life to protect her. "Ready?" she whispered.

"Yeah. Be careful."

You too. Nodding once, she opened the door. Immediately a blast of icy air hit her, momentarily stealing her breath. She hugged the wall, her gaze pinned to the tree line on the opposite side of the driveway, about twenty yards away. That familiar tingle started up at the base of her neck, warning her that danger was nearby.

Careful to keep her steps quiet, she eased her way to the edge of the far wall and paused to look back. Matt had mirrored her movements, was poised at the opposite end of the house. At his nod that everything was clear on his side, she swung her head back around. Keeping to the shadows against the house, she moved in a crouch, weapon up and ready, finger resting on the trigger guard.

Through the night-vision scope the landscape was revealed in bright green, allowing her to see every detail clearly. Across the wide expanse of lawn separating the house from the road, nothing moved except the tree branches swaying in the wind, the snow falling heavy and thick around her. As she moved she zeroed in on where the trespasser had been. There were no tracks in the snow but whoever it was could be hidden in the trees, watching for her. They might have a vehicle stashed nearby.

Her jaw tightened. A surge of righteous anger swept through her at the thought of her own agency sending someone to snuff her. And here, in her safe haven.

No one's taking me out.

She'd worry about the who and why later. Right now she would fight to the death to protect herself, and Matt. She trusted his skill implicitly.

Briar eased into position behind a stack of firewood for cover and stared through the scope at the far tree line. Long minutes passed while she waited. The wind picked up, allowing the cold to penetrate her clothing, already beginning to numb her hands and feet. Whoever had come here might have already left the area, but she didn't think so. No, they could simply be biding their time, staking the place out and being patient, waiting for the right moment to attack.

They would discover she wasn't an easy target.

The wind howled and moaned over the frozen landscape. Just as the first shivers began snaking through her, a flash of movement to the west caught her attention.

Briar swung the scope to the left in time to see someone moving back in the trees. The trunks made it hard to see the person but Briar kept staring through the high-power scope, surveying the area.

Damn. She wished she had an earpiece or some other form of comms to contact Matt with. Had he seen it too? Was there anyone else moving in on his side? God, she'd just never expected anyone to be able to follow them here. They'd been so careful, gone completely dark. How the hell had this person found them? Now she was more worried than ever about Janaia—

There it was again. More movement.

Briar followed the shadowy outline with the scope, her breathing slow and steady. The person was moving with measured treads in the trees, definitely heading north. Trying to reconnoiter the house? Or circling it, looking for a way to sneak up?

Not happening, asshole.

Briar began shifting to the right with the person, inching her way along the side of the house, toward the carport. The bastard wasn't getting any closer to this place. This was Janaia's refuge, *Briar's* refuge, and no one was taking that away from her.

She'd made it a third of the way to the carport when she heard a faint hissing noise and caught a streak of movement in her peripheral vision.

Shit!

She hit the ground, barely covering her head before the grenade detonated and the SUV exploded into a ball of fire.

****

George lowered the rifle and jerked back behind a solid tree trunk as the vehicle burst into flame. Fanned by the wind, the fire quickly spread, engulfing the entire body. The diversion served two purposes. It eliminated the target's means of escape, and, if she was still inside the house, it would help flush out both her and the HRT member with her. If not…

I'm coming in after you.

Exposed by the flames, a human shadow was silhouetted against the wall. George eased down and peered through the scope, finger curved around the trigger.

Gotcha.

Breaths slow and easy, George waited, ready to time the shot in between heartbeats. No clear shot yet, but it would come. Patience was the key. Just one movement, one mistake, and the target would be dead.

You're mine.

A shot suddenly cracked into a branch overhead. What felt like fifty pounds of snow crashed to the ground.

An exploratory shot, meant to expose an enemy position. Cursing silently, George shook off only the snow on the riflescope with minimal movement and searched for the target before she took another shot.

Nothing moved against the house, and there was no further hint of the shadow that had been behind the woodpile. Twenty-five yards of open ground between the trees and the house. Too far to run without being fully exposed.

Another bullet slammed into the tree, lower this time, sending down a cascade of snow. Then another round hit the ground, slicing into the snow just inches from George's head. Ducking and rolling slightly to make a smaller target, the weapon slipped. It fell to the ground and was buried by the snow.

Footsteps came from the left. Quiet, moving fast.

Shit, where the hell is my rifle? As George scrambled to find it another round hit the tree, sending up an explosion of bark and snow.

And then George understood.

The shooter hadn't missed by accident, but on purpose. That last shot had been a clear warning. The last warning.

"Hands! Show me your hands!" a female voice shouted, only yards away.

George dug hurriedly in the snow, searching for the rifle.

"Hands up, *now*!"

Just as George's fingers touched the barrel, a shot thudded into the ground inches to the right, sending up another small spray of snow.

From the right of where the female target was.

Fuck. Two shooters.

The woman's footsteps kept coming. Close enough for a pistol shot now. George reached for the weapon in its thigh holster.

Too late.

A sudden impact in the chest as a bullet hit the Kevlar vest. The force knocked George down, giving the target just enough time to make the tackle. They went down with a thud, falling through the snow, hitting the frozen ground beneath it in a tangle of arms and legs.

George managed to block the first blow to the face, got in a solid shot to the jaw but missed the second. A starburst of pain flared as a fist cracked against bone. They grappled in the snow. Even through the Kevlar the pain of the bullet impact site made it hard to breathe.

The woman's surprisingly strong hands grabbed both wrists, then a cold, deadly male voice came from nearby in the shadows, carrying over the wind.

"Fucking move another muscle and I'll put a bullet between your eyes."

George froze, panting, brain struggling to process what was happening.

Caught. Fucking *caught* during an op. It was both unthinkable and humiliating.

Seconds later the man materialized out of the darkness. He moved with a menacing stealth, death written all over him, a pistol in his grip. "Put your goddamn hands where I can see 'em," he growled.

Still on top, the female agent relaxed her grip then let go of George's wrists. But even with both hands free and the pistol mere feet away there was no way out of this. No way but death, and that wasn't happening.

Fuck. Me.

Burning with rage that was at least half self-directed, George reluctantly rolled to her stomach and raised her hands above her head.

Chapter Nine

Matt buried his rage at seeing Briar tangling alone with the sniper and kept his finger steady on the pistol's trigger. The bastard was small, with a slender build. He was facedown in the snow, both hands now behind his back as Briar secured them with a zip tie, but Matt didn't trust him not to try and attack them both. Cornered animals were the most dangerous.

"You all right?" he asked Briar without looking at her. When he'd seen her tackle the guy he'd thought his heart would stop beating.

"Yeah." She straddled the shooter's waist and grabbed him by the shoulders to flip him over. Climbing off him, she rubbed a hand over her jaw, keeping an eye on him. "Got a light?" she asked Matt.

Holding the pistol steady, he stepped closer to cover her and reached one hand into his jacket pocket to take out a flashlight, aiming the beam at the tango's head. The guy was clean shaven, and blinked against the brightness of the beam as Briar pulled off his knit cap and NVGs.

Her shocked gasp made every muscle in his body tighten.

In the sudden silence that enveloped them, Matt took his first good look at the tango's face and did a mental double take. A woman? What the *fuck*? How the hell many female assassins were working in Colorado right now?

The woman had blond, shoulder-length hair and light blue eyes that were narrowed to slits as she glared defiantly up at Briar. There were two large bruises forming on her face, one on her right cheekbone and the other on the left side of her jaw. Briar kept staring at her, seeming too stunned to move.

Before Matt could say anything, she reached down to the woman's waistband and yanked the left side down a few inches, exposing her skin. Whatever she found, it made her gasp again and jerk her gaze back to the woman's face. "Georgia?" she said, clearly astonished.

Matt stared at them, a sense of foreboding sweeping over him. They knew each other?

The other female's expression turned shocked, then wary. But she didn't answer.

Briar tried again. "Georgia, it's me. Wardah."

Wardah? Arabic for rose. Was that Briar's real name?

Georgia seemed to blanch slightly at the announcement. She frowned in apparent confusion and peered harder up at Briar, shaking her head in adamant denial.

"Yes," Briar insisted.

"No. No fucking *way*."

Briar's hands curled into fists. "Are there others? Here with you?"

The woman glared at Briar. "You know how we operate," she muttered.

Briar leaned closer and grabbed the woman by the nape, forcing her to hold her gaze. "Who sent you here? How did you find me?"

Georgia darted a distrustful look at Matt before her gaze flicked back to Briar. "You know who."

Briar's face tightened. "Why? Tell me *why*, dammit!" The pain in her voice was real and it set off a jagged twinge in Matt's chest. She was strong and tough, and seeing her hurting made him want to gather her up in his arms so he could make it better.

Georgia's lips thinned, her nostrils flaring. "It was a contract job."

"You're an independent contractor now?"

She nodded.

"What was the contract? Just me? Or him, too?" Briar gestured to him.

"You." She glanced his way. "Him if he got in the way."

Briar shook her once, her expression a mix of fury and determination. "*Why*?" she demanded.

The woman's jaw flexed and she was silent a long moment before she finally answered, her willingness to say anything surprising Matt. "Why the hell do you think? You think you could just go rogue and no one would notice?"

Oh, fuuuuuck.

At that Briar's face went slack with shock. She recovered fast, methodically searched the various pockets on the woman's utilities and patted her down. "She's clean."

Slowly, she climbed off Georgia and pushed to her feet. "Help me get her inside," she mumbled to him, the haunted look on her face making him want to hold her and somehow fix all this. Unfortunately that was impossible and they didn't even know who the hell they were dealing with, except his gut said it had to be someone in the CIA behind everything.

Holstering the pistol, he reached down and hauled Georgia to her feet. Briar tied a scarf around Georgia's eyes to act as a blindfold. He was ready for a fight, expected it, but the woman surprised him again by walking beside him without resistance back toward the house. He didn't relax his grip and didn't let his guard down. If she was anything like Briar she'd be able to do significant damage even without a weapon, given the chance.

Snow continued to fall around them like a thick veil, the wind swirling it in every direction. In the carport the SUV was still burning but the flames were dying out now and luckily hadn't spread to the house. Out in front Briar trudged through the snow and stopped in the carport to grab a fire extinguisher from the wall. She aimed the nozzle at the vehicle and shot retardant into the interior. Within a minute the fire was out.

"Let's go," she snapped, then stomped up the back steps and entered the combination on the keypad, putting her palm to the biometric scanner.

Matt escorted Georgia up the stairs into the kitchen, following Briar into the great room. "Sit her down here," she said, indicating one of the leather couches before the fireplace.

What, she was their guest all of a sudden, because Briar thought she knew her?

Not liking it but sensing Briar must have her reasons for this, Matt forcibly pushed Georgia down on the couch. He stepped back to keep watch, folding his arms across his chest as Briar removed the blindfold and faced her. Georgia blinked and looked around, her expression unreadable. Definitely unafraid, when Matt would have preferred she was the exact opposite.

Briar pulled off her knit cap and ran a hand through her hair. "So when did you get your orders?" Her voice and expression devoid of emotion.

Georgia studied the room more thoroughly, then Matt for a few seconds before answering. "Two days ago.

I was given a file on a rogue agent named Rosa Massoud. You." She turned her eyes on Briar.

An alias she used?

Briar's face tightened. "My name is Briar now. Who authorized it?"

Those cool blue eyes measured her. "The usual people. I don't have names. You know how it works."

"Yeah, and so I know it's different for contract agents." Briar exhaled and shook her head slowly in denial, jaw set. "You're the one who shot me last night?"

A nod, but there was a slight twinge of remorse in the woman's expression. Matt assumed her acting abilities were every bit as good as the lethal skills she possessed, so it was probably fake.

"Shit." Briar dragged a hand down her face then put her hands on her hips as she stared at Georgia. "You still don't believe I'm Wardah, do you?"

The woman dragged her gaze up and down Briar once more, her eyes full of distrust. "I remember the name, vaguely remember what she looked like back then."

Back then? When? Matt added those questions to the mental list he'd compiled, which he'd ask the first chance he was alone with Briar.

Briar shifted slightly, unzipped her jacket then raised the T-shirt he'd given her a few inches with one hand and pulled the waistband of the sweats down to expose her left hip. Matt followed her movements, his eyes settling on the small tattoo on the side of her hip.

Whatever it was, it was enough because Georgia sucked in a breath, her eyes flaring wide before they jerked up to Briar's face. "Shit, I didn't know." She shook her head, horror on her face. "I didn't know, I swear." She suddenly looked pale, shaken. "Jesus, I'm so sorry."

Matt had had about enough of the acting.

Briar let her clothing fall back into place. "You were

three years ahead of me. I've changed a lot since then and it's been a long time. I guess I'm not that surprised that you didn't recognize me in the file."

Three years ahead of her where? In the military? Matt eyed Briar, waiting for her to look at him and explain, or at least elaborate. She cast him a quick glance out of the corner of her eye but didn't say anything. He shifted his stance, his patience running thin. He wanted some fucking answers, but not in front of the prisoner. Or old college pal, or whoever the hell Georgia was to Briar.

Georgia still seemed a little shaken by whatever the tat meant as she spoke to Briar. "There will be others coming."

The ominous tone had Matt cranking his head around to stare at her, his body bristling at the knowing tone. "Did you lead them here? Are they tracking your location?"

"No and no. But they'll be coming. If I found her, they will too."

"How *did* you find her?" he demanded.

She shrugged. "Little detective work."

He gave her a cold smile to remind her he could stop playing nice whenever he chose. And that could happen soon. "Elaborate."

"Simple. I knew she'd been taken prisoner—"

"How?"

She slanted him a bland look. "How do you think?"

Through your scope. She'd been watching Briar the entire time. Briar had been damn lucky to get off that mountain alive. "And?"

"With her wounded and the highway shut down I knew she'd need help and wind up stuck in town for the night. I called around to local motels asking about a group of men staying together with one woman. Wasn't hard."

Matt's jaw flexed. He and his team had been guarding Briar, but they'd actually helped lead Georgia right to her despite the precautions they'd taken. "Then what?"

"I followed the trackers on your vehicles."

There was no fucking way. "We swept them for bugs."

Her expression turned flat. "Apparently you missed them."

Shit, so she must have tracked all three vehicles and followed his and Briar's when the others had turned off the highway. He pulled in a deep breath, tamped down his rising anger. "So can it still transmit?" The SUV was a smoldering pile of metal and plastic right now, but he didn't know what type of device she'd used or what it was made of.

"With a fire that hot? Please."

He relaxed a fraction and did another visual sweep over her body. She had a compact build and was a few inches taller than Briar. Briar had patted her down but might have missed something critical. No way to tell if she had another transmitter somewhere unless they strip-searched her.

"Don't even bother."

He looked back up to find her giving him a warning glare. Before he could say anything she switched her attention back to Briar, staring at her with an odd kind of approval, as though she was a long lost relative Georgia had just been reunited with. "You need to contact your handler."

"I was supposed to meet her here. This is her house. She should have arrived hours ago." Briar drew a deep breath, squared her shoulders. "What are the charges against me?"

"You seriously don't know?"

"No. So tell me."

Georgia sat very still. "You've been disavowed."

Christ. Matt looked at Briar, saw her shock and disbelief, the blood drain from her face as the ramifications hit home.

"The Director signed off on it?" she asked, her voice slightly husky.

Georgia nodded. "They've got evidence against you for the murder of two Company assets who died after meeting you."

Briar's jaw flexed. "Let me guess—one in Baton Rouge and the other in Boulder, right?"

"Yeah."

"What kind of evidence have they got?"

"I don't know."

That Matt believed. The rest of this scenario? He didn't know what to think. This changed everything though. If it was true that she'd been officially disavowed, Briar was technically no longer under his protection. His superiors would want him to bring her in.

He couldn't do that. Not if she was innocent and someone was truly setting her up. Her life would still be in danger.

Briar glanced over and met Matt's gaze. "They're setting me up." She swallowed, looking scared for the first time since he'd met her. He felt his own heart rate kick up in response. "Why are they setting me up?"

To take the fall for someone else's shit.

His gut said she was innocent. Protocol dictated he take her into custody and contact his superiors. Or he could let her go.

Matt wasn't ready to do either.

"You need to break radio silence and get hold of Janaia," he said. "Now." Hell, there might be teams already dispatched to come after her. Possibly his own guys, since they had the training for this type of op and were still in the vicinity. Wouldn't that be fucking ironic? The one time he'd gone dark and they had no way to contact him. And until he knew more about the so-called *evidence* against her, he wasn't risking calling them.

Briar nodded and turned her attention back to Georgia. "So The Company hired you on a contract for this?"

"Yes."

She set her hands on her hips. "Do you still have a handler?"

A slight hesitation. "I still keep in touch with my former handler. He contacted me about the job."

Briar walked away, disappearing into an adjoining room that he knew was an office before shutting the door. Matt turned to face Georgia with a hard stare. "What the hell is going on?"

She shook her head. "I truly don't know."

"How do you two know each other?"

"I can't tell you that."

He raised an eyebrow and withheld a snort. She had to know who he was, or at least that he was with HRT. She'd know about his security clearance. "It's classified?" he mocked.

Rather than answer she looked away, toward the office door. "God, I can't believe I almost killed one of us…"

One of *us*? His patience snapped. "Enough with the fucking riddles and non-answers. You're coming with me," he said, grabbing her by the upper arm to yank her off the couch and towing her to a corner where a pipe emerged from the wall. He tied her ankles together and secured her bound hands, still behind her, to the pipe before straightening. "I've got no ties to you, no loyalty. You do anything to endanger her or me, and I won't hesitate to take you out." He didn't need to explain further. "We clear?"

Glaring up at him through cool blue eyes, she snorted. "I'm not a threat to her anymore, and I'm only one to you if you try to hurt her."

Nice line, sweetheart. He wasn't buying it. "Don't

move."

Chapter Ten

Matt stalked over to the office and opened the door without knocking. A small lamp shone in the corner of the room. Briar turned to look at him, a cell phone he assumed was a burner to her ear. He shut the door part way to allow him to maintain a visual of Georgia and still give them some privacy. Then he waited.

A few moments later Briar ended the call and lowered the phone, a worried frown on her face. "She's not picking up. I don't want to call her house because someone's probably monitoring the number and I don't want to worry Barry. But something's wrong. Really wrong. I feel it."

Matt nodded, searching her eyes. For an instant she let her guard down enough for him to see uncertainty there, as though she felt lost. Then it was gone and she was back to unreadable again. He hated the damn shields she kept putting up around him. Hadn't he proven himself to her by this point, that she could trust him?

She had a bruise forming on her cheek from when

she'd tussled with Georgia. His fingers itched to touch it, soothe both the mark and the worry in her dark eyes. He kept his voice low so Georgia wouldn't overhear. "What the hell was that all about back there?" He nodded toward the great room.

Rather than dodge the question Briar blew out a breath and looked down at the surface of the desk. Then her shoulders seemed to sag a little as she set the phone down and perched on the corner of the desk. "We were both trained together."

He'd gathered that. "When? Where?"

"It started back when we were all kids." She rubbed a hand over the back of her neck, looking wearier than he'd ever seen her. "I told you I was orphaned when I was young. I had no family to take me in so I was put into foster care. When I was twelve I moved in with a woman and her husband. She was really nice, put me in private school and really looked after me well." Her eyes met his, the slight pause making him brace for whatever was coming next. "But it turned out she wasn't just a regular foster mom. She was a recruiter for a secret CIA program called the Valkyrie Project."

He frowned. "What the hell's that?" He had Top Security Clearance and he'd never heard of it. Sounded like something out of a freaking sci-fi TV series.

"They recruited orphaned girls who showed the right aptitudes for certain desirable skills they could hone and funneled us into the program without us realizing it. They measured our abilities on various things like problem solving, reaction time, critical thinking skills, and gave us individualized programs that played to our strengths. The more…technical stuff came later, during and after college. We've all got the same basic training but then we all moved on to become specialists in our own fields." She shrugged, like it was no big deal, when it was anything but. "Georgia and I were trained primarily as snipers.

Some of us were trained to kill by more up close and personal means. Others are elite hackers or experts at seducing information from targets before killing them. Some are a combination of all that."

What. The. Actual. Fuck. A secret program full of deadly female assassins, sanctioned by the U.S. government? Briar's expression told him she was dead serious and everything she'd said certainly explained a lot.

"By the time I hit college I was an expert marksman, trained by guys like you. My instructors were former Marines, SEALs, Delta. I guess you could say they kind of reprogrammed us. Since it all started when we were young, it was easier to condition us. I was hired by the CIA straight out of college—not that there was ever any doubt I'd go elsewhere, since they'd been grooming me for it since twelve—and did my first solo op at twenty-two."

Matt absorbed all that, staring at her like he'd never seen her before. And he hadn't, he realized. Not the real her.

This was one hell of an eye-opener. He didn't know what to think or what to make of it, but he believed every word of the story.

She sighed and rubbed at her jaw. "I know. It's a lot to take in."

Yeah. And he wasn't a man who was easily surprised, yet he was momentarily at a loss for words. "The tats," he said after a moment. "They're a symbol or something?" They held significant meaning to those who had them, that much was clear.

"Yes. We all got them when we graduated college." She turned to the side and pulled the waistband of her sweats down to reveal a tattoo about the size of a silver dollar on her left hip. It showed what appeared to be a black crow with a sword held in its talons and *Valkyrja* written inside a stylized scroll under it.

"Valkyrie," he murmured.

Briar nodded. "It means 'chooser of the slain' in Old Norse. Legend holds that the Valkyries sometimes disguised themselves as ravens."

A fitting name for a group of female assassins. "How many of you are there?"

She shrugged. "When I was in the project it was in a test phase. I don't know if it's still operating, but during my time there were fourteen of us."

Holy shit. This was unreal. Matt rubbed a hand over his face and blew out a breath before facing her once more. They were in this together now. It was time for her to come clean before anything else she'd been hiding got them both killed. "What else don't I know about you that I need to?"

She thought about it for a moment. "I'm fluent in Spanish and Arabic, with a working knowledge of Urdu and Pashto. And I have a bachelor's degree in political science."

Of course she did.

Matt shook his head at her in wonder. But even though she was the most fascinating and complex woman he'd ever met, they had one hell of a problem on their hands. "Georgia's right. If you've been disavowed, teams will be searching for you, if not already, then as soon as they realize you're not dead. We can't stay here." Risking a call to the outside world, even to one of his guys, might lead whoever was tracking her right to them. Anyone skilled in SIGINT could trace them.

But he didn't see any other way around it. Maybe he could call one of his guys and get a feel for what the situation was. He could call Tuck from a burner phone, then ditch it.

She lowered her gaze. "I know." A long silence filled the room before she looked at him again. "I didn't kill those assets. No matter what evidence they think they have against me, I'm innocent."

Matt nodded once. "I believe you." She might be a trained killer, but she played by the rules. He'd seen enough to convince him of that. And she'd seemed truly stricken by the news that her own agency had turned on her.

Surprise and relief flashed in her eyes. "Thank you."

Matt inclined his head, then hesitated, trying to figure out the best course of action from here. "Is there anyone else you can contact? Someone else you can trust?"

"Just Trinity and I never know when she'll be online so it's kind of pointless to reach out to her now. But maybe…" Her gaze strayed to the door.

"What?"

She looked up at him. "Georgia could contact her handler, see if they know anything about my case or Janaia."

"You mean, call the same person who sent her to *kill* you?" he said, disdain dripping from every word.

Her eyes flashed with anger and her expression closed up. "The handler will be on top of the situation and know what's going on a hell of a lot better than the rest of us. And now that Georgia knows who I really am, knows I'm one of us, she won't sell me out."

He raised an eyebrow, incredulous. "You willing to bet your life on that?"

Her chin came up, conviction and defiance written on her face. Strong, proud and deadly in her own right. He would never have thought that combination would work for him but Christ, she was so fucking gorgeous when she looked like that, it made him crazy. "Yes. We'd never turn on one of our own. *Never*. We take an oath."

"So do the people you worked for."

Her eyes clouded over for a second at his use of the

past tense. "There must have been a mistake. Whatever evidence they have, it's all a misunderstanding." She said it as though she was trying to convince herself of that.

He held her gaze for another few seconds, debating her words, then nodded at the phone on the desk. "Is that a burner phone?" When she nodded, he continued, all his protective instincts burning hot. "Georgia makes a single call to her handler, finds out what she can and then we leave here together. Immediately." They'd go on foot until they could find a vehicle. "I don't care how much you think you can trust her, I was tasked with protecting you, and I don't trust her as far as I can fucking throw her. So she stays in my custody until you and I part ways with her, and that's gonna be real soon. Got it?"

Briar nodded. Matt turned and reached for the doorknob but her voice stopped him. "You asked me if there was anyone else I can trust."

He turned back to her, waited.

Looking straight into his eyes, she gave him a nod that was full of respect. "I trust you."

The simple statement slammed into Matt's chest like a punch. He knew what a rarity it was, for her to believe in someone else, to trust them, and how much it took for her to say it.

Her trust in him was his undoing.

He took a step toward her, then another, closing the small space between them, unable to keep his distance a moment longer. The danger she'd unwittingly dragged him into didn't matter. The twelve year age gap between them didn't matter. All that mattered was now, and this primal need to touch her. To show her that he cared, that he wanted her.

Briar never moved, never backed away or tried to avoid what was coming. He stopped in front of her, only inches separating them. Reaching up to cup her cheek with one hand, he swept his thumb gently over the blue-tinged bruise forming on her cheek.

She drew in a swift breath. Her pupils expanded as she stared up at him, skin like warm velvet, silky soft.

"I'm glad you do," he murmured.

In the stillness Briar's gaze flicked to his mouth before moving back to his eyes. The pulse point in her throat beat faster. An electric current seemed to crackle between them in the taut silence. Desire shot through him followed by an intense possessiveness, fed by the answering heat in her gaze and the trust she had in him.

In that moment he realized he would do fucking anything to protect her.

They were the same in so many ways, she and him. Trained by the best in the world to take a life with a single pull of the trigger, and driven to protect the innocent. They'd both known the brutal pain of loss and found the strength to keep on living. They were warriors with a strong moral compass. Both loners.

Until now.

He curved his palm around the side of her face, driven by the need to protect, to imprint his touch on her body. "You don't have to do this on your own anymore," he murmured.

Briar held his gaze for a long moment before turning her face into his palm in a nuzzling motion and closing her eyes. Accepting both his touch and his protection. Something squeezed in his chest.

Sweetheart, you're mine.

The thought came from the most primal part of his brain, raising the hairs on the backs of his arms. She was his and he wanted her to know it.

Matt reached back with one foot and closed the door fully. Keeping his hand on her face, he leaned down and covered that tempting mouth with his. She let out a soft gasp, then her lips softened beneath his and she slid a hand around the back of his neck. Her touch was light, almost tentative, but it sent a shiver rippling through him.

Needing more, he tipped her head back with his hand and increased the pressure of his mouth, letting his tongue glide along the seam of her lips, needing to taste her, get inside her even in this small way. Her fingers tightened on his nape and then she parted her lips, her tongue touching his almost shyly.

Blood surged to his groin. He drove his tongue into her mouth, slid it along hers, getting lost in the feel and taste of her. She made a soft sound in the back of her throat and stroked his tongue with hers, pressing that lithe, lean body against him. Matt was already hard, aching for her, imagining the moment when he finally got to peel away her clothes and see her fully naked. He would touch and taste every inch of her, make her writhe and beg before sliding his tongue, then his cock, inside her.

But there was an unwelcome guest in the next room and a new threat hanging over Briar's head.

With a silent groan he pulled back and searched her eyes. They were hot with desire, a little glazed, and all he'd done was kiss her. Shit, his objectivity on this protective detail was shot to hell and he didn't even care that he could face disciplinary actions for helping her from this point forward. "I'm not gonna let anyone hurt you."

Her answering smile was warm, and full of pure, smug confidence. "I won't let anyone hurt you either."

The sassy response pulled a chuckle out of him, though he had no doubt she could back it up. That was new and surprisingly sexy. He lowered his hand, immediately mourning the loss of touching her skin. "Let's make that call before I lose my head and get you naked on this desk."

Her eyes flared and she licked her lips. "Maybe you can do that when this is all over."

Maybe? No maybe about it. "Oh, honey, that's a

promise." Once it was over and she was safe, he was going to have her naked and under him, her legs wrapped around his back, her hands holding his head close as he drove her out of her fucking mind with pleasure.

Mentally switching gears to slow his racing pulse, he opened the door and stood close by as she explained the situation to Georgia, still secured to the pipe in the corner.

The woman nodded. "I'll try. Frank might not pick up if he doesn't recognize the number though."

Briar raised the phone. "What's the number?" When Georgia gave the digits she punched them in and put the call on speaker. The moment the call connected Matt's stomach tensed. The clock was ticking now, even faster than it had been before. Every second from here on out might bring the people hunting Briar closer.

A man's voice came through the phone. "Yeah."

"Frank, it's me," Georgia said, her eyes meeting Briar's. "Is this line secure?"

"It is. Got any news?"

She hesitated for only a heartbeat. "The package has been eliminated."

Briar, she meant. Interesting, that she'd cover for her.

"You got proof to send me?" Frank asked.

"I'll send it ASAP. Any word from her handler on the situation?"

Frank grunted. "No. She's dead."

Briar sucked in a breath, took a step back. Even from where he stood Matt saw her face drain of all color.

"What?" Georgia asked, expression tense.

"A woman matching her description died at the Denver airport this morning. They've taken her to the morgue to await official identification."

Briar turned those dark eyes on him and the utter devastation in them hit him like a kick to the gut.

"An accident?" Georgia asked, watching Briar.

"Doesn't look like it, but I haven't been able to find

anything yet." The gravity of that statement seemed to resonate throughout the cavernous room. "You watch your back out there, you hear me?"

"I will. You too." Georgia looked shaken as the line went dead. "I'm sorry," she murmured to Briar.

Briar lowered the phone. "Not Janaia." She shook her head, her expression almost pleading. "Not her."

The desolation on her face sliced him inside. Without a word he crossed to her and pulled her into his arms. She shuddered and slipped her hands up to rest on his back, her head on his shoulder. She was stiff, her whole body taut. Shock and denial.

Matt hugged her tight, spoke into her hair. "We don't know if it's true."

"I have to see her," she mumbled against his jacket. "I have to know if it's her."

"You've just been reported dead," he reminded her. "If it's her and it wasn't an accident, then whoever killed her is at least as close as Denver. You can't risk it."

She lifted her head, gazed up at him with heartbroken, dark brown eyes. "I *have* to, Matt. I'll change my appearance—"

"With what? We have to get out of here and can't risk going into a store to buy anything."

"I can help with that," Georgia said.

They both looked over at her.

"What kind of evidence are you going to send Frank about her?" he demanded.

"The usual. Pictures, fingerprints and some DNA. I'll need to do it soon. We could go to the morgue and do everything there after we see the body."

"I can't go there without blowing my cover," Briar said.

"Yes you can. I've got a disguise and a fake ID in the vehicle I drove here. Left it about a mile from here, on an access road."

Matt still didn't trust her, even if she'd covered for Briar and bought them some time. "And why would you do all that?" he asked, the steely edge to his voice unmistakable.

Georgia's expression turned hard. "Because if they framed Briar for crimes she didn't commit and potentially killed her handler, then it means someone's trying to cover up their tracks and was trying to use me to do it. Think about it. They're eliminating everyone involved with her." She looked from Briar to him and her blue eyes went glacial. "Whoever's behind this is working their way down a hit list, and my name will be on it."

Chapter Eleven

T he Denver county morgue was quiet when they arrived at a little after eleven p.m. The storm had caused multiple road closures and forced them to take a long, circuitous route into the city. Briar dreaded going inside, while at the same time she just wanted to get this part over with and behind her. Not knowing was worse than the possibility of finding Janaia in there.

On the trip from Glenwood Springs they'd come up with a plan of sorts. She was careful to keep her face averted at a slightly downward angle in case there were any security cameras around. The light brown, shoulder-length wig hid her ears and the green contacts changed her eye color. The Denver PD uniform Georgia had loaned her would give her a false identity for the time being, but it didn't grant her complete anonymity because of the facial recognition software used by various intelligence agencies. With her ears hidden by the wig, the cotton rolls she'd inserted under her cheekbones to help change her features might help confuse the software even more.

Matt kept pace with her, one step behind as they

headed down the hallway that smelled of antiseptic. Knowing what she was likely going to face in a few minutes, Briar was glad to have him here. His calm, take-charge attitude had been a huge comfort to her over the past few hours. What she'd said was true, she did trust him, even though her logical brain was having trouble coming to terms with that.

Georgia stayed a few paces farther back, acting as rear guard and lookout, dressed in a light gray business suit and carrying ID that named her as a Denver PD detective. Once inside the room Briar would look at the murder victim. Whether it was Janaia or not, they all had roles to play after that. Somehow Briar had to stay tough and not show any emotion if it was her dearest friend lying in that refrigerated drawer.

A set of wide double doors stood at the end of the hall, one security guard in a chair beside them. He rose when he saw them. Matt took out his badge and held it up as they approached. "FBI. They're with Denver PD," he said, indicating her and Georgia with a jerk of his chin. "We're here to examine a victim."

The guard studied Matt's ID for a moment, then Briar's and Georgia's. He briefly looked at their faces, then nodded and opened the doors for them. "Right this way."

The medical examiner, a male probably a few years younger than Briar, was over at a small table set at the back of the room, eating a sandwich. He set it down and wiped his hands on the paper towel serving as his napkin, frowning at them. "Can I help you?"

"FBI agent and two Denver PD members here to examine one of the bodies," the guard said.

The ME's eyes widened slightly. "Oh. Sure. Who do you want to see?"

Briar braced herself and kept silent, letting Matt do the talking. Her heart drummed a hard rhythm against her ribs, dread curling in her stomach. She'd seen death many times, sometimes up close. But seeing the body of someone she cared about would never get any easier.

"The woman from this morning at the airport," Matt said.

The guy stood, frowning again. "Her identity is still classified, because of an ongoing investigation. Do you have the paperwork with you?"

Matt pulled an envelope from his inner jacket pocket containing a court order they'd forged before leaving the safe house and handed it over. The ME took out the letter, scanned it, then handed it back. "She's right over here." He strode to one of the stainless steel cabinets lining the right wall and gripped the handle.

Briar forced herself to take a quiet, deep breath and not dwell on the possibility that her best friend and mentor was lying in there as he pulled it open. A zipped-up, black body bag lay on the shiny stainless steel surface. She braced herself as the ME undid the zipper with a quiet rasp, pushed back the flaps and stepped aside to give them room.

Her eyes locked onto Janaia's static face.

A hot, searing pain tore through her chest. Horror flooded her, then grief, so intense it stole her breath. For a moment it felt like her heart had imploded.

Her hands curled into fists, her nails digging into her palms. She welcomed the pain. It was all the reaction she could show without making herself look suspicious.

Digging deep, she studied Janaia's face. Her skin still had telltale signs of red on it.

"Cyanide," she murmured, her voice raspy because her throat was suddenly so thick. There was no Y-shaped scar on her naked torso, no slice near the hairline that signaled the marks of an autopsy. At least her body hadn't been defiled that way.

Yet.

A deep, burning rage took hold. Whoever had done this would pay, she vowed to herself.

Dearly. Briar would make sure of it.

"Yeah, that's right," the ME said in surprise, looking at her with a newfound admiration. Briar couldn't have cared less what he thought of her, as long as he didn't remember her face when she was gone. "Potassium cyanide, to be exact. We've taken blood and tissue samples to confirm but we were ordered not to do the autopsy. You guys are supposedly sending in your own pathologists to do it in the morning," he said to Matt.

"How was it administered?" Matt asked, moving a step closer to her so that their arms brushed. She knew he'd done it to comfort her, make her feel less alone, and she appreciated the gesture, knowing he'd be holding her right now had he been able to. But God, she couldn't tear her eyes from Janaia's face while the image seared itself into her memory forever.

"We think the killer rubbed it onto the steering wheel and gearshift. The victim took off her gloves when she got into the vehicle and came into direct contact with it that way. You guys are sending more forensics people to look at the Explorer tomorrow as well. We also found this." He took a sealed evidence bag from beside Janaia's body. Inside it was her inhaler. "Using her ID we accessed her medical records to confirm she had asthma. She might have thought she was suffering an attack initially, especially since it's so cold out. You can see the marks on her neck and chest, from where she scratched herself."

While she'd been desperately fighting for air.

Briar blinked fast in an effort to hide the tears burning her eyes. For Janaia to die like that, panicking and clawing at her own skin while she suffocated...

She turned away, pretended to be disinterested with the remainder of the ME's explanation as she looked around the rest of the room, not really seeing anything.

The only image in her mind was of Janaia's face as it must have been during the moments before her death, slowly turning cherry red from the cyanide, her eyes bulging, her skin coated with sweat. Had she realized it wasn't asthma before she'd died? She must have been terrified.

And she'd died alone. It broke Briar's heart.

"From the concentration of the potassium cyanide, the time of death would have been less than three minutes from the first exposure to the victim's skin," the ME continued.

Long enough that her suffering would have been excruciating.

Briar's hands curled into fists as the rage pulsed inside her, bright and hot. She swallowed, staring blindly across the room at the long stainless steel table and the drains beneath it. Tomorrow the pathologists would put Janaia on it and cut her open, remove her internal organs for further examination.

Briar's stomach pitched at the thought.

"Any other evidence that might give us a starting point?" Matt asked, though he knew as well as she did that this had been a professional hit. Slick and ballsy, right out in the open. Definitely a trained operative. Probably CIA contracted, to ensure the op was off the books. Easier to hide that way.

Whoever had ordered it had considerable power. That narrowed the field of possible suspects considerably, but even she didn't have a list of names or faces to go on.

What Briar wouldn't give to review the security footage from the airport and help bring everyone involved to justice. She couldn't do that or risk reaching out to any of her contacts if she was supposed to be dead, but maybe Matt could help her. He'd said he believed her, was still helping her even though he was no longer obligated to and might even be risking his career in doing so. He would know people who could help find the answers she needed.

"People from the local field office were already here this afternoon to go over everything," the ME said. "A whole team's coming with the pathologists in the morning. Who was she, anyway?"

Was.

The word reverberated through Briar's skull. Because Janaia was gone forever.

She hitched in a breath as a sob strangled her. She covered it with a cough and dug deep for her resolve, fighting for control. But she felt like a pressure cooker inside, ready to explode. The walls of the room seemed to close in on her, the smell of the antiseptic and formaldehyde sickening.

Breathe. Calm down. You have to maintain your cover. She caught Matt watching her from the corner of her eye and knew he was worried about her.

At least he didn't have to worry about her blowing their cover. She forced her shoulders back and regrouped, mentally compartmentalizing Janaia's death. There would be plenty of time to think about it later.

"Can you give us a minute?" Matt said to the ME.

"Sure—"

"No," Briar managed, her voice hoarse. Leaving the room now or asking to be left alone would tip the man off that something was wrong and increase the chance that he would remember her. They couldn't afford that.

The weight in her chest had coalesced into a searing ball of pain. She exhaled, forced it down deep as she faced Matt. "Get whatever else you need. I can wait."

He gave her a single, searching look then focused back on the ME. Folding his arms, he studied the other man for a long moment, until the ME began to feel uncomfortable and averted his gaze, shifting his feet. "As you know, this investigation is classified. We need to discuss some things privately. If you wouldn't mind stepping outside, the officer will provide security while we talk." It wasn't really a request.

Matt cut her a sidelong glance and ushered the clearly interested ME to the door. When the man was outside in the hall with the security guard, Matt shut the door after himself and Briar stepped closer to Janaia.

She stared down into her friend's face for a full minute, aware of Matt and Georgia standing behind her, watching her. She tried to see past the blue tinge around the eyes and lips and the red staining that signified how Janaia had been murdered. What would Barry and the kids do without her? It would be hell for them, finding out Janaia had been murdered this way. Worse, Barry would have to hear it from the Feds because as much as Briar wanted to be the one to break the news, she couldn't. She had to be long gone before the agents showed up tomorrow.

Unable to touch Janaia or zip up the bag without leaving fingerprints, she had to make due with staring into that still face. Tears could come later, when she was alone and out of danger of being discovered. For now, a promise was the best she could do.

I'm so sorry, J. I'll miss you like crazy, but if it's the last thing I do, I'll find out whoever did this and make sure they pay.

Pulling in a deep, shuddering breath, Briar made herself turn and walk away from the drawer, giving herself a mental kick as she crossed to the others. *Game face. Get it together.* She could grieve later, once she'd found justice for her friend.

"You ready?" she asked in a brisk voice that belied her emotional turmoil.

Matt's gaze didn't move from her face. "I'm sorry for your loss."

"Me too," Georgia said, sympathy in her eyes.

Briar nodded, set her jaw. She didn't want their sympathy, she wanted to find Janaia's killer and whoever else was behind this.

That too, would have to wait. Right now they needed to get the forensic evidence Georgia had promised her handler, in the form of blood samples and the staged pictures they'd taken of Briar lying dead in the snow back at the safe house. "So let's do this."

In the eyes of The Company, she was already dead. All she had to do now was disappear and find out who had torn her world apart.

And once she found them, she'd make them regret their actions.

****

Will sat in his favorite tufted leather armchair in his mahogany-paneled study, his feet on a matching leather ottoman as he enjoyed the fire crackling in the hearth and the thirteen-year-old scotch he was sipping.

It was a rare night off for him, rarer still because it was early December and his social calendar for the entire month was overflowing with Hanukah, Christmas and New Year's functions. Barbara was out at a fundraiser for a local Children's Hospital and he had the house to himself. He was taking the time to savor some peace and quiet in the haven he'd created for himself, in this wood-paneled room filled with pictures of him and his former teammates in Central America and the Middle East.

Those had been the toughest and yet most rewarding years of his life. They'd forged him into the man he was now.

Outside the window, the naked branches of the cherry tree near the sidewalk swayed in the cold night air, the glow of the streetlamp across the street casting a warm light that spilled through the panes into his study. The lampposts were all decked out in strands of white lights and a wreath with a red ribbon at the base graced the top of it. Their entire neighborhood was festooned that way, resembling a postcard come to life. He loved this time of year and the prevailing mindset of goodwill toward men.

The liberals had all but ruined this country with their bleeding heart policies that had watered down good, old-fashioned Christian American values and sent the country into a pitiful tailspin. School kids unable to say the Pledge of Allegiance or pray because it might offend an immigrant family of a different religious persuasion? What bullshit.

Things had to change and he was going to ensure they did. If he had to use morally questionable methods to do so, well… That reckoning would come between him and God on Judgment Day. But Will was absolutely certain in the righteousness of his path, and his cause. The conservative right had to stand up and take the country back, by storm if necessary.

He took another sip of his scotch from the crystal tumbler, studying the way the firelight sparkled against the lead crystal. He'd earned each and every luxury in his life, having started out in a three-room shack in a tough working class neighborhood of Detroit. Now look at him. Sitting in this beautiful study in Georgetown, about to make his mark on American politics. He was living proof that the American Dream was alive and real, for those who wanted it bad enough.

The scotch burned down his throat and set off a pleasant warmth in his stomach. There was so much still to plan, and several things that had not yet fallen into place, a few of which were worrisome. He wasn't a patient man and waiting was hard, especially for word about the ops he'd privately sanctioned recently.

His cell buzzed on the massive walnut desk across the room. A text message.

He ignored it for a few minutes, allowing himself the luxury of finishing his drink in peace. Only when he had finished the last sip did he rise and cross the room.

He picked up the phone. The message was a single plus sign, the caller unknown.

But it was enough.

Will breathed in deeply, let the air fill his lungs before exhaling. Rounding the desk, he selected a disposable phone from a locked drawer and activated it. He dialed the number from the text using his other phone, glad once again for his privacy.

"Yes?" a female voice answered. He knew her name but George didn't know his, only that she was to call him once the target was eliminated. And apparently Jones had been.

"I need proof." He only hired the best, but George wouldn't get the other half of the money until she gave it to him and he verified the kill.

A slight pause. "I'll send you some pictures. I'm shipping the samples to you in the morning."

"Good. I'll be watching for the package." She had strict instructions for handling that as well.

He ended the call and dismantled the phone. In a while he'd walk the dog and make a stop at a Dumpster a few blocks over, behind a row of restaurants, and toss the phone pieces in there.

With Jones and her handler both dead, two more obstacles standing in the way of his plan to reach the Senate had been removed. Soon another would be taken care of as well, when George met the same fate tomorrow. The Valkyrie Project agents were all skilled and fucking smart. He should know, since he'd once been part of the program in its infancy. Will wasn't leaving anything to chance. Every one of them involved in this case had to be eliminated.

Which meant he had more calls to make.

On his way to the door he snagged another burner phone from the desk drawer and glanced back at the armchair. Firelight flickered invitingly over the butter-soft leather, the crystal of his tumbler catching the glimmers of gold and orange.

One more drink, he decided, snagging the bottle of scotch from the built-in bookcase next to the door. He'd earned it. Knowing Jones was dead called for a celebration.

Chapter Twelve

Matt cast a sideways glance at Briar as the cab drove them away from the airport. Georgia had left first in another cab, leaving them with the number for a burner phone she was carrying. They'd gotten the samples Georgia needed to submit to the man who'd ordered the hit on Briar, and until they figured out exactly what was going on, both she and Briar were going to ground. Matt prayed the other woman wouldn't betray her fellow Valkyrie.

Briar sat next to him in the backseat, staring out the window at the darkened, snow-covered landscape. She'd been silent ever since they'd gathered the blood samples and cheek swabs back in the morgue. From what he could tell she wasn't shaky or in shock. At least, if she was, it didn't show on the outside. He hated that she was in pain and there was nothing he could do to ease it.

"You want me to grab us something to eat on the way?" he asked her quietly. They were on their way to a motel where they'd spend the night coming up with an action plan.

"No, I'm good," she said without looking at him.

Although there was a lot Matt still didn't know about her, he knew enough to understand that losing Janaia must have devastated her. Confronting the evidence that she'd been poisoned couldn't have been easy. Any other woman would have been shaken up, crying and grieving. Briar hadn't made a sound.

He was worried about her. On top of all the rest of this shit with the CIA, this blow was too much for her slender shoulders. As strong as she was, she couldn't bury her grief forever.

When she didn't say anything else, just kept staring into the darkness as they sped down the interstate, Matt felt helpless to ease her pain. He reached for her hand, laced his fingers through hers and squeezed. She looked over at him, face solemn, squeezing in return before looking away.

Matt maintained that simple link with her all the way to the motel they'd stopped at in Aurora. He paid cash for the room and they carried their bags to the second floor. Just like the last time they'd roomed together, this place had two double beds. Matt wanted her in his, wrapped up in his arms for the night.

The lamp set on the nightstand between the beds glowed softly. He set his duffel over in the corner and faced Briar, who was sitting on the foot of one bed. She'd pulled off the wig and taken the contacts and cotton rolls out. Though it looked like she was staring into space, he could practically hear her brain humming from where he stood.

"What are you thinking?" he asked.

She focused on him, dark eyes intense. "That I'm going to find whoever did this and make them pay."

The deadly resolve in her voice took him off guard, it was so incongruent with her calm expression. Her reaction didn't surprise him in the least though. He understood it perfectly, so he nodded. "You were really close to her."

Now the anger burst into flame in her eyes. "She was the only family I've had since my parents died." Before he could say anything else she stood and began pacing back and forth, as though the emotions roiling inside her were too much to contain and she had to keep moving to burn off the tumultuous energy seething inside. "I've been trying to figure out who's behind this. If this was someone in The Company there'd be paperwork involved, official signatures needed. Even if this was done off the books or something was forged, it has to be someone with a lot of authority and know-how. There has to be a trail to follow."

Matt studied her for a moment, sensed there was more she wasn't telling him. "And?"

She took a deep breath, released it, some of the anger evaporating from her expression. "When I was on a job I only had contact with Janaia, and whatever assets I used for any given op. I rarely had dealings with anyone else in the agency, due to protocol and security reasons. I've been trying to think of links between the dead assets and Janaia and me." She paused, sharpening Matt's attention. "There's one thing I keep thinking about."

He waited, unwilling to push because he knew it wouldn't do any good. If she wasn't ready to tell him, nothing he said would make her divulge it. It was frustrating. By not turning her in and helping her fake her death, he'd stuck his neck out for her. Way out.

On top of what he'd already done to protect her, he didn't have to prove himself anymore and wasn't going to try. At this point she either trusted him fully or she didn't.

Briar rubbed a hand over the side of her jaw. "I've done a lot of ops overseas, mostly in the Middle East and Central and South America, because of my language skills. I met Jerry in Syria about a year ago."

The guy who'd died in Boulder.

She hesitated a moment before continuing. "He told me there was a rumor floating around about American weapons being sold to the rebels and other terrorist organizations in the region. As long as groups were fighting against the regime and would pay the money, the arms found their way into their hands. I looked into it briefly, but never found enough to confirm it was actually true. I reported it to Janaia, who passed it on to her boss."

She stopped walking, turned to face him across the room and put her hands on her hips, her expression hard. "I was told there wasn't enough evidence to pursue it, and since it wasn't my problem, I let it drop. But Jerry brought it up again when I saw him the other night. He said he thought there was a massive cover-up happening, because whoever had set up the weapons deals didn't want the world to know the U.S. was arming terror groups."

A prickle of alarm touched him. "Did anyone follow you to that meeting?"

"No." She shook her head, adamant. "I was careful."

"Could Jerry have been wearing a wire?"

"Doubtful, given what we talked about. He was scared enough just meeting me. And if the killer wanted me dead too, then why not target me along with Jerry? Easier to get us both when we were leaving the bar, rather than try to take us out separately afterward."

"Because they didn't want to seem too obvious. And the agency knew you were going after Ramadi, so they wanted to wait until after you took him out." Bastards. Letting her do the hard part, then turning on her once she'd served her purpose.

A muscle in her jaw flexed. "Yeah. What Georgia said about the hit list makes sense. Whoever's orchestrating this whole thing wants to wipe their slate clean. My gut says it has to do with the arms deals."

"What about the other asset, the guy in Baton Rouge? Did he know about any of this?"

"We never talked about it, but it's possible he knew about it. The group he was involved with operated along the Lebanon-Syria border and in Iraq. If he didn't know the details about the weapons, someone in his circle would have." She shrugged. "It's the only connection I can think of that makes any sense."

Matt resisted the urge to rake a hand through his hair. This shit was whacked and way more complex than he'd ever imagined.

"Do you think I'm crazy?" she asked him softly.

"No." She was many things, but crazy wasn't one of them. "If someone at the agency was pulling that kind of shit behind the scenes, then it makes sense they'd want to cover it up at all costs. Including taking out anyone you might have talked to about it, and anyone else who might have figured out what was going on."

"Janaia was just doing her job," she said angrily, hands curling into fists at her sides. As he stared at her, her eyes filled with tears. "I can't believe she's gone." Her voice cracked on the last word and she bit her bottom lip, blinking as she looked away quickly.

Matt closed the distance between them in three strides. Briar looked up at him, the pain clear in her beautiful dark eyes, now wet with tears. That she was letting him see her with her guard down told him everything he needed to know and he couldn't stand to see her hurting like this.

Without a word he wrapped his arms around her and pulled her close. She was stiff initially, but as he curved his body around her and pressed her face to his chest with a hand on the back of her head, she wound her arms around his ribs and held on tight.

Matt rested his chin on the top of her head, not saying anything. Her shoulders shook in a silent sob, then another, and he wished she'd just let go. The way she struggled to hold back her tears and catch her breath was more heartbreaking than if she'd wept openly. He knew how strong she was, how strong she'd had to be to become the woman in his arms, but he needed her to know she didn't have to prove anything to him.

"Don't stop it," he murmured against her hair, squeezing her tighter, more relieved than he'd ever admit when she didn't push away. He understood what that kind of raw grief felt like, wished he could do something to dull it for her. But if she continued to hold it inside the pain would eventually cause her to explode. "It's just me. It's okay to let it go."

She remained stiff in his arms for another few seconds, then, as if his words had unlocked them, her tears poured forth. Again, she barely made a sound as she cried, burying her face into his chest while the silent sobs wracked her. She felt so small, so fragile in his embrace, when he knew the opposite was true. Her arms tightened around him, holding him as if he was the only thing keeping her upright.

Matt closed his eyes and savored the feeling of her needing him, trusting him this much. He didn't say a word as the awful spasms tore through her, her tears dampening the front of his T-shirt. He stood unmoving, never lessening the pressure of his arms as her grief ran its course and eventually left her leaning against him, little hiccupping breaths stuttering through her.

When she gave a tired sigh he relaxed his grip and ran one hand up and down her spine, the other smoothing over her hair. Briar exhaled a long breath and dropped her arms from his back, easing away. But rather than duck her head or try to turn away, she gazed up at him as she wiped her face with the heels of her hands.

"I'm so sorry," he told her.

She nodded, hitched in a little breath as she dried her tears. "Thanks. I know you get it."

He did. And so he knew exactly how raw and

exhausted she must be right now. "It's late." Or really early, depending on how she wanted to look at it. "Let's get some sleep, okay? We'll figure out where to go from here in the morning."

Briar slid a hand into his, looking into his eyes. "I'm tired."

"I know, honey." They both were.

"No, I mean, I'm *tired*. Of…a lot of things. But mostly right now I'm tired of being alone."

It was like kryptonite, that rare glimpse of vulnerability she let him see. He could almost feel himself melting inside. "You're not alone." He squeezed her hand.

"Stay with me."

He didn't think she meant stay in the room, because she couldn't seriously think he'd leave her right now. The only other thing she could mean was to crawl into bed with her, and as much as he wanted that, he wasn't going to take advantage of her when she was torn open like this. "I'm not going anywhere."

She didn't let go of his hand as she turned away. Matt followed her over to the bed, stood there with his heart hammering while she pulled off her boots and coat, then turned down the covers. She crawled in, fully dressed, and turned onto her side, watching him expectantly.

Even though he knew it was likely asking for trouble, there was no way Matt would turn down the invitation. He dumped his jacket and boots onto the floor and got in the opposite side, a squeezing sensation tightening his chest when she instantly pressed against his front. The feel of her small, firm breasts flattened to his chest and her hips cradling his, knowing this was Briar in his arms and wanting to be there, had the inevitable result.

He set one arm around her waist, high enough not to touch her stitches, and eased his hips back a little, putting some distance between her and his growing erection. Briar made a sound of protest and wiggled closer, pushing her body flush to his.

Withholding a groan as her lower belly settled against his swollen dick, Matt rolled slightly and reached past her to turn off the light. In the darkness they lay together, him enjoying the feel of her in his arms, listening to the sound of her even breaths.

She shifted again restlessly, trapping his cock between them and he tightened his hold on her to keep her still. In the near darkness she tilted her head back and set a hand on the side of his face, her fingertips stroking over his whiskers. Then she leaned up and touched her lips to his jaw in a lingering kiss that fired the lust he was trying so hard to ignore.

Her mouth sought his, a soft press of lips on his, her tongue flicking out to tease him. He gave a throttled groan and opened, touching his tongue to hers. Getting more involved than he already was probably wasn't the smartest idea he'd ever had, but he was already attached to her, already insanely protective of her. If this was what she wanted to help dull the grief, he wasn't going to stop it.

Chapter Thirteen

B riar made a murmuring sound and slid her hand around the back of his head, deepening the kiss. Matt's heart pounded, everything in him wanting to roll her onto her back and cover her, thrust into her and hear her gasp, feel her tremble around him. But she was sore from her wound in addition to just having gone through an emotional meat grinder. He was used to taking control of every aspect of his life, most definitely including his sex life, but she seemed to need to be in charge right now though. He was going to let her set the pace here, even if it killed him.

Within seconds the kiss turned hot and heavy, an urgent melding of lips and tongues as she strained to get closer. Matt kept one hand steady between her shoulder blades, the other beneath her head as his fingers gripped a handful of her hair. With an impatient movement she reached for the hem of his shirt and stole beneath it, running her hands over his bare chest and belly, the little purr of female satisfaction she gave making the throb in his groin a hundred times worse. She tugged the shirt up his ribs and he released her only long enough to peel it over his head, flinging it to the floor beside the bed.

Briar took advantage of the position and straddled his thighs, leaning in to nuzzle his throat. She hummed against his suddenly hypersensitive skin, her tongue trailing over it seductively. She scooted to her knees and kissed her way down his chest while he cupped the back of her head in one hand and fought to stay still. Then her hand brushed against his covered erection and he struggled to stay coherent. It'd been around nine months since he'd last had sex, but even though he was desperate for this, knowing it was *Briar's* hand wrapped around him, Briar's mouth trailing lower and lower with each kiss, had every muscle in his body taut with anticipation.

She fumbled with the fastening on his cargo pants for a few seconds until he reached down and undid them for her, the sudden release of pressure on his throbbing cock a huge relief. Her fingers curled around him through the thin cotton of his boxer briefs and he couldn't help closing his eyes and lifting into her touch. It felt so damn good, he wasn't sure how long he could hold out once she touched him without his underwear in the way. Even as the thought penetrated the fog of lust, he cursed himself. He was fired up and ready to go but he had no idea if she was even half as aroused as him.

Wrapping his fingers around hers to still the way she was squeezing him, he reached his other hand up to trail his fingertips down the side of her face. She seemed to freeze in place, her gaze locking on his as though the tender touch surprised her. Matt maintained the contact. He didn't want to fuck her, he wanted a much deeper connection. Did she?

Needing to see her face, he reached over and flipped on the bedside lamp. Briar flinched at the sudden brightness and averted her eyes. Again he drew his fingertips over the silky soft skin of her cheek, bringing her gaze back to his. The expression in her eyes was wary.

Unsure. "What, honey?" he whispered.

As he watched, a blush bloomed in her cheeks. She broke eye contact, ducked her head a little. "The light."

"I want to see you."

A pause. "I'm...more comfortable in the dark."

It surprised him that she was shy about her body. "Why's that?"

She blew out a breath, gave a taut shrug. "It's been a long time since I last did this and I'm...a little out of practice."

Now it was his turn to stare. "That's okay."

She cast him another uncertain glance. "I don't have a ton of experience."

Her unexpected innocence and awkward confession were so adorable he felt his heart squeeze. "It's been a while for me too," he told her.

She met his gaze fully now. "Really?"

He nodded, tucked a lock of shiny dark hair behind her ear. "Better part of a year, and it was a one-time thing." That wasn't for him. He'd felt emptier afterward than he had before, the loneliness sharper, and now that he'd found Briar he wouldn't settle for a fuck that merely took care of a base physical need. He had his own hand for that.

And he wasn't going to let her make this just about sex either.

She seemed to relax at his words, relief bleeding into her expression. "Longer than that for me. My kind of work makes it hard to date."

Matt huffed out a chuckle, amazed at the turn of conversation and his ability to find humor in this when his cock was aching this badly. "Yeah, I'll bet." He understood that she wouldn't trust anyone easily given her line of work, especially the kind of trust that sex required. Good sex, anyhow. Had she experienced this sort of connection with anyone else before?

Her hair was shiny and cool to the touch. Felt good between his fingers. Then a disturbing thought occurred to him and he stilled. "You're not just looking to escape right now, are you?"

"No," she said, her tone adamant. "You make me feel things I…" She trailed off, a slight crease wrinkling her forehead, as though she didn't understand her reaction to him.

"C'mere," he whispered, cupping her cheek as he lifted up enough to kiss her, wanting to get her out of her head. She responded with a sigh and parted her lips to the stroke of his tongue. He seduced her with the kiss, caressing the inside of her mouth with soft licks, delighting in the tiny murmurs of pleasure she made and the way she wriggled impatiently, setting his body afire.

Easing away he curled his fingers into the hem of her shirt and slowly pulled it upward, holding her gaze the entire time. Briar was already breathing faster, face flushed. She helped him ease the shirt over her head then pulled off her bra. She didn't shy away or try to cover herself as he stared at her naked breasts, small and round with chocolate-brown nipples that tightened under his gaze.

God. He'd fantasized about her ever since meeting her in New Orleans, and the reality was a hundred times sexier than his imagination had ever been.

With a growl of need he cupped the firm mounds in his hands, gently squeezing the soft flesh. Goosebumps broke out on her skin, her nipples pebbling tighter and when he slid his thumbs over the hard tips she gasped, her spine pulling taut. Matt couldn't wait a moment longer to taste her. Holding her in his palms he leaned up and closed his mouth over one rigid center.

Briar moaned and gripped the back of his head with one hand as he curled his tongue around her, her hips shifting restlessly against his thighs as her other hand pulled his underwear down to grip his naked cock. He groaned against her breast and sucked her nipple, wanting to give her the same pleasure she was giving him.

Her little whimper of need sliced through the room, making him desperate to get inside her, watch her face go soft with pleasure as he took her to heaven and back. He switched to the other nipple, giving it equal attention, learning what pressure and rhythm she liked, giving her a slow suckle and a firm flick of his tongue. Her fingers dug into his scalp, urging him on, but he needed no further encouragement, removing his hands from her breasts to slide his fingers into the waistband of the sweats he'd loaned her.

"Lift up," he rasped out against her nipple, gliding his tongue over the tip.

Briar squirmed and helped him shove the pants over her hips, shifting to the side to strip them down and off her legs. Before they'd hit the bed she straddled him again, fully naked, and Matt drank in the gorgeous sight of her lightly bronzed skin, satin smooth over a build lean with muscle, the row of stitches an abomination on her beautiful body.

Her abs flexed as she moved, and he could clearly see the definition there, his gaze zeroing in on the dark triangle of hair between her toned thighs. Those pretty folds were already flushed and glistening with arousal. His mouth fucking watered at the thought of tasting her, sliding his tongue deep into her while he held her down and she writhed and begged for more.

"Wait," she whispered, surprising him when she shifted off him. She bent over the side of the bed, giving him an incredible view of her tight, rounded ass as she dug into her pack for something and came up with a condom. "Grabbed them from the house, just in case."

Knowing she'd been planning for this, maybe even hoping for it, pushed his arousal to a whole new level. She blushed more, making him want to flip her over and overpower her with his strength before lavishing her with every bit of his skill, show her why giving up control to him was worth it. Somehow he remained still.

Briar straddled his legs again and took out the condom, fumbled to put it on him. The soft touch of her hands on him made him suck in a breath, her awkwardness flooding him with tenderness. He took over for her, rolling the latex down his length and gripping the base of his cock as he reached for her hip to guide her into place, careful to keep his hand away from her stitches. With one hand he cupped her mound, savoring her quiet intake of breath and the feel of her slickness as he softly rubbed his fingers against her slippery folds.

Briar sat up tall, licking her lips as she brought the head of his cock to her opening and began a smooth, downward glide to take him inside. Matt held his breath at the feel of her enveloping him, all sleek, soft heat.

Briar drew in a sharp breath and paused when he was halfway inside her, her lashes fluttering down for a moment before she opened her eyes fully and gazed down at him. He set his hands on her hips, squeezing the supple flesh.

Bracing her hands on his shoulders she moved up slowly, then down, giving a little hum of satisfaction as she finally took him deep inside her. Sweat broke out across his skin at the incredible sensation. He reached up to cup one side of her face and curved his other hand harder around her uninjured hip, helping her with the movement. Her eyes glowed down at him, hot with desire, but they weren't glazed with the look of a woman on the verge of impending orgasm.

He was going to fix that.

Lowering the hand on her cheek, he wrapped his fingers around one slender wrist. He brought it to his mouth, stared into her eyes as he kissed her fingertips, flicked his tongue against them then slid two between his parted lips. Her eyes flared and she let out a tiny gasp. Sucking gently, he caressed her fingertips with his tongue and pulled her hand free, leaving them glistening.

"Stroke yourself," he murmured, guiding her hand between her legs. As much as he wanted to do the touching, he wanted his hands free to guide her more, and be able to watch what felt best for her. She hesitated a moment, but when he leaned up to capture a hardened nipple between his lips, she sighed in pleasure and began stroking her clit. He could hear the slick sound of her caressing fingers and his cock sliding in and out of her core. Matt closed his eyes in pleasure and sucked tenderly, rubbing his tongue against her.

A soft sound of enjoyment spilled from her throat as she found a motion she liked, her hips moving smoothly. Soon her breathing turned shallow and rapid, her eyes half-closing as she stared down at him. Matt lay back against the pillow and adjusted the tilt of her hips with his hands, changing the angle, seeking the one that would make it even better for her.

"Oh," she moaned and stopped, eyes fluttering shut as though she was savoring the sensation.

Perfect. Matt's heart pounded out of control, his breathing rough. He kept one hand on her hip and reached the other up to brush a lock of hair back from her cheek, then cradled the side of her face, forcing her to maintain eye contact. "Stay right there and keep touching yourself," he commanded in a low voice.

Her eyes opened and she focused on him, skin flushed and her eyes aglow. With her poised atop him, he increased his grip on her hip and took over the motion from beneath, watching her eyes, his hand on her face forcing her to keep the intimate connection between them. He drove up into her and withdrew in a slow, steady rhythm, watching her expression, using it to guide him.

When he shifted the angle slightly once more, her lips parted on an almost soundless gasp of pleasure. Shock flared in the depths of her eyes, then something like awe, as though she couldn't believe what she was feeling. He felt the answering tremor race through her body, felt the tingles race up from the base of his spine.

Right there, he thought in satisfaction, pumping into her at that same angle.

Her body automatically took over the motion, hips rocking as she sought her pleasure, going after it with single-minded intent, fingers rubbing her clit in tight circles he memorized. Her eyes fluttered closed, as though the sensations were too exquisite to bear. "Oh, Matt," she moaned, her face awash with ecstasy.

God, he fucking loved the idea that she'd never felt this with another man. It made him insanely territorial and protective, but more than that he needed to watch her come apart for him, while he cupped her cheek and drank in every shifting expression on her face. Her fingers moved faster over her clit now and a frown creased her forehead, a quiet whimper escaping as she climbed toward release.

Matt stared up at her and let her move how she wanted, his cock sliding against that sensitive place on her inner walls with each downward stroke. Her sex gripped him, the delicate muscles rippling around his throbbing cock and it felt so good he couldn't hold back a groan of pleasure. Briar moaned in answer, her head falling back as she rode him. So fucking beautiful he knew he'd never forget the sight of her like this.

His hand on her hip tightened, fingers digging in as he pushed her toward orgasm. Again and again he drove up into her, her tightening expression telling him how close she was. She gasped and seemed to hold her breath for a moment, her entire body drawing taut, spine arching back, then her husky cry of release rang through the room.

The walls of her sex milked him as she came, the sounds of her pleasure filling the air, raking over his raw nerve endings. Matt gritted his teeth and held on, the need to come flaying him.

Finally she stilled and opened her eyes to stare down at him, panting, eyes heavy with satisfaction, cheeks pink and her lips flushed. She turned her cheek into his palm and kissed the heel of his hand, holding his gaze as she rocked again, the movement languorous and sensual. Matt growled deep in his chest and drove upward, so desperate to come he was trembling.

Something predatory flared in her eyes. Grabbing his wrists she pushed his arms upward, toward the pillow. "I want to do it," she whispered, that hungry look in her gaze driving him fucking insane. Muscles rigid with need, he allowed her to pin his hands on either side of his head and watched her ride him while the pleasure built and his heart tried to pound its way out of his ribs.

She rode him in a slow, sensual rhythm, her eyes drinking in his every reaction as she took him apart. The pleasure coiled higher and higher, tearing helpless moans from his throat, every muscle locked. She was killing him in the best way possible, and clearly loving every second of it. Matt laced his fingers through hers and gripped hard as he moved with her, plunging up as she sank down, his cock swelling inside her as release loomed.

Too much. Too good. He couldn't hold on anymore.

"Briar," he croaked, eyes squeezing shut as he gripped her fingers tight. She murmured something and leaned down to place a soft kiss on his lips, teasing him with a flick of her tongue. Before he could deepen it she sat up again.

Still holding his hands she rocked faster, harder, making him see stars until he surged into her and the orgasm finally exploded. His body shuddered as wave after wave of sensation careened inside him, wiping out everything else.

Briar gradually slowed to a stop as he sagged against the bed and eased her grip on his hands, sighing in contentment as she bent to kiss him, her lips and tongue lingering on his. Matt groaned into her mouth and kissed her back, trying to catch his breath.

When she finally released his hands and cradled his face between her palms to keep kissing him as though she never wanted to stop, he felt his heart wave its little white flag in surrender. He was done for, and was man enough to admit it to himself. But not to her, not yet, because he had a feeling it would make her bolt. All he knew was, he was staying at her side throughout the rest of this, no matter what happened, and then he wanted *her*.

After a few minutes Briar's lips left his to kiss the tip of his nose, his forehead. She leaned back slightly to look into his eyes and the softness he saw in her expression filled him with peace. "That was so good. Thank you," she whispered.

He gave her a tender smile, ran his fingers through her jaw-length hair. "It was my pleasure, sweetheart."

At the endearment she searched his eyes for a moment, then returned the smile and stretched out along his side, tucking one thigh over his and nestling her head into the curve of his shoulder. "Pretty sure it was at least half mine." She sounded supremely satisfied about that.

After ditching the condom, Matt reached over to turn off the lamp and wrapped both arms around her. He'd given her pleasure and a measure of peace, and it was enough for now.

Holding her close in the darkness, he listened to the sounds of her even breaths and the beat of her heart, waiting until she'd drifted off before allowing himself to follow.

Chapter Fourteen

A s he left his second meeting of the day Will checked his phone and discovered a message from the lab. He waited until he was alone in his car before using the burner phone to call them back. "This is Will Balducci. You have some results for me?"

"Yes," the male voice replied. "The samples are a perfect match with the ones in our database. They definitely came from her."

Some of the tension in his shoulders eased. Briar Jones was dead then. "Best estimated cause and time of death?"

"Based on the photos, two gunshots to the chest, time of death around six p.m. last night, as your contact told you. Without a body to examine it's impossible to be a hundred percent sure, but those wounds are definitely fatal. The victim would have died within minutes, if not sooner."

"Thanks for letting me know."

"You're welcome."

He drove back to his office at CIA headquarters in Langley, still not entirely satisfied with the situation. To deal with Jones and her handler he'd been forced to handle it privately and use outside contractors. He'd hired George not merely because of her formidable skill, but because he knew she would think like Jones.

Without a body it's impossible to be a hundred percent sure.

Exactly. That's what was bothering him the most right now.

George had informed him she'd dumped Jones's body in a lake near the safe house in Colorado, where it would be unlikely anyone would stumble upon it, at least not before fish or other scavengers had ravaged her beyond recognition. The handler was currently in a Denver morgue. A team of Feds had been sent there to investigate, but they'd never be able to trace her death back to him.

Thing was, he didn't trust George. Until this was all nailed down and he was officially in the clear, he wouldn't be able to relax.

In his office he logged into his computer and checked his e-mails. Five minutes in, someone knocked on his door. He looked up to find the Deputy Director of Counterterrorism standing there. "You got a minute?"

Will waved him in. "Sure."

Rob closed the door behind him and lowered his weight into a chair opposite the desk, glancing at the framed photo of Will and some of his teammates back in his Navy days, their faces covered in camo paint, fresh back from an op. Then his attention switched to the martial arts trophies lined up on the shelf, and finally down to Will's hands and the fresh abrasions on them. "You still at that?"

"Three times a week." And twice weekly at the range, where he could still put a grouping dead center in the target from seventy-five feet with a pistol.

"You just got your third degree black belt, right?"

"Fourth."

Rob smiled. "Admit it, you've still got the itch to be out there, rather than working behind that desk."

"Never denied that," he said with a grin, leaning back in his chair. He and Rob had worked together for almost eleven years total, a span of time that included some of the most important ops in the agency's history. They worked well together, trusted each other.

And yet, however closely they worked together, Rob had no idea about Will's side ops, but they were few and far between anyway, and something told Will that Rob would understand the necessity of them should he ever find out.

"You heard the news yet?" Rob asked.

"Just got back from a meeting. What's up?"

"One of our Clandestine Services Operation officers is dead. Janaia Miller. She was a handler. FBI team in Denver says she was killed in a professional hit. Cyanide."

Will kept his expression blank. "When was this?"

"Yesterday morning. And the operative she handled is missing now too. The one who did the Ramadi hit. She's been AWOL ever since. She was in the area, and might have killed her."

This was working to his benefit far more than he'd anticipated. Will took that moment to pull up the message he'd seen in his e-mail folder. "You mean Briar Jones?" He turned the screen so Rob could see the picture of her.

"Yeah." He frowned as he peered at the screen, reading the notes there.

"I just got off the phone with our forensics people twenty minutes ago. Jones is dead, as of last evening. Sniper got her."

Rob glanced at him in surprise. "Was it one of ours?"

He was asking because those agency-sanctioned ops almost always required at least one of their signatures on the orders. "No." *One of mine.* "Any leads yet on Miller's case?"

Rob's mouth tightened. "Zero. Security footage from the airport apparently isn't that helpful. But if Jones and Miller are both dead, there may be others involved." He shook his head. "Bet you're glad you're leaving, huh?"

He was mostly glad he'd hired the right man for the Miller job. The Feds would never find the guy now, not with him having this much lead-time. In addition to making things untraceable, another benefit of hiring outside people was that they tended not to ask questions. As long as the money was good and showed up in their bank accounts on time, they did the job and disappeared into whatever new life the payout afforded them. "Moving on to bigger and better things."

Rob smiled. "Yeah. Got the paperwork on that other op we were working on last night?"

"Already sent it to you and the Director."

"Great." Rob stood, put his hands in his pockets. "Let me know if you hear anything more about Jones or Miller."

"Will do. Hey, you coming to the fundraiser tomorrow night?"

"Wouldn't miss it," he said, eyes twinkling at the lie. Everyone knew how much Rob hated social functions and avoided them whenever he could. "See you then."

"You bet."

As Rob closed the door behind him, Will mentally let out a sigh of relief. He'd always been careful whenever he'd sanctioned private ops, making sure there were no paper trails and using his offshore accounts to fund them.

Four people who might have exposed his extracurricular activities were now dead. Three for sure. He wanted to see Jones's body though. George had once worked for The Company, before she'd gone off the grid and become a mercenary.

She'd be hard to track now that she'd done the hit, but Will was very familiar with her file and knew how close she was to her former handler. He could use that to his advantage, kill the two of them and seal this entire thing up tight.

His position and the powers that came with it gave him many advantages, including access to a long list of people who could help him out of this current predicament.

He pulled up his contact list, searching for the name of someone he'd used once before. The man was a stone cold merc, quiet and absolutely lethal. A former Mob hit man. He didn't care who the target was as long as he was paid well. Expensive, but worth it because of his reliability and speed. Will would call him on his way home tonight, have the standard fifty-percent deposit ready to wire by this evening. The remainder was always due after proof of the target's death was established.

That was one more thing he needed to button up.

So close now, he thought as he reviewed more e-mails concerning his current load of on-the-books ops he was involved with. If all went well, he'd work his last day Friday and move on without the worry of past threads tripping him up.

****

Briar woke suddenly when a vacuum started up next door. Her eyes flew open to find gray light seeping in from around the edges of the blinds, her body automatically tensing as she registered the motel room, the hard, warm body spooned against her back.

Matt.

She relaxed. He shifted and tightened his arm around her ribs and she allowed herself a few minutes to lie there and enjoy the peacefulness, the feel of him. Even as the

memory of Janaia's face at the morgue hit, having Matt
holding her like this took the sharpest edge of the grief
away. It'd been so long since she'd stayed the night with
a man. Not since her ex-boyfriend, the user loser. It went
against her nature to let her guard down like this but she
already had last night so she didn't see the point in
worrying about it now.

And Matt…he was a good man. Being with him like
this made her wonder what her life might have been like
if her parents hadn't died when she was so young. She'd
have grown up secure and loved, protected and doted on
by her parents. Would she have gone to college, found a
normal job, then eventually met someone and settled
down?

A tiny, secret part of her still wanted that. A family
of her own, a place where she belonged.

"Morning," he whispered, his voice a sleepy rumble
against the back of her shoulder.

"Morning." God, he was so warm and solid. She
couldn't remember ever feeling this safe.

"Get any sleep?"

"A bit. You?"

"Best sleep I've had in a while." He hugged her
closer, making her vividly aware of how big he was, how
hard all over compared to her as his erection swelled
against her rear. "And you feel so damn good I don't
wanna get up. Well, most of me, anyway." She heard the
smile in his voice. Heat spread beneath her skin at the
evidence of how much he wanted her, his breath fanning
the back of her neck. It was such a relief that he wasn't
letting things be awkward between them this morning.

As much as she longed to turn off her mind, ignore
the danger they were in and give in to another taste of the
oblivion he'd showed her last night, she knew she
couldn't. Not without losing more of herself to this man,
and she'd already lost more than she could afford. "I've

been thinking about what I should do."

He went still behind her and she continued. "I'll make my way south, maybe head into Mexico. And with me officially declared dead, you won't be under suspicion. You can go back to Virginia—"

"No."

She turned her head slightly on the pillow, trying to see him. "What?"

"No," he repeated, his tone firm. Gripping her shoulder, he turned her to face him. Briar laid her head on the pillow to find him staring at her, a fierce frown on his face. "We're not splitting up now."

He couldn't mean that. "You've already gone above and beyond for me. You'll hurt your career, your reputation."

"Not if we clear your name. And I'm not walking away from you. We're going to find out who's done all this. Together."

The way he said it put a knot in her throat. How could he lay everything on the line for her, a virtual stranger, and a dangerous one at that? She had enemies, people in the government who wanted her dead. Sure they'd just slept together, but that didn't necessarily mean anything to him. She swallowed. "I can't ask that of you."

"Fine. So I'm volunteering."

She shook her head. "Matt—"

"I love the way you say my name, but the answer's still no. I'm sticking with you. Or you're stuck with me. However you want to look at it."

The man was unbelievable. She looked away before he could read the emotions she was trying to hide. "I don't want to ruin your life."

"You won't, and this is my decision. Have some faith in me, okay?"

She looked back at him. "I do have faith in you. More than I have in anyone else."

He smoothed a lock of hair away from her cheek, his expression so tender and possessive it sent a thrill through her. "Then let me help. I have friends who I can contact. They'll keep everything off the record, and I won't tell them you're still alive. All we need is one good break to start hunting, then we'll nail whoever's done this."

A funny squeezing sensation in her chest made it hard to breathe for a moment. Reaching out a finger, she toyed with his HOG's tooth, suspended from a cord around his neck. The bullet was smooth, warm from his body heat. She prayed it did its job and always protected him from an enemy's bullet.

"All right," she relented. "But if things get worse, I won't let you sacrifice yourself for me." She cared about him too much, wanted him to be happy and safe, for him to go back to saving the world with his HRT guys. If she had to walk away and lose him forever to keep him safe, she'd do it no matter how much it hurt.

His hand trailed down her jaw to her neck, smoothed over her shoulder and down her side. She suppressed a shiver of longing at the heat in his eyes. "Not your call. And don't even think about doing something stupid like running, because I'll only come after you."

She believed he'd actually do it, but it was still incredible to know he cared so much. "Why? Why would you do this for me?"

"Because you've been wronged and innocent people have died. And because I care about you."

Something inside her melted at his words. She glanced down at his HOG's tooth again, afraid to look into his eyes in case he saw her growing feelings for him revealed there. This was even more dangerous. If it came down to it, she wasn't sure she'd have the strength to walk away from him. Not even if it was for his own good. He deserved better, someone like his late wife. Briar was the furthest thing from domesticated.

Matt leaned in and pressed a kiss to her forehead. "You told me how you got into this line of work, but not much else. Ever been in combat?"

"If you mean in a conventional sense, no. I almost always work alone."

"When did you start taking ops?"

This was easier. Changing the subject, shoving aside the tenderness she felt for him. "You'll tell me yours if I tell you mine?"

His wide shoulders moved in a half-shrug. "If you wanna know, sure."

She remembered it with vivid clarity. "It was a hit on a major arms dealer in Bosnia. Real piece of shit who was into human trafficking, sex slavery as well as arms dealing. Solo op. I waited for two days out in the hills above his villa. Did it with one shot and walked away. Nice and clean. That was seven years ago." She'd been twenty-two, fresh out of college. It had never bothered her, taking a life when she was told to. Not surprising given her training and the kinds of people she'd been sent to eliminate. "What about you?"

"God, that was a long time ago now."

She snorted. "Yeah, cuz you're ancient compared to me."

In retaliation he ducked his head to rub his whiskers against the curve of her neck, making her squirm. "Not ancient. More experienced, is all." He pressed his hips against her belly, the solid length of his erection impossible to miss. More heat slid through her, tempting her with the promise of what he could make her feel with his hands and mouth, his magnificent body. She could stroke all those muscles for hours and never get bored.

"Mmm, I like that about you," she admitted. "It works for me."

His chuckle ruffled the hair at her temple. "I'm glad it does."

She reached behind him and smacked his butt. "Stop distracting me. You were telling me about your first time."

"Her name was Sally," he said, his voice heavy with reverence, "and it was in the back of my dad's Mustang."

"Ew! No, you know what I mean." She didn't fight her smile and it felt good. As though a weight had loosened inside. God, when was the last time anyone had made her smile like this?

He nibbled at the side of her neck for a second, then stilled as he grew serious and drew his head back to rest on the pillow. He played with her hair some more as he spoke. "Iraq, outside Fallujah. It was a teenage kid on a motorbike, approaching an American convoy with a claymore strapped to his back. I barely saw it in time under his jacket."

Briar sobered at the image. She'd never had to take the life of someone so young. "Was it hard?"

"No." He paused, as though waiting for her response, but if he was waiting for her to judge him, he'd be waiting a long time. "I knew it was either him or however many Marines were in the vehicles close to him when he blew himself up. Once I got clearance my training took over and I did my job."

She drew her fingertips across the back of his hand, stroking gently. "What about after?"

He sighed. "His age bothered me for a long time. I wasn't much older than him at the time. Intellectually I knew I'd made the right call, but later I kept seeing his face in my mind. Maybe because he was my first, I don't know. He's stayed with me though. I still think about him."

She nodded. "Some are harder to forget than others."

"Yeah. And I never thought I'd ever be having this conversation with a beautiful woman, especially in bed."

She felt her cheeks warm at the compliment. "Does

it bug you that I asked?"

"No, because I know we think the same way. We had similar training, operated in some of the same places. And I have to say, it's fucking hot to know you're that good with a long gun. I'd like to see you shoot sometime."

She grinned, feeling him relax again. "Maybe we'll have a contest someday."

"I'm up for that."

"As long as your ego can handle losing to me."

He arched a brow. "Pretty sure of yourself."

"Yep. And I'm still active, unlike you," she teased, feeling freer and more alive than she had in forever. "Shooting's a perishable skill. Not sure how you'd do against me on a range now that you drive a desk for a living."

Chuckling, he cupped her face and leaned in to kiss her softly on the mouth. "I can hit any target I set my sights on, sweetheart," he said, gliding his hand over her rear in a caress meant to underscore that he'd set his sights on her.

I love being in your crosshairs, she thought, parting her lips for him, sinking into the kiss.

A knock sounded on the next motel room door over. "Housekeeping."

Briar tensed. "We'd better get moving."

He hugged her close one last time. "Yeah. Much as I'd love to just stay here with you for a couple days instead."

Sounded like heaven.

Releasing her, he turned away, giving her an eyeful of his muscled back and the tattoo on his right shoulder blade as he sat up. A skull wearing a boonie hat, one of its eye sockets fashioned out of a crosshairs, and crossed rifles beneath it. "Very sexy," she murmured, tracing a fingertip over it.

He looked back at her over his shoulder, his eyes

smoldering. "Want to join me in the shower?"

"Don't tempt me."

He grinned and rose to his feet, turning as he stretched his arms over his head, giving her an eye-popping view of his muscled physique. Good God, he was gorgeous. It was hard to believe that body had been on hers, beneath her, inside her, giving her such incredible pleasure and security. Whatever else happened, what they'd shared last night had been real and no one could take that away from her.

Seeing her staring at him like a starving woman, he smirked before heading for the bathroom. "I'll be fast, then you can take your turn and I'll start making some calls."

Chapter Fifteen

M att waited until he heard the shower running in the bathroom before digging out a burner phone they'd taken from the safe house, and dialed Tuck. It was almost eight, and two hours later than that on the East Coast. If his team was even back there yet.

"Tucker here."

The rush of relief at the sound of his team leader's voice surprised him. "Hey, it's Matt."

"Matt, how the hell are you? You okay?"

"Yeah, I'm good. Where are you guys?"

"Better question is, where are you? We were told to stay put after the order came down yesterday morning to capture Briar."

Whoever was after her hadn't wasted any time in sounding the alarm. "She's dead."

"What?"

"Within a few hours of me leaving her. Sniper took her out, I just got word a few hours ago." He felt guilty lying to Tuck about it, but he couldn't risk her safety by telling the truth, not even to one of his most trusted guys.

"Oh, man, I'm sorry to hear that."

"Yeah. I am too."

"You still in Denver?"

"Yes. Gonna take a few days off though. Just need some time to myself after all this."

"I get it. Guess we're heading back to Quantico in a couple hours then. Can I do anything?"

"Yeah, actually." Matt put one hand in his pocket and kept watching the bathroom door. "I'm gonna talk to Celida about it too, but this stays between us for now. Totally off the record. Is this a good time?"

A pause. "Gimme a minute to find us some privacy. Schroder's a nosy bastard." Matt imagined Tuck saying it within earshot and the answering scowl on the medic's face, undoubtedly a raised middle finger in there as well. Team banter was part of the reason the guys were so tight.

He heard footsteps on the other end of the line, then the sound of a door opening and closing. "Okay, I'm alone. What's up?" Tuck asked.

Matt knew Tuck's phone was encrypted, so he didn't worry about anyone being able to trace their conversation, and he would ditch his own before leaving the motel. "Something I learned while I was with her. It's something that needs to be looked into real carefully and kept off the books. No one can find out we're digging."

"Sounds intriguing, and you know how Celida loves a challenge." Tuck's voice held a resigned, sardonic edge and Matt understood why. Celida didn't back down from anyone or anything. She and Briar had that in common. "Does it have to do with Briar?"

"Yes. The CIA must have evidence against her to have been able to order the disavowal. I want to know what it is. Two agency assets in two different cities died the same night they met with her. She swore she was innocent. My gut says she was telling the truth, and the agency's trying to set her up to cover something else. Something big. I'd like to find out what really happened and clear her name if possible. I feel like I owe her that much."

Tuck was silent a moment. "You seriously believe her?"

"Yeah, I do. I'll understand if you don't want to be involved though, in which case we'll just pretend this conversation never happened."

Tuck gave an irritated grunt. "You know me better than that. If you say she was set up, then I'm willing to believe it. Want me to talk to Celida about this?"

"No, I'll do it. Just wanted to give you a heads up and let you know what I was planning."

"I appreciate that. Anything else the guys and I can do?"

"Tell them to have a beer for me and I'll see you all in a few days. And I need you to text me Celida's cell number."

"Will do. Call if you need anything though, okay?"

"You know I will." After hanging up he called Celida. He filled her in on the situation, held a finger to his lips to warn Briar to keep silent as she exited the bathroom. She was still wearing the T-shirt and sweats he'd loaned her. The primal part of him liked the sight of her in his things but they'd have to get her more clothes.

"Can you look into this without tripping anyone's radar?" he asked Celida.

"I'm gonna have to figure out how I can minimize the chances. I can't guarantee someone won't get flagged. The systems are really sophisticated."

"I know." It was a huge risk for her to take. Could potentially end her career if things didn't work out the way Matt hoped they would. "If I'm wrong and it's nothing, then it's nothing. But I think this is something big that needs to be uncovered."

"Okay. Can I bring Travers in on this, or no?"

"Just you. The fewer people involved, the better until

we know if this is even worth pursuing."

"Dammit, now I just want to dump my other cases and focus on this."

Matt smiled. "So you're in?"

"Totally in." There was no hesitation in her voice.

"I was hoping you'd say that."

She chuckled. "You know I love a good conspiracy theory. I'll look into this in a little bit. If I find anything, how can I reach you?"

"I'm not sure where I'm going yet, but it'll be safer if I contact you." They still had a few more burner phones left.

"Okay. I'll start this as soon as I can. Hopefully I'll have something for you when we talk next."

"Thanks for this, I really appreciate it. Good to know I've got people I can count on to have my back."

"And vice versa. Take care."

"You too." He hung up, smiling at Briar's questioning look. "Got someone over at counterterrorism looking into this."

She frowned, combed her fingers through her damp hair. "Just like that?"

"She's engaged to one of my team leaders. She's solid and a former Marine. She knows the risks involved and is going to do it anyway."

The suspicion on her face morphed into mild surprise. "You have nice friends."

"I do."

She cocked her head a little. "So if not Mexico, where are we going? And how are we getting there? Driving's too risky, and flying's worse."

Not if we take the right flight. "Got one more call to make. I'll take care of it." He dialed the number from memory and the man answered on the third ring. "Hey, it's DeLuca," he said. "I need a really big favor."

****

Two hours later Briar stood next to Matt at the end of a small airstrip outside of town as light snow fell from the leaden sky. She kept her hands in her coat pockets, their breath forming vapor in the cold air as the sleek little jet did its final approach and touched down on the far end of the runway.

"You sure about this?" she asked him. Little late to be bringing it up now, but she was already unsettled by being out in the open like this, and waiting for whoever Matt had called. Too many people for her liking knew she was still alive. Adding more just seemed like asking for disaster.

Matt wrapped his arm around her waist, still careful of her stitches, and gave her a squeeze. "Yeah. Don't worry, it'll be fine."

She couldn't help the rigid set to her muscles as the jet taxied toward them and parked close by. The engines began powering down and a minute later the forward door popped open. Matt kept his arm in place as a man appeared in the opening, tall, with graying brown hair.

Alex Rycroft.

Startled recognition flooded her and a wide smile spread across her face. "Alex." She waved, got a grin and a wave in return before she looked at Matt. "Why didn't you say anything?"

He shrugged and pulled her tighter into his side, his voice a low murmur. "Wanted it to be a surprise and I knew you could probably stand to see a familiar face right now. I love seeing you smile."

She wound her arm around him and squeezed him in silent thanks, resting her head on his chest for a moment. His thoughtfulness touched her deeply.

Alex called out from the jet doorway. "You guys coming aboard, or what? It's goddamn freezing out here."

Briar started toward him without hesitation, still smiling. She'd dealt with Alex a few times over the years and Janaia had been a huge fan of his, so at least Briar didn't have to worry about her safety being in a stranger's hands. She trusted him to a certain extent, and his reputation as both an operator and an intelligence officer were unparalleled. Her boots clanked on the metal steps leading up into the jet.

"Good to see you again, Briar," Alex said, holding out his hand.

"Likewise." She shook it, feeling so much better about this plan all of a sudden. "Thanks for the lift."

"You're welcome. Matt, how are you?"

"Better now. I appreciate this," he said, shaking Alex's hand.

"I'm happy to help. Especially if we can expose someone's corrupt ass over at The Company." He turned and led them into the interior. The Learjet was very high end, the seats leather and comfortable-looking. Briar's steps faltered when she saw the woman seated near the back. Around her age, her bronze skin and dark hair similar to Briar's, of Middle Eastern or South Asian descent. Their eyes met, held, the other woman's greenish gaze arresting against her dusky complexion.

Matt set a hand on her lower back and waited, the pressure of his palm steady and reassuring through her jacket. Alex looked back and paused when he saw that she'd stopped.

"Zahra's here at my request," he said, gesturing for them to follow. "She's my secret weapon."

Another female assassin? Briar stayed a few steps behind Alex as he led them to the back and made the introductions. Zahra's smile was warm, her gaze intent as she studied first Briar, then Matt. Briar took the aisle seat, giving Matt the one beside the window. It made her feel less trapped.

One of the pilots came out for a moment and when Alex nodded at him, he closed and locked the forward door and disappeared back into the cockpit.

"So, where are we headed?" Matt asked.

"Lake Placid," Alex said. "Upstate New York."

Briar's attention sharpened. She lived only a couple hours from there. "Why there?"

"I own a place on the ski hill. It's out of the way and private, plus the security's good. It's as safe a place as any for you two to stay while you're off the grid, which hopefully won't be for too long." He handed them both a bottle of water and eased back into his seat, the elegant dress shirt and slacks doing nothing to diminish the razor sharp edge about him, his gray eyes alert. The man was in his early fifties and still a capable operator, his posture, bearing and confidence a testament to his years served in SF.

"I brought Zahra along because I've asked her to help with the digging on this. If there's information out there, she'll find it. But first we need a list of possible suspects."

He obviously trusted Zahra implicitly to bring her in on this, but Briar could tell there was more to their relationship than met the eye and she was curious about it. There was an almost fatherly vibe coming from Alex, which she found interesting. He looked at her. "Who are you thinking?"

Briar still wasn't thrilled about discussing this in the open, but she didn't have much choice and it would be stupid to refuse his help, especially after all the trouble he'd gone to in coming to get them. Whether taxpayer dollars were funding this or not, hiring a private jet was not cheap and it helped to know that he was with an entirely different agency. "Has to be someone with insider knowledge of paramilitary operations. That narrows it to a smaller pool, anyway. We should start with my direct chain of command, specifically with who my handler reported to, and go from there."

"I was very sorry to hear about Janaia," he said, expression somber. "From what I've heard and know, she was a good officer."

Briar nodded and glanced toward the window. "Yes, she was. Thank you." It was still so hard to believe she was gone. She hadn't been able to process the loss fully yet. Every time she thought about Janaia, it made her either numb or angry.

"If you can give me some names, I'll start doing my thing," Zahra said, setting her laptop in her lap.

Briar shrugged and looked at Alex. "You've probably got a better idea of names than I do. I reported directly to Janaia. I never got to see the paperwork and never knew who had sanctioned the ops."

"We'll work from the bottom up to the top of the food chain. My bet is we're looking at a big fish here."

While she was extremely aware that people were messed up, Briar found it abhorrent that someone high up in The Company would abuse their authority to this extent. "Could be a network of people. Would be hard for one person to keep this all under wraps."

"I don't think so," Matt said. "Way harder to keep others quiet. I think we're dealing with a lone wolf. We need to find out who, and why."

"Let's start with Janaia then," Alex said to Zahra as the pilot taxied the jet to the end of the runway. "We'll have about four and a half hours in the air to work on this."

Zahra smiled at her. "Can you give me her phone numbers and e-mail accounts? I can start there and see if anything turns up that's worth looking into further."

Briar had no clue how the woman knew how to do all this, but she was NSA, so there was probably a whole arsenal of software on that innocuous-looking laptop. She gave her Janaia's cell and landline numbers, and the two e-mail accounts she knew. There were bound to be others though.

"What's the plan for you two?" Alex asked as Zahra started working.

"We lie low until we know who we're targeting," Matt answered. Briar glanced at him, running her gaze over his face as the jet's engines roared and the plane shot forward down the runway. The light coming through the small window illuminated the thick growth of whiskers on his face, showing golden highlights in the dark hair. He had his Chargers cap pulled low on his forehead and was leaning toward her so that they touched from shoulder to elbow.

She knew it wasn't accidental and she liked knowing that a lot, which was crazy. The more time they spent together, the more he went out of his way to help her, the harder it was to keep her emotional distance from him. Every day she fell a little more for him. She was already dreading the day when this was over and she had to walk away from him.

The plane lifted off and soared skyward. "Once we have a name and enough evidence to get a conviction, we'll get the warrants in place and move in for an arrest. I want my guys to do it," Matt said.

"I'm going in with them," Briar announced. In a case like this they had the jurisdiction and they certainly had the expertise, but she was going no matter what.

The others all looked at her but she stared back at Matt, letting him see her resolve. Whoever was behind this, she was going to be there to see them brought down, and to be part of it.

"We'll see," was all he said. She opened her mouth to argue but he switched his attention to Zahra. "What are you looking for?"

"I'm starting with phone records to see who she'd been in contact with the day before and the day of her murder." Her green gaze flashed up to Briar's. "Sorry."

"It's all right. It's the truth." The fucked-up, horrible truth.

Zahra went back to searching through her program. The jet broke through the clouds and sunlight streamed in the windows. Zahra reached one hand over and lowered the shade so she could see her screen better. "There are lots of incoming calls to her cell phone from southern Michigan."

"She lived there with her family. Her parents and siblings are there too." And God, what they must be going through right now. It weighed heavy on Briar that she couldn't be there to help with the funeral arrangements, give comfort to Barry and the kids. Would they ever know how Janaia had died? The CIA would no doubt make up some kind of cover story to conceal the truth and keep the story from going public. They'd probably tell Barry she'd had a severe asthma attack that led to a heart attack, might not even mention the cyanide.

"There are two other calls from two different numbers the night before." Zahra typed some more commands in, a slight frown creasing her brow. Everyone was silent as she investigated more.

The jet leveled off as it reached cruising altitude above the clouds, a ding from overhead signaling that they were free to get up and move around the cabin. "They're definitely burner phones," Zahra added. More typing. "Calls were made from northern Virginia."

CIA headquarters were there, at Langley. And it was close to D.C.. Briar's hands tightened on the armrests. "Can you tell from where?"

"Gimme a minute." Her fingers raced over the keys and a satisfied smile curved her lips. "Alexandria."

Briar leaned forward. "Both calls?"

"Yes."

"Can you triangulate the area?" Alex asked.

"I'll pull it up on Google Earth." *Tap, tap, tap.* "Here." She turned the laptop so the rest of them could see. It showed an industrial area of town.

Briar's pulse accelerated. This was a possible lead for them. "Any CCTVs in the area? Maybe we could see someone or a car around the time the calls were made—"

"Already on it." Everyone watched her intently as she worked for the next few minutes. Then she shook her head. "It'll take me a while to search all these. I'll keep looking into this, but is there anyone else you want me to check?"

Of the names Alex mentioned, a few were familiar to Briar. Men she'd heard of during her tenure with the CIA, but had never met or dealt with directly. Goldstein. Smithers. Balducci. Harding. All people involved with paramilitary ops.

"Those are a start. If we need to go higher after we check them, we will," he added.

"I recognize those names. Balducci and Goldstein were both trainers." She felt Matt watching her and met his gaze. "I remember their names, vaguely recall their faces. One was former Navy and the other a Marine scout sniper."

"What do you mean, trainers?" Alex asked.

Where to start, she thought with a sigh. "They both trained operatives I knew years ago." Including Trinity and Georgia. Briar would ask Trinity about them.

Alex looked intrigued by that but didn't press for more. The Valkyrie Project was top secret, but it was possible he knew of it. "Balducci was in Naval intelligence before he joined The Company. And Goldstein's been with them forever."

"I seriously doubt either of them are involved." It would be too complicated for them, opening up the possibility of sealed records being declassified and unleashing a shit storm that would end their careers and land them in jail for the rest of their lives. "Let's start with Smithers and Harding."

"I know Harding personally," Alex said. "I highly doubt he'd be involved with anything like this, but we'll check him and the others out anyway."

Briar relaxed her hold on the armrests and took a calming breath. All this would take time. There were so many people to investigate, so many threads to pull on. She had to be patient, the same as when she waited in a sniper hide with her scope to her eye.

But with so much at stake it was hard.

After a while Zahra shifted in her seat and grimaced slightly.

"Stretch your legs for a bit," Alex told her, taking the laptop away. Zahra shot him a narrow-eyed look then grudgingly pushed to her feet. She moved awkwardly into the aisle and when she walked Briar noticed a pronounced limp. Zahra glanced over her shoulder and caught her looking. Rather than being offended, she smiled.

"Hip doesn't bother me as much as it used to, but it's still a pain in the ass. Literally."

"You mean, more than your husband?" Alex said dryly.

At that Zahra grinned. "Yep. But he's a close second." She glanced Briar's way again, and something in the other woman's eyes told her she'd been through her own personal hell. "I know all about having a score to settle. That's why I'm going to do all I can to help you find whoever did this."

The heartfelt words surprised Briar. She inclined her head. "Thank you."

Matt reached over and took her hand, lacing his fingers through hers. His hand was so large compared to hers, so strong, yet he'd always touched her with such gentleness. Until him, she'd been convinced men like him existed only in fairy tales. "We're going to find them. I promise."

She squeezed his hand in return, thankful he'd called in backup because she was all too aware that she was going to need all the help she could get.

Chapter Sixteen

⟿

A jolt of fear shot through Will as he gripped the phone in his left hand. "What?" he demanded, praying he hadn't heard the man right. This wasn't just a headache; it was a potentially life-ending catastrophe.

"You heard right."

Will dragged his hands through his hair and leaned against the front of his desk. Barbara was out of the house for the day so he was alone and there was no risk of anyone overhearing. "You're sure about this?"

"I just texted you the images from this morning. This software doesn't lie. I'm sure."

Sure enough, his other phone chimed with an incoming text. He checked the three images showing a man and a woman approaching, then climbing into a taxi waiting at the curb. One look at them and he knew it was true.

His heart careened inside his ribcage as he confronted the awful truth. Not only was Briar Jones alive, but DeLuca was with her. Obviously in on this cover up and likely still guarding her.

Goddammit!

This couldn't be happening. He'd been so careful, and all he needed was to tie up these last loose ends and he'd be in the clear for good. "Did you follow them?"

"You're joking, right? I literally just found this footage ten minutes ago. Do you know how hard it is to search through all the hits I got with the program? We're lucky I found them at all, let alone this fast. And I had to use all sorts of other tricks to tighten the resolution on them, that far away from the camera. These guys know what they're doing, they made sure they stayed away from buildings and any security cameras when they got in the cab."

Fuck, he had to calm down. Calm was a hallmark of leadership and it was contagious. He needed to get his shit together.

Will forced himself to take a deep breath, slowed his racing mind. He could still fix this. It wasn't too late. "Where was this taken?"

"Camera is installed outside a little coffee shop in Aurora."

"Call the cab company and find out where they went."

"Already did," the man said, sounding annoyed that Will was ordering him around. "Driver took them to a small airport outside of town. I'm waiting to hear back from someone about the flight logs there, but the guy I spoke to said there've only been a dozen or so flights in and out this morning because of the weather. All privately owned aircraft so far. There's little to no security there and I'm sure they avoided areas that might be on camera whenever possible. I'll need to check each of the flights, find out where they originated and where they're going before I can get anything else."

Yes, this was going to work. It had to.

Keeping his voice calm, Will added, "I'll double your fee if you find them and take care of this within the next twenty-four hours." Hell, he'd pay ten times the fee if it would help make this all go away that quickly.

"Well then let's hope I get lucky with a lead."

Yeah. That his entire future was currently hinging on something as fluky as luck or fate just made him sick to his stomach. The biggest night of his life was coming up in a few days' time. A scandal like this one would make everything blow up in his face. It wouldn't matter how much money he had or how powerful his friends and supporters were. He had to keep this secret at all costs.

The last thing he wanted was to be branded a traitor, thrown in prison and maybe even wind up facing the death penalty for what he'd done to earn the money he'd socked away in the Caymans. Money earmarked to launch his political career and pay for his comfortable retirement. "Call me as soon as you find something. I'll have this phone with me."

He ended the call and tossed the phone onto the walnut desk. The clatter startled his black lab awake, who was lying on the bed next to the fireplace. Patriot blinked sleepily at Will a few times, ears back, the tip of his tail thumping feebly as though he wasn't sure whether Will was angry at him.

"Not mad at you, boy. Got myself in a tight bind," he told the dog.

Patriot perked his ears and thumped his tail harder, seeming to understand that he wasn't in trouble.

Sighing, Will crossed the room and sank onto the leather ottoman at the foot of the easy chair, absently scratching the dog's silky ears. There were too many things beyond his control, it made him feel frantic, a totally foreign sensation. He hated it.

Georgia had lied to him. Or maybe she *had* thought Briar was dead and dumped her body someplace, but he doubted it. And she was still out there too.

Had she and Jones recognized each other from before, perhaps? The idea was a stretch but it sent a wave of cold through his body anyhow. He was more convinced than ever that Jones had found out about his side ops. She could have told George. They might both be working with the HRT commander now, trying to bring him down.

Shit. He closed his eyes, one hand still on Patriot's head. He'd never felt this scared before. Everything he'd worked for now dangled on the edge of a sharp precipice. All because two female assassins had so far gotten the better of him.

For the first time in recent memory, he wasn't sure what to do. A dark hole of doubt opened up inside him, a place he always refused to acknowledge and couldn't now.

Locating Georgia and sending someone to deal with her would involve yet another person and increase the likelihood of a leak or something else going wrong. But he'd lied to her about who Jones was. If she knew the truth she might come after him, or at least try to expose him given the chance. And Jones would want her name cleared. They would both be after him. His best hope lay with getting rid of them.

If just that much could go right, everything would be okay. Once the other two were dead, even if Georgia knew about his illegal deals overseas, it would be her word against his. A lone female contract agent who'd officially left The Company years ago under a dark cloud that had stained her reputation and would follow her for the rest of her life.

He could easily handle her. His tenure with The Company had given him the best possible preparation for the shark tank that was Washington politics. She'd be dead before long anyway. It would all work out. He'd weathered far more severe storms than that before in his career and come through okay.

Not like this, you haven't.

Shoving aside that dark voice and the wave of anxiety rising inside him, he rose, looking down at the dog. He had a last resort backup plan in place of course, but he didn't want to have to use it. Enacting that would signal the death of everything he'd worked for. "Should we go for a walk?"

Patriot's eyes lit up, ears perking and he got to his feet, his fourteen-year-old body struggling with each movement. He stood there with his back end wiggling from the force of his tail whipping back and forth.

Will took the leash from the basket by the door, hooked it to the collar. Might as well go get some fresh air and a brisk walk to help relieve the stress. There was nothing else he could do now but wait, and pray his sins didn't catch up with him.

****

Briar didn't know what to expect when Alex led them into the two-story timber lodge built right on the ski hill, but it wasn't anything this luxurious. He took them through the newly renovated kitchen and through the open-plan living room that overlooked a ski run, then upstairs where three bedrooms and two baths were located. All newly renovated, the décor warm and cozy and fresh. The curtains were all drawn, she noted with approval, and there were security cameras discreetly mounted in places that allowed for the best coverage.

Back downstairs he flipped on some more lights and set about making a fire for them in the fireplace. "Grace wanted gas but I like the feel of a real fire better." He glanced over his shoulder at them. "We were planning to come up this weekend to put up and decorate a tree but Grace got called overseas last night so we might not get here over the holidays after all."

"That's too bad," Matt said. "It's a great place."

Alex shrugged and started crumpling some newspaper to put beneath the logs he'd set up. "We still might. Just depends."

On whether or not she and Matt were still here? "We can go someplace else," Briar said. Alex had already done more than enough and she could find another place to hole up in without taking his vacation home away from him over the holidays.

He waved her words away and added more kindling beneath the split logs. "Don't worry about it. I'd rather someone use it anyhow, to justify all the property management fees and taxes we've paid this year," he added dryly.

"You bought it?" she asked him, a little surprised. He wasn't the sort of man to slow down and take vacations, let alone often enough to warrant buying a place like this. Grace's influence had obviously been good for him. Briar knew how much of a toll it took for someone to devote his or her life to their country. She loved the idea of Alex scaling that back, reclaiming his life for himself and enjoying all the time he had left with his new wife. Someday she hoped she got that chance too.

"Last year. Brought Grace here to unwind after the incident in Karachi and we both fell in love with it."

He meant when Grace had nearly died in a chemical attack there. Janaia had told her about it and just the thought made her insides shrivel. Briar was much more comfortable dealing with rifles and bullets, or a blade if necessary. Chemical weapons were so evil and cruel she wished they had never been invented. "I can see why." The place was cozy with lots of character, and all the modern conveniences to make it comfortable.

"I've canceled the weekly cleaning service until further notice, so do me a favor and make sure you wipe all the fingerprints off the stainless appliances or Grace will freak." Alex lit the fire and adjusted some logs before climbing to his feet. The flames crackled and snapped, filling the room with a warm orange glow. "You guys hungry? Zahra should be back with the groceries soon, but I'm sure we've got some stuff in the pantry still."

"No, I'm good," she said, glancing at Matt.

He was looking around the great room, studying the beams in the high ceilings as he answered. "I'm good too."

"Go ahead and get settled," Alex told them. "I'll get the computer set up in the den."

Briar took her ruck and the small bag of clothes Zahra had brought for her up the stairs, aware of Matt close behind her. She was still a little uncomfortable with staying at Alex's private vacation place, mostly because of him and Zahra being here. Socializing always made her anxious and as much as she appreciated their help, she was looking forward to them leaving so she could be alone with Matt.

Although that was a double-edged sword in itself because spending more time alone with him was both enticing and flat out dangerous to her. He kept slipping past her defenses at every turn. At this point she wasn't even certain that she wanted to keep him out anymore.

You're so fucked-up.

Ignoring her internal voice, she pushed open the first door on the left in the upper hall, taking in the queen size bed with a blue and white patchwork quilt spread over it. She set her ruck down and emptied what little she had in there into the dresser, placing a pistol and an extra magazine in the top drawer of the bedside table before taking out her meager toiletries. Because, priorities.

She heard Matt moving around in the other guest room across the hall and a strange feeling of disappointment hit her. They likely wouldn't have much time left together, at least not if the investigation moved quickly. She'd assumed—okay, had been hoping—they'd share a room and a bed together tonight. Was he playing it like this because Alex was here? Or maybe he was going to start distancing himself from her now because he knew as well as she did that there was no future for them.

Her heart sank.

Taking her toothbrush and razor into the bathroom across the hall, she stopped when she saw Matt there, placing his shaving kit on the counter next to the sink. He glanced over at her, his gaze traveling down the length of her body and back up. The unmistakable male heat in his eyes made her blush and shake her head. She was the furthest thing from attractive right now. "I'm wearing a shapeless T-shirt and sweats that are about ten sizes too big for me."

"They've never looked better. And on you, they're not shapeless. Trust me."

Flustered, she stepped up beside him and laid out her two items on the opposite side of the sink.

"Alex said you could take the master bedroom, you know. It's got a connecting bath in there. I figured you'd want it."

She wanted to say she'd stay there if he did too, but wasn't going to wave her growing feelings for him around out in the open if he was deliberately pulling back. "My room's fine."

Matt set a tube of toothpaste out, then his own razor and a can of shaving cream. Briar snuck guilty glances at him in the mirror, trying not to be obvious. This close, with the scent of his soap intensified by his body heat and all that rugged power wrapped up in such a protective, sexy package, she was having trouble remembering why she shouldn't get more attached to him, let alone why she couldn't get her hands on him again.

What would he do if she shut the door, pushed him

up against it and kissed the breath out of him, then undid his pants and sank to her knees to take him into her mouth?

Arousal slid through her, languid, like warm honey, igniting a delicious throb between her legs. She imagined the way his eyes would smolder down at her, all heavy-lidded with desire and anticipation as he clenched his hands in her hair and pushed his cock into her mouth. Taking what she was more than willing to give. And the sound he'd make as she sucked on him, a low, rumbling groan because he just couldn't hold it back…

God, she could practically hear it vibrating in her ears.

She'd never been the seductive-type, but man, that fantasy was so freaking hot her skin was growing more sensitive by the second, her nipples hardening against her bra. Matt glanced up, caught her looking and smiled at her in the mirror. A knowing, seductive smile that told her he knew exactly what she was thinking.

And that he liked her train of thought as much as she did.

Embarrassed, she looked away, her gaze snagging on something in his open shaving case. A small, framed photo.

Her heart did a funny little kick, the sharp stab of pain catching her off guard as she stared at the picture of him and his wife.

Following her gaze, he reached in and pulled it out of the kit.

Briar resisted the urge to turn away, uncomfortable with having to confront the image yet unable to make herself look away.

"It was our wedding day, just before the reception," he said quietly, setting the photo upright on the counter for her to look at.

For some reason Briar's throat thickened at the sight

of them together. Matt looked outrageously gorgeous in his tux, and Lisa was stunning in her ivory wedding gown, a delicate veil spilling down her back. Her long brown hair curled slightly at the ends so that it flowed around her shoulders in silky waves, her head leaning on her new husband's shoulder. They looked so happy together as they stared into each other's eyes and smiled, a secret smile between the two of them. Her throat tightened.

"I started taking it with me whenever I went away for work. After she died I couldn't break the habit because it felt like one of the only pieces of her I had left, aside from my ring. Like leaving it behind would be as bad as forgetting her, somehow. Stupid as that probably sounds."

"It's not stupid." Not by a long shot. What would it be like to love and be loved that way, only to lose it forever? "She was beautiful."

"She was. Inside and out."

Her heart ached for him. How he must have suffered when he'd lost her. "What did she do?"

"She taught ESL to kids and teens."

Of course she did.

Briar drew in a slow breath, pushed back the growing ache in her chest. This picture was yet further confirmation that she and Lisa were polar opposites in every way. The woman in the photo was loving, gentle and maternal, the kind of person Matt deserved. Briar didn't have a domestic bone in her body and had spent the better part of her adult life either taking or aiding in the taking of lives, not helping people. Unless she counted helping the greater good by eliminating potential threats to the United States and its people. But Briar didn't consider herself a hero. Not by a long shot.

"I just can't bring myself to stop carrying this with me," he said. "I don't ever want to forget her."

"Of course not. She's a part of you and always will be." God it was stupid to feel this raw. She was never this emotional, let alone insecure. Must be the stress and lack of sleep over the past few days catching up with her.

Not knowing what else to say, Briar started to turn away with the intention of heading back downstairs but Matt reached out and snagged her hand. She stopped, met his eyes in the mirror, almost dreading what he'd say next.

He nodded once, his expression grave. "You're right, she will always be a part of me. I'm a better man because of her. I'll always love her, always miss her, but losing her also taught me a lot."

She waited, shoving back her emotions and the need to press against him, to feel those strong arms wrap around her and allow herself to imagine for just a moment that he wanted her as much as she wanted him.

His fingers tightened around hers, his gaze direct and sincere. "There are few things I regret in my life, but they almost all have to do with her. Looking back, I wish I'd paid more attention to the little things. I knew what I had, knew what she meant to me, but I took it for granted. Didn't mean to, but it still happened and I've got no excuse."

Briar swallowed, found her voice. "What little things?"

His shoulders moved in a slight shrug. "God, a million little things. Being more affectionate. Putting more effort into our marriage. Telling and showing her I loved her more often. Sending little texts for no reason except to let her know I was thinking of her. Buy her flowers because I knew how much she loved them, take her dancing even though it's not my thing. Just ways to show her what she meant to me, that she mattered. She put up with me and my crazy training and work schedule and hardly ever complained that she was alone so much. I owed her more than what I gave her, but it took me losing her to recognize it. I got lazy, and if I could go back and do it all over again, that's what I'd change."

Oh...wow. His words left her speechless. Most people lived their whole lives without ever gaining that insight and maturity.

"But I also learned another important lesson." When she didn't respond he continued. "Losing her was so sudden and unexpected, it taught me to always live in the moment, never pass up the opportunity to tell someone I care." His thumb moved across the back of her hand in a slow caress, sending sparks up her arm. "I care about you, Briar. A lot. And I want to see where things go between us once this is all over."

She stared at him, having no idea how to answer that. The lump in her throat was so huge she could barely get a full breath of air. She struggled to speak past it. "Matt, you don't know what you're saying." She nodded at the picture of him and Lisa. "I'm nothing like her. Nothing. You deserve that kind of normal, happy life, with someone stable who wasn't groomed to be a killer." All the things she secretly craved and was afraid she'd never have.

"I was trained to do the same thing, but that part of me doesn't define who I am and it doesn't define you either," he said, his tone stern.

For her, it did. She shook her head. "I'm not like you." She was terrified that she didn't have what it took to make a relationship work, let alone be what he needed. That there might be something lacking inside her, that she might be broken in ways that could never be fixed. She would die before voicing that fear to another living soul though. "I'm no good for you."

A hard hand cupped her chin and lifted it, forcing her gaze up to his. His expression was fierce, his green eyes burning with intensity. "I'll decide what's good for me. And you're selling yourself way short by saying bullshit like that."

Something close to panic skittered inside her. She

shook her head again, her chin rubbing against his palm. "I have no clue how to make a romantic relationship work." She'd only done it once before and had wound up crushed by the experience.

"I do."

The words, the quiet conviction behind them, hit something buried deep inside her, the most vulnerable place she'd consciously guarded her entire life. They slid past every defense she had, unleashing a yearning so strong that she ached. She desperately wanted what he was offering, wanted to believe it might work. To her horror, tears flooded her eyes.

Instantly his expression softened, his grip on her chin gentling. He slid his thumb over her cheek, his gaze sincere. "All I'm asking is for you to give us a chance."

She pressed her lips together and blinked fast, too afraid to speak in case a sob came out instead.

That strong hand moved to settle against the side of her face, his fingertips playing in the hair near her temple. "Do you trust me?"

The answer was immediate. She pulled in a shuddering breath as she fought for control and nodded.

"Then give us a chance."

There was no way she could refuse him. Or herself, no matter how terrifying the prospect of failure was. "Okay." It came out raspy and hoarse, the bubble of hope trapped in her lungs growing bigger and bigger.

A dimple appeared in his scruffy cheek and his eyes glowed with triumph, along with a flash of raw male hunger. Heat bloomed deep in her abdomen, the promise of what would happen when they were finally alone helping erase the threat of tears. "Thank you." He dipped his head, his lips pressing against hers in a soft, slow kiss that set off a delicious curling sensation in her belly.

Briar closed her fingers on his shoulders, sinking them into his sweater. He made a hungry sound and wrapped an arm around her rear, pulling her into his body. She hummed at the feel of his erection trapped between them, her mind slipping back to the fantasy about pinning him to the door. His earlier words echoed in her head, about living in the moment and not wasting the opportunity to show someone she cared.

She would show him exactly what he meant to her.

With one hand she reached back and shut the door, locking the rest of the world out. Matt kissed her harder, deeper, sliding his tongue into her mouth.

Gripping his shoulders she used leverage and the element of surprise to hook a leg around one of his and twisted him around, pushing him up against the door. He stiffened in surprise for a second then groaned his approval into her mouth and fisted a handful of hair at the back of her head. The show of need, the slight, delicious burn on her scalp only shot her arousal higher.

Her hands slid down the front of his body to the waistband of his pants. This time she got them undone without fumbling and reached inside his underwear to grip his cock with her fist. His groan vibrated through her as she freed him, her fingers curling around his hot, thick length.

Ignoring his firm hold on her hair, Briar nipped and kissed her way down his chin, his throat, pulling against his grip as she went to her knees. He hissed in a breath and she paused to look up the length of his body, the molten desire in his gaze sending another wave of heat through her. She wrapped both hands around his cock, pressed her lips to the tip of the flared head. Matt plunged both hands into her hair and gripped her head, fingers flexing against her scalp, his entire body taut, breathing roughly.

She wanted to devour him, make him writhe and beg. She'd never felt so sensual, so powerful as she knelt before him and parted her lips to take him into her mouth.

Matt let out a guttural growl and tightened his hands in her hair, his hips flexing in helpless response. She let him slide deeper inside her mouth, swirling her tongue around the sensitive underside of his cock before pursing her lips and sucking slowly.

"Ah, fuck, *Briar*."

Her body tingled all over, her sex already swollen and wet as she drew on him, savoring his salty tang on her tongue, the desperation in his voice, the grip of his hands. She slid her fists down his length a little, allowing her to take more of him in her mouth, and swallowed.

"Jesus Christ," he groaned, his hips moving again, as though he couldn't help it.

She wanted to make him lose control, leave him sweating and trembling and weak when she was through tormenting him and swallowed his release. It wasn't something she'd ever found the least bit sexy before, but now the mere thought of doing that to Matt had her trembling.

He groaned through clenched teeth as she moved her hands and mouth up and down him, savoring every twitch of his muscles, every hitch in his breathing. "Sweetheart, stop or I'll come," he warned.

No way. She was going to destroy him with pleasure first. She sucked slowly, humming with pleasure as she twirled her tongue around him.

With an unintelligible sound of denial he suddenly clenched his hands tight in her hair and pulled her off him. Briar eased back onto her heels and stared up at him, her own heart pounding at the sight of more than two hundred pounds of prime, aroused alpha male gazing down at her, his eyes blazing with lust. Before she could move he grabbed her shoulder and hauled her to her feet, spinning to pin her to the door with his body. His hands gripped her thighs as he lifted and wound them around his waist.

His mouth slammed down on hers, one of his hands

now gripping a fistful of hair at her nape, holding her there while his tongue plundered her lips and he rubbed his rigid cock against the throbbing apex of her thighs. Briar let out a broken moan that he smothered with his kiss and ground against him, her entire body on fire, need like she'd never experienced clawing at her. She wanted him to take her right this instant, right against the door and she didn't care who heard them.

Straining in his solid grip, desperate for more, Zahra's voice suddenly called out from downstairs. "Hello?"

They both froze. Matt jerked his head back and they stared at each other, breathing hard.

"Guys, I'm back! Where are you?"

"Ah, shit, really?" Matt muttered, closing his eyes as he leaned his forehead against hers. Briar did the same, struggling to get her raging body back under control. "Rain check," he said softly.

"I've got food, so who's hungry?"

Briar stifled a whimper as Matt released her and let her slide down his body until her feet touched the floor. Oh, they were both hungry all right. Starving. And unfortunately they were both going to have to wait to satisfy their true appetite.

Chapter Seventeen

M att peered over Zahra's shoulder as she pulled up a list of possible suspects on Rycroft's computer in the den, trying to give her his full attention while every cell in his body was attuned to the woman standing next to him. It was pure mental willpower that allowed him to concentrate on what was being said while his body was still burning with sexual frustration.

As soon as they were alone tonight, he was going to turn the tables on Briar and make her scream with pleasure as she came against his tongue and around his cock.

Not helping the situation.

With a mental shake he focused on what Zahra had on the screen. A list they'd compiled of people who might possibly be involved with the illegal arms deals and also connected to Janaia, Briar and the dead assets.

It was a long fucking list. They'd opted to begin searching at the bottom of the food chain and work their way up, to try and avoid flagging anyone in the CIA about their digging.

A few minutes later the encrypted phone Rycroft had given him rang. Matt pulled it out, saw Celida's number and answered. "Hey. What's up?"

"I've been tracking the contacts both dead assets had been in touch with recently. Mostly men involved with militias back in Syria. I'm sending you guys pictures. Can you see if any of them look familiar to Briar?"

"Sure." They'd had to let her and Tuck in on the fact that Briar was still alive. He didn't have any reservations about it because he trusted them both implicitly and knew they wouldn't tell anyone else, not even the rest of the guys on the team. Celida was working on this in secret, on her own time, and covering her tracks. She was a hard-nosed investigator with the reputation of being a bulldog when she sank her teeth into something, and that's exactly what Briar needed right now.

He put Celida on speaker so they could all hear her. Zahra opened the file she sent and began scrolling through the photos.

"Abdul," Briar said, pointing to one man about three-quarters of the way down the second page. "I've met with him a couple times in the past."

Rycroft peered at the information beside the photo. "He's a low level arms dealer."

"Yes. He should know about the arms deals in the area."

"Abdul's been in contact with a few people in the U.S. recently," Celida informed them. "Including a few in and around the Washington D.C. area. Zahra, can you check his bank account records?"

"Sure can." The female analyst opened up another program and began a search using his name, birthdate and place of birth. She checked various accounts, stopped on one in particular. "This could be something. There've been a few good-sized fund transfers out of his account over the past ninety days, the last one eight days ago."

Matt leaned forward to look at the sums. Good-sized was an understatement. Five electronic fund transfers, each ranging from two hundred to over eight hundred thousand U.S. dollars. "Who were they transferred to?"

Zahra opened another screen and began searching the account number. "Registered to a Free Enterprise Investments, Limited. U.S. company."

She found it online, but there wasn't much information. It seemed shady, even to him. The company definitely existed, at least on paper, but the lack of info hinted that it could be a front for a sophisticated cover-up operation.

"It's a solid thread," Rycroft said. "Keep pulling on it." He glanced at Briar. "Anyone else you recognize in that list?"

Zahra pulled up the original screen and Briar studied it. "Him," she said, pointing to another man, this one who looked to be in his late fifties or so, balding. "He was a lawyer I met once in Iraq, who gave me intel on a militia leader I was tracking. Said he was investigating funding for several groups fighting in the area, and mentioned the American weapons."

Accessing his financial information, Zahra grunted. "I'll bet he was, since he was apparently a major funder himself." She leaned back to let everyone see the financials. Again, several six-figure EFTs had been sent from his personal account to others. "Here's another American company," she said, pointing to the name of it, different from the first. "I'll check it too."

Briar continued looking through the list but didn't recognize anyone else.

"I've got to get some things cleared off my desk before I head home, but I'll try to work on this some more tonight or before I head back in tomorrow," Celida said. "And Tuck says hi."

"Tell him hi back," Matt said. "And thanks again for

all this. I appreciate it."

"You bet. Just hope we find the asshole responsible so we can get moving on this."

"I hear you." They ended the call and Matt tucked the phone back into his pants pocket. "Any other angle you want to try?" he asked Briar.

She was staring thoughtfully at the screen, her arms crossed loosely beneath her breasts. Breasts currently outlined in a distracting way now that she was wearing a shirt that actually fit her instead of his XXL T-shirt. The black V-neck sweater hugged her curves and slender waist, ending at her hips that were now encased in snug, dark denim.

He couldn't wait to strip everything off her and get his hands and mouth on all that bronzed, silken skin.

"I'm trying to think what the hell these guys had to do with my assets and Janaia, but other than the weapons I just don't see a connection."

"Zahra, you'll keep looking into the financials of those companies? See if you find more leads?" Rycroft asked.

"Yes." She didn't glance up from her laptop screen.

"Okay, we'll get dinner together then." He waved Matt and Briar into the kitchen and they threw together a salad, some pasta and garlic bread from the groceries Zahra had picked up earlier. They ate together in front of the fireplace while Zahra picked at her food one-handed while reading whatever she'd pulled up on screen.

"Is she a hacker or something?" Briar asked Rycroft, slanting a glance at the woman through the open office door.

"She can do that too, yeah," he said, taking a bite of the garlic bread and talking around it. "Her real specialty is SIGINT. She's a cryptologist by trade, can break codes, translate Urdu, some Pashto and Arabic." He glanced at Briar. "I hear you're not bad with the languages either."

She shrugged, forking up some salad. Matt got distracted watching her lips close around the fork, glistening from the oil in the dressing as she chewed, and was reminded all over again of the sight of those shiny lips wrapped around his cock.

His fingers tightened around his fork and he shifted on the couch in a futile effort to relieve the pressure increase in his groin. He'd taken a separate room from her earlier because he hadn't wanted to simply assume she'd want him staying with her, and because he'd wanted her to come to him next time. Now that she had, damn near bringing him to his knees in that bathroom, he wasn't sleeping anywhere but beside her. Not that either of them would get much sleep tonight.

"Just Arabic and Spanish, mostly. But I'm not bad with Urdu and Pashto either," she said to Rycroft. Setting her fork down, she looked at Matt. "I want to contact Georgia, make sure she's okay and see if she's heard anything. Can I borrow a burner phone?"

"Sure." He jogged upstairs to get one from his duffel and came back down with it. Once it was activated he handed it to her and she texted Georgia a message. When no response came she set it down on the wood coffee table and resumed eating her dinner.

The fire was still crackling cheerily away in the hearth and Matt wished like hell they were alone. Oh, the things he'd do to her in front of that fire while the reflection of the flames flickered over her naked body...

"This is interesting," Zahra called out from the den, causing all of them to look toward the doorway. "Both these companies seem to be fronts. I can't find anything substantial behind them. No tax returns, no useful information."

Matt set his plate aside, excited at the prospect of having a solid starting point. "Like shell companies?"

"Could be," she answered. "And by the looks of it,

someone else has been trying to access the account information. Last time was about an hour ago." She tucked a lock of hair behind her ear. "I'll keep digging."

He exchanged a look with Briar, then Rycroft, and he knew they were all thinking the same thing. Those U.S. companies could easily be fronts for someone into shit they didn't want anyone tracing.

Like illegal arms deals.

A moment later, the burner phone on the coffee table chimed with an incoming text. Briar picked it up and read the message, her expression tightening, shoulders turning rigid. Before he could ask what was wrong, she pushed out a breath and shook her head. "Frank's dead."

Cold settled into Matt's gut. "Her handler?"

She nodded, put the phone to her ear as she dialed Georgia. "She found him two hours ago dead at his house outside of Cheyenne." A few moments passed before she lowered the phone. "Just goes straight to voicemail."

Rycroft grabbed it from her, hurried into the den and handed it to Zahra. "See if you can trace this number."

Seeming totally unflustered at having her work interrupted, she opened up a new program and typed in the number Georgia had given Briar. While they waited, Rycroft made a call of his own to verify. "Frank's definitely dead," he confirmed when he hung up, face grim. "More cyanide. An anonymous caller reported it a couple hours ago, I'm betting Georgia. Time of death estimated at around eight hours ago. Same M.O. and near enough to Denver that it could be the same killer who took out Janaia. I'll update Celida, see if she's heard anything."

"Just another minute," Zahra murmured, almost to herself as she worked her magic. "Here. Looks like Georgia's text came from the Wyoming-Colorado border."

Not far from Cheyenne. Briar was worried about her.

Rycroft glanced at her. "Any idea where she's

going?"

"No. I'll ask but I doubt she'll tell me." She took the phone back and texted another message. The reply came back a moment later. Briar shook her head and read it aloud. "Sorry. Going off grid. Will contact you at this number when it's safe. Watch your six. They're getting closer."

Matt didn't blame her for not divulging her location or plans, and he didn't want her knowing where he and Briar were either. He hoped like hell the encryption on the burner phone was good, and that Georgia wasn't as talented with electronics as Zahra. Even if they were in New York State, she could still potentially leak their location and help someone else find them.

Rycroft straightened from the desk, his mouth a flat line. "This is way the fuck out of control." He ran a hand through his hair, sighed and shook his head. "Much as I want to call some contacts and bring them in on this, we're gonna have to do the legwork ourselves for now. With Celida's help," he added.

Frustration and anger built inside Matt. Someone with power in the intelligence world was out there playing cat and mouse, ordering hits on government operatives, and they'd locked his or her crosshairs directly on Briar.

His jaw flexed. No one was fucking touching her while he was still alive. She stood beside Zahra looking at the laptop, appearing totally calm, but he knew this latest news had shaken her no matter how well she hid it.

He closed the distance between them and curled an arm around her back to draw her to his chest, glad that she didn't shove him away. Better yet, she rested her head against him and exhaled, relaxing into his hold. Rycroft was watching them but didn't say anything and Matt didn't give a shit what he thought about them being together. All he cared about was helping Briar, making sure he was there for her to lean on, protecting and shielding her as best he could.

Not that she was the kind of woman who would want to be shielded. That was actually part of the reason he was falling so hard for her, despite all his protectiveness. "We'll just have to keep digging," he murmured to her. She nodded but didn't answer and he could practically hear the wheels in her head turning as she tried to piece this all together.

They each took some financial information and began sorting through it. Just after midnight they hit a brick wall that prevented Zahra from delving any deeper into the shell companies' histories.

She let out a frustrated sigh and drummed her fingers on the desk, a frown on her face. "I'm not sure what else I can do. I've tried everything I can think of without going so deep that I trigger warning bells anywhere." She looked over at him and Briar, now seated on a couch set against the wall, looking through reports she'd dug up on the men Briar had earmarked for further investigation. "We need to bring more people into this to help find that money."

"Not yet," Rycroft said. "If we can't crack this thing ourselves by the time we leave, I'll see what I can do on my end once I get back to Fort Meade." He checked his watch, frowned. "We won't be flying out of here until morning now." He glanced over at Matt. "Guess you're stuck with us for the night." A hint of rueful amusement lit his eyes, as though he knew it was the last thing Matt wanted to hear.

"No problem. Hell, it's your place. I'll—" He was about to say he'd stay with Briar, since he had no intention of sleeping anywhere else, but then stopped when he saw the expression on her face. Discomfort, and maybe a little embarrassment. Shy at the thought of the others knowing they were sleeping together? He knew she didn't have much experience with this kind of relationship, so maybe she didn't want the others to know about them.

He could have told her that Rycroft was well aware of what was going on, but that would likely only embarrass her more. "I'll take the couch in the living room," he amended, "and Zahra can have the other guest room upstairs."

Although he was disappointed that he wouldn't have Briar curled up naked in his arms, he didn't want to make her uncomfortable and couldn't very well drive her to screaming orgasm when Rycroft was in the next room and Zahra across the hall. Considering how hot she made his blood run, there was no way he could take her slow and sweet next time. After they'd both come at least twice, but maybe not even then.

"You two go ahead and call it a night," he said to Briar and Zahra. "Alex and I'll make sure everything's buttoned up tight."

Briar shot him a narrow-eyed look at the dismissal and stood. "I'll help."

Matt hid a grin but didn't argue, knowing she'd be offended if he didn't treat her as an equal. It was rare that he met someone who could match his skills in the field or with a firearm, but Briar could and that made her a thousand times hotter than she already was. "Sure."

Together the three of them checked the lodge again and took a thorough look outside. No one found anything that raised any concerns or led them to believe that anyone had been skulking around. Still, there was no way to tell for certain whether their location had been leaked.

They came in the back door and took off their snow-covered boots. Briar's cheeks and the tip of her nose were pink from the cold. Alex mumbled a good night and left them in the foyer, heading upstairs to the master bedroom.

In the silence they stood staring at each other, and it was clear from the hunger glowing in her dark eyes that had they been alone here, she would have jumped at picking up where they'd left off in the bathroom. Suppressing a groan of frustration, Matt slid a hand into her hair at the back of her head and wrapped his other arm around her ribs, tugging her close.

He hugged her tight to his chest, closing his eyes as she held him just as hard. "Try to get some sleep," he murmured against her hair, all shiny and smelling of shampoo. "We'll hit it again in the morning."

"Yeah. Hope you get a good night's sleep too." She gave him one last squeeze and released him, stepping back to give him a sexy half-smile that made his pulse pick up. "I really liked doing that to you in the bathroom. I look forward to that rain check, except next time I want to finish what I started."

Ah, hell, the thought of her finishing him off in her mouth made his heart rate double. It was torture having her this close without being able to do more, but her sauciness made him chuckle. "Can't wait. Know what else I'm looking forward to?"

She lifted an eyebrow.

"Burying my tongue inside you."

Her smug expression evaporated, replaced by shock and then desire as her cheeks turned pinker. That blush was fucking adorable but he was now stuck on an image of her naked, thighs parted for his mouth while he teased and tormented her with his tongue. Until her hands were clenched in his hair and she was pushing against his mouth, begging for him to let her come.

"I'm not ashamed of what we're doing or of being with you," she said quickly, surprising him. "I don't want you to think that's why I don't want to share a room with you. It's just…with the others here I felt weird about it." She glanced away.

"It's all right," he said, and waited for her to look at him again before continuing. "Thanks for telling me."

Briar pushed out a shaky exhalation and gave him a

soft smile. "So we'll finish what we started later, then." There was a hint of uncertainty in her eyes that he wanted to erase.

"Honey, we definitely will," he promised. "Sleep well." He watched her walk away, through the kitchen and up the stairs, a slender shadow moving without any sound. Even after spending the past few days with her she was still a mystery to him in so many ways. A fucking sexy one. He looked forward to peeling back each layer and discovering what lay underneath.

Stretching out on the long leather couch in the living room a few minutes later, he stared at the darkened high ceiling as the silence settled over him and realized that despite all the shit going on with Briar's safety, he felt more at peace than he had since Lisa's death. He'd never stop loving or missing her, but the loss no longer felt like a leaden weight in his chest. Because of Briar.

He was ready to move on and wanted her to be part of his future. How far she'd let him in, he wasn't sure, but he hoped she would make good on her promise to give them a chance. He was finally ready to let a woman into his heart and give himself permission to be happy again. For the longest time he'd refused to allow it, out of guilt and an effort to honor Lisa's memory.

Not anymore.

Lisa wouldn't have wanted him to remain alone, she would want him to be happy if the right woman came along. And she had, in the most unexpected way imaginable. He would fight to help Briar regain her reputation and freedom, and then he would fight to stay by her side. Although he hoped she didn't make him fight very hard on the latter.

With the hush of the house surrounding him and Briar safe upstairs in her own bed he allowed himself to drift off, but his eyes snapped open in the darkness sometime later when a sound woke him. He bolted upright, paused to get his bearings and caught a glimpse of a shadow at the top of the stairs. Tiny digital displays from various electronic devices around the room gave him just enough light to see its shape.

"Out back." Briar's whisper barely carried down to him. "I checked through the window. There are ski tracks leading to and from the west side of the house."

Matt grabbed his pistol from where he'd placed it on the coffee table and rounded the end of the couch. Another shadow joined Briar at the top of the stairs, a full head taller. Rycroft.

"Zahra, stay in your room," he murmured quietly, his tone commanding despite the low volume. "If we're not back in fifteen minutes, call the cops." Then he came downstairs with Briar.

Another sound came from outside. Matt paused, straining to hear the muffled slide of something moving in the snow. He glanced back into the kitchen, at the stove's digital clock. Almost one-thirty. Could be someone coming back from a late night celebration in the village, or maybe an animal of some sort.

It could also be a trained assassin sent to kill Briar.

So not fucking happening, asshole.

In full operational mode Matt hurried to the foyer and put on his jacket and boots. Rycroft and Briar were right behind him, carrying M4s. "Briar, stay here and guard Zahra."

"No," she whispered back, handing him one of the two rifles she carried, and an extra magazine. "If someone's here for me, I'm taking them down. And I'm not letting you risk your life for me without backup."

Before he could argue she hurried into the great room, her boots silent on the carpet, weapon up and ready.

Rycroft eased into place next to him and stood on the opposite side of the door, rifle in hand. There was a small bathroom just off the mudroom to the left, with a window there. Rycroft headed for it. "I'll check this side. If it's clear then I'll head upstairs and act as lookout. You go with her."

Tamping down his anger at the idea of Briar putting herself in danger, Matt hurried into the great room. No matter how well trained and experienced she was, anything that put her in harm's way brought every single one of his protective instincts blazing to life.

He found Briar hunkered below the large window on the east side of the room. She'd pulled the drapes back a few inches and eased the blinds up a fraction to see outside. He pressed up against the wall on the other side of the window while she did a visual sweep.

"I can see ski tracks leading around to this side from the trees out beyond the backyard." She eased back and they both paused there in the darkness, listening. There was no further sound from outside, but that didn't mean that whoever had been here was gone. Briar's breathing was slow and steady as they waited.

Matt didn't like this, not one bit, even though he knew they couldn't just sit back and let someone attack if that's what they were planning. They had to go out and make sure there was no threat, and eliminate it if there was. He knew Briar could absolutely handle herself tactically, but he didn't *want* her to have to. That primal part of his brain that he couldn't shut off wanted her hidden upstairs with Zahra, as far away from this new threat as he could get her.

He also knew that if he pushed her on this, he risked having her pull away from him, maybe even losing her.

Fuck.

"I'm going out to check. I'll take the right side," she whispered, carefully unlocking the window. "You take the left." She slid it open a few inches, letting in a wave of cold, dry air, and waited. When nothing happened she pushed it open a little more, waited again. Still nothing.

"West side is clear," Rycroft said quietly as he came in from the kitchen. "I'll take lookout from Zahra's room."

"Ready?" Briar asked Matt.

Since he had little choice in the matter he nodded and she eased the blinds up slowly, silently, until she had enough room to slip out. With her rifle in hand, her profile illuminated by the sliver moon hanging above the tall evergreen trees, she eased up enough to put a hand on the windowsill then paused again.

No sounds from outside, no movement and thank God no shots.

She swung one leg up, gripping the window ledge for support, shifting at the last second. Her booted foot had just cleared the frame when a bullet buried itself in the wall where her head had been an instant before.

Chapter Eighteen

B riar jerked back but Matt had already grabbed the back of her jacket to yank her inside.

Son of a bitch almost got me.

She stumbled and caught herself against the wall, quickly regaining her footing and putting the butt of the rifle to her shoulder. Her pulse throbbed in her ears as she ducked low and slammed the window shut, sneaking another peek through the edge of the blinds.

The threat was real. Now to determine how many tangos were out there, eliminate or capture them.

The riflescope afforded her a crystal clear view of the hillside. She couldn't see any movement outside, but that shot had definitely come from south of where the ski tracks had stopped.

"You see him?" Alex called out from upstairs.

"Negative. Shot came from our two o'clock," she answered. The shooter was likely moving to another position now. "You?"

"Negative. Moving to the master bedroom now."

They needed another set of eyes up there. "Be right back," she said to Matt. Without waiting for a response she sprinted upstairs to take up position in the guest bathroom, being as quiet as she could.

She knew the layout of the house and the surrounding area by heart because she'd memorized it on arrival. It was something she did everywhere she went, so ingrained she didn't even have to think about it. There were three possible escape routes the shooter could take away from the house. They had to seal them all off.

"Are you okay?"

She turned her head to find Zahra peering at her with wide eyes from the partially open doorway of her room across the hall. "Yeah, I'm good. Just stay there, shut the door and don't come out until we tell you." She didn't want Zahra or either of the others getting hurt because of her.

"You got a visual yet?" she called to Alex.

"Nope. My side's clear. I'll head back down, check the front again."

In the guest bath she stood to the side of the window and eased the blind aside enough for her to get a clear, bird's eye view through her scope. The ski tracks definitely broke off partway between the house and the nearest group of trees to the north, but even from this vantage point she couldn't see where the tracks led because of the undulating topography. The shooter had used that benefit to their advantage. That told her the tango had training, and it upped the threat level against them all.

Lowering her rifle she stepped back and charged downstairs, careful to keep away from the other windows even though the blinds were still closed. Matt hadn't moved from his spot beside the long window, his back to the wall. He was a big, lethal shadow there in the corner, poised to react to any further threat.

Raising her M4 into position against her shoulder, Briar headed for Alex's office at the rear of the house,

Matt right behind her. There was a big enough window there for them to climb outside. She crouched beneath it, stole a look. An instant sense of calm overtook her, the weight and feel of the weapon familiar and comforting in her hands.

"See or hear anything while I was gone?" she whispered to Matt.

"No."

She scanned the part of the backyard she could see through the scope. "Shooter moved from the trees and around the side of the house, then stopped to take the shot but I can't see him because of the terrain so we'll have to do more recon from outside. Cover me while I run to that stand of trees to the southeast."

"Fuck that," Matt whispered back. "You—"

"Just cover me," she snapped, annoyed that he'd pull macho, protective bullshit now. They didn't have time for it and she was more than capable of running a counter-sniper mission and had done so alone on more than a few occasions. He might be the one wearing a HOG's tooth but she'd earned the equivalent of a true one several times in her career by taking out enemy snipers. And besides, this shooter was after *her*. It was personal and she wanted to finish it, so if anyone was taking the risk of going out first, it was going to be her.

She eased the window open, paused to ensure the shooter didn't have a bead on her, then started to push through it.

A shot hit the front of the house.

Alex.

She pulled back and whipped her head around to stare toward the front door, just out of view through the kitchen. "Alex?" she called out, loud as she dared.

No answer.

Briar gritted her teeth. *This ends now.*

"I'm going."

Before Matt could argue she levered her body through the window and dropped the few feet to the ground, quickly rolling behind the hot tub set on its concrete pad beneath the upper balcony. And waited. There were no more shots, nothing moving on the hill behind the house or in the shadows. She looked back at the window to nod at Matt, still mostly hidden from view.

Taking aim at the spot where those ski tracks disappeared around the side of the house, she set her finger on the trigger. Matt slid through the window and raced to her, skidding to his knees beside her in the snow.

"Nothing more from out front," he whispered.

Briar frowned. Was Alex pursuing the shooter? Or had he been hit?

"You take point and I'll watch those trees," Matt said, pointing to where the shooter had come from. There might be more hidden in the shadows. "All right," he said, face grim in the low light. "Let's find out what the hell we're facing."

She nodded once, geared up for the short dash to the side of the house and took off, her boots sinking in the snow. At the corner of the house she stopped and waited for Matt. He set a big hand on her left shoulder, a standard reminder of his position but it felt good. His touch centered her, strengthened her resolve. She was going to nail this bastard and find out who had sent him here.

"Our six's still clear," Matt murmured.

Briar's attention was focused on what was happening around the side of the house, where the tracks led to and away from it. "Ready?" she whispered.

"Yeah."

She drew in a breath, let it out slowly. *Three. Two. One...*

Briar whipped around the corner of the house, rifle up. She found nothing in front of her but smooth, pristine snow. The ski tracks leading from the upper tree line stopped halfway to the house before veering away back toward some trees a dozen or so yards up the slope to the east. As though the shooter had suddenly changed course.

Then Briar noticed a line of footprints leading from the tracks to the south, toward the front of the house. "This way," she whispered and crept forward.

Alex must have heard them coming because he called out in a low voice that would be deadened by the snow. "Saw him take off south toward the village. Pretty sure he's alone."

Just one shooter, moving to the south. Those were good odds for them. "Coming up on your six," Briar called back. Within seconds she'd reached the front of the house and found Alex crouched behind the SUV they'd arrived in.

He picked something up from the ground and held it in the faint moonlight so they could see it. "Timer and fuse he was going to use to blow the C-4 I found attached to the side of the house. Enough to take this whole place down."

Shit, he could have blown the house to pieces and them with it if they hadn't heard him earlier.

Lights suddenly switched on at the eastern exterior of the closest house down the hill. Security lights triggered by the man who'd been about to blow them all up? Using rocks and trees for cover along the way, Briar surged toward the house at a run. Matt and Alex were close behind her, and she knew they'd be watching for more threats. She was so used to operating alone, it felt good to know she had such formidable backup.

Sticking to the shadows she tracked her quarry, aware that her prints in the snow were a dead giveaway but there was no help for it. The moon was bright enough that the shooter wouldn't need night vision equipment to see her. Luckily, whoever had been hunting her had left tracks of their own. She locked onto the path, followed it down into a hollow, then paused. Matt and Alex joined her a minute later.

Hidden by shadows she scanned the wide ski run before her, crisscrossed by thousands of ski tracks and footprints. Going up the rise to continue following would make her a clear target. She had to approach from a different angle and hope she could catch the shooter by surprise. The three of them were on the hunt now, and the prey was close.

After a short conversation they came up with a plan of attack and split up, each going in a different direction but staying close enough to one another to provide covering fire if necessary, the goal to encircle or at least cut off the shooter. Matt and Alex covered her while she darted from their position into the next house's yard, at the base of a rise farther down the hill.

While she was scanning the slope she caught a glimpse of movement downhill. Automatically she tracked it with the barrel of her weapon, staring through the sight. A man, moving fast. Too concealed to tell whether he had a weapon or not and she wasn't going to risk shooting an innocent civilian. Damn she wished she had comms with the others right now, they might have a better line of sight.

Knowing they'd see her and follow, she broke from cover and chased after the man. Maybe fifty yards ahead of her he veered into a stand of trees along the near side of the ski run and disappeared from view. Briar slowed as she approached where he'd turned, keeping to the shadows cast by the trees, being as silent as possible as she moved through the snow.

Her heart rate was calm, her breathing steady despite the rush of excitement in her veins. *Almost got you.* All she needed was for him to hesitate, make one mistake.

Another glimpse of movement in the trees, down and to her right. She swung around the tree trunk she'd been standing behind and followed. This time when the man appeared between the trees ahead she clearly made out the shape of the rifle slung across his back.

Taking a shot from here was possible, but risky. The report would give away her position and even though she was an expert shot, she couldn't guarantee hitting him in the arm or leg at this distance. It had to be a non-lethal shot because dead men didn't talk. No, she was going to take this bastard alive and extract every single piece of intel he had.

She ran after him, her boots plunging into the snow, dodging branches as she went. The village wasn't far now, the edge of it no more than a hundred yards away to the south. The shooter seemed to be headed for it, probably had a vehicle waiting there. She had to stop him before he reached it, and before anyone heard or saw them and called the cops.

If they haven't already.

At the last line of trees before a long stretch of open ground, she paused, watching the area downhill. The lights of the village twinkled below in the darkness, looking like some kind of fairytale town in all its Christmas glory. Completely at odds with what was playing out on this ski hill.

Stealing a glance over her shoulder she looked for any sign of Matt or Alex. Although she couldn't see either of them or their tracks she knew they were still close enough to give her covering fire. They had to have seen the shooter and would be pursuing him as well.

When she swung her gaze back toward the village, she saw the figure dart out from behind the covering shadows of a distant house. Briar raced after him, her thighs burning as she sprinted to make up the ground between them. The shooter slipped on something and went down, tumbling in the snow. She readied her rifle and took aim but before she could lock onto him he gained his footing, scrambling through a yard and into the next.

The mistake she'd been hoping for.

Gotcha, you bastard.

The yard was completely enclosed on three sides by a good-sized wooden privacy fence. There was no way out except over it or back the way he'd come, and he'd never risk retracing his steps. She saw him look around frantically for an escape.

There wasn't one.

Briar moved in closer, only a few dozen yards separating them now. She took aim as he ran up to the fence. When his hands caught the top of it, Briar fired one shot, hitting the back of his right shoulder where even a Kevlar vest wouldn't protect him.

The shooter arched back with a muffled cry and dropped from the fence. Briar took three quick steps forward, prepared to fire again but he'd rolled out of sight into a dip and she didn't have a shot. She went to one knee and waited for him to move, caught a glimpse of motion and instinctively dropped to her belly just as she saw the muzzle flash. A round smacked into a tree behind her, passing so close she heard its whine.

One of the guys behind her returned fire, two rapid shots to pin the shooter in place. Briar took the opening that gave her and sprinted for the closest house on her right, diving behind a stone retaining wall lining the backyard.

Staying low so she could use it for cover, she ran toward the thin stand of trees blocking the view of the house from the ski hill. The shooter was still pinned down, wounded, with nowhere to go. But the shots had attracted unwanted attention. Lights in the house nearest her and several others nearby were coming on, people emerging out on their balconies and doorsteps to see what was going on.

Briar's mouth thinned. She was going to finish this

right now.

Knowing the guys had her back, she gathered herself for one final advance and broke from cover. The shooter had gotten to his knees.

"Freeze!" she yelled, keeping her pace slow enough that her aim didn't waver.

He didn't. Instead he threw his left hand up to grasp the top of the fence and began to haul himself up. Briar swore and tightened her finger on the trigger, then suddenly another shot rang out from behind her, hitting the target's left shoulder. The angle and force of the impact knocked him forward. He wobbled, managed to fight gravity long enough to pitch his weight forward and topple over the other side of the fence.

He was *not* fucking getting away.

Briar raced for that fence. She heard the thud of running feet behind her, knew Matt and/or Alex were right on her heels as she sprinted for it, heart drumming against her sternum. She could hear the shooter moving as she ran, his muffled grunts of pain giving his position away.

Things were about to get up close and personal.

She slung her rifle across her back to get it out of her way, grabbed her pistol from her waistband. Catching the top of the fence she used her momentum to swing her legs up and over the top, bringing her weapon up as she cleared it. As her boots hit the ground she stumbled but gained her footing and locked her sights on the man lying bleeding in the snow. She aimed dead center at his forehead, prepared to kill him if necessary.

He was half propped up on his back in a spreading pool of blood, both arms hanging useless at his sides. He glared up at her in the moonlight, his pale eyes glittering with an almost feral light.

"Who sent you?" she demanded, her voice so low it came out almost like a growl.

His jaw flexed once and his nostrils flared but he didn't answer, instead turning his gaze several feet behind him where a sharp drop-off marked the edge of the upper limit of the village below.

"I want a name," she demanded, finger firm on the trigger.

The man still didn't answer. He struggled into a sitting position and as much as Briar would love to shoot him again there was no point. He was no longer a threat to her and she needed the information he had, so putting him in more pain that would make him incapable of talking was plain stupid.

The running footsteps behind the fence came closer and a moment later a big shadow sailed over the top. Matt landed with a soft thud, his body coiled tight as he brought his pistol up, sparing her a quick glance before zeroing back on their target. A few seconds after that Alex appeared on her right, having gone around the houses to block the shooter's escape.

"There's no way out," Matt told the shooter, his expression hard in the moonlight. "Cops will be coming any minute. Tell us what you know."

The man's breathing was harsh and ragged as he glared at them all, then focused solely on her.

Briar's patience snapped. This guy had come to kill her, might have killed Janaia and Frank. He wasn't going anywhere and he'd never do another hit again. "At best you're going to jail. At worst you'll wind up facing the death penalty once they disavow you like they did me and uncover all your kills that they'll call unsanctioned. I know that makes you want to get back at whoever sent you. Tell me their name."

The man's mouth twisted into an ugly smirk as he stared back at her, the smell of his blood rising in the cold air.

Alex made a snarling sound and stalked forward,

clearly intending to grab the guy and force the information out of him.

Without warning the shooter suddenly twisted toward the edge of the drop off, too far away for Briar to stop him. Matt swore and lunged for him but it was too late.

Briar watched, frozen, as the man deliberately launched himself off the edge of the precipice and plunged out of sight. She stepped to the edge just as he hit the ground some fifty feet below with a muffled thud, feeling almost numb inside as she stared at his unmoving body. From this height the hard-packed snow had done little to cushion his fall. If he wasn't dead already, he would be soon.

He lay on his back with his broken arms outstretched, eyes open and staring sightlessly up at her, blood pooling around him like the wings of a macabre snow angel. They had no answers and no time because from the faint voices floating down from up the hill, more and more people were coming out to investigate the shots.

Cursing, Alex whipped out his phone and put it to his ear. "Zahra, we're all clear but we need an emergency evac. Get everything out of there and pick us up at the south end of the lower village in ten minutes. Move." Lowering his phone, he shook his head in disgust. "Thought we had him."

Yeah, she had too. But he'd chosen death over a life behind bars or on death row. Or maybe he'd been even more scared of whoever had hired him, that he or she would make him pay for his failure and kill him regardless. Briar couldn't really say she blamed him.

"We've gotta move," she muttered. They had to be long gone before the cops arrived and started asking questions, began tracing their movements. She couldn't let them or anyone else see her.

Matt holstered his pistol and surprised her by

reaching out to grab her, pulling her up hard against his chest, his heavy arms slipping beneath her rifle to band around her back. She returned the fierce embrace, feeling the ragged inhalation he took, the way his muscles slowly relaxed as he breathed out. "You're okay?" he asked against her hair, voice rough.

"Fine," she said, taken aback by how worried he seemed. She wasn't some clueless civilian running around with a firearm and hoping to get a lucky shot. "I'm good, Matt. I know how to handle myself."

"I know, but… Fuck, I hated watching you charge after that guy while I was too far away to get to you if anything happened."

She tightened her arms, touched by his concern. He wasn't questioning her ability, just worried he might lose her. "Well I'm okay."

He sighed and released her but grabbed her hand and started walking at a fast clip after Alex. Together they hustled along a narrow, snow-slick path that snaked back and forth down the steep hillside. It would take a while for the cops to piece everything together and follow their tracks. By then Briar planned to be long gone.

When they finally made it to the road Zahra was just pulling up in the SUV. They jumped in and she hit the gas the moment they slammed the doors shut.

Chapter Nineteen

B riar's eyes snapped open when the jet's landing gear came down. She lifted her head from Matt's shoulder and rubbed at the tight muscles in the left side of her neck. Out the window the sky was still black.

"We'll be landing in a few minutes," he murmured, lifting his arm to wrap it around her shoulders. She leaned into him once more, enjoying the closeness as they descended into Tipton Airport, at Fort Meade, Maryland. She'd slept for most of the flight but it hadn't been enough and now she was groggy as hell.

The jet touched down and taxied to the end of the runway where it turned and parked close to the small terminal buildings. Alex and Zahra disembarked first. Briar went next, Matt following. When she stepped off the plane into the cold night air she saw a big, dark-haired man approaching with a cane, a severe limp in his gait.

She relaxed when she saw Zahra lower her bags and race toward him. The man dropped his cane and caught her in his arms, hugging her tight as he lifted her off the ground, his face buried in her hair.

Briar shouldered her ruck and followed Alex, who was smiling at them. The man holding Zahra set her down gently and put a hand on the side of her face, his expression intent as he said something. She nodded and twined her arms around his neck, squeezing tight. After one more hug he released her to slide one arm around her waist and turned to face the rest of them.

"You said she wouldn't be in any danger," the man said to Alex, his tone and expression full of hostility.

"I wasn't expecting any trouble," he said. "But it's all good because we had lots of backup." He nodded to her and Matt.

The man's dark gaze landed on her, did a quick once-over before settling on Matt. "And *they* are?"

"Matt DeLuca," Matt said, stepping up and offering his hand. "You must be Dunphy."

The man lost his hostile edge, his eyebrows rising slightly. "You were FORECON, right?"

"Yeah." He turned to her. "This is Briar." She was glad he didn't give her last name.

The man held out his hand to her. "Sean Dunphy. I'm Zahra's better half."

"Um, you've still got that backward," Zahra said with a laugh, resting her head on his chest. "And if they'd known you for more than five minutes, they'd never believe it."

Briar shook Dunphy's hand. "Hey."

"Hey," he echoed, still assessing her as though he didn't know what to make of her. "Why do I get the feeling this had something to do with you?"

Briar didn't feel like answering and was grateful when Alex spoke. "The others here?"

"Yeah, waiting out front." Dunphy bent to pick up his cane but Zahra scooped it up and handed it to him.

Wait, others? Briar glanced at Alex, who was watching her.

"It's okay, I've just brought in some reinforcements for the time being."

Matt wound his arm around her waist. "I met a couple of them in New Orleans. We can trust them."

"When did you guys decide on this?" she asked under her breath, annoyed that she hadn't been included in the decision.

"When you were out so hard on the plane that you drooled on my shoulder," he answered with a grin, and started walking with her toward the terminal.

Briar pulled the hood of her jacket closer around her face and kept her head averted slightly as they entered the small building, to help avoid a good shot of her by security cameras. She vaguely recalled the murmur of male voices on the plane when she'd dozed off. Just went to show how exhausted she was, to have missed all that.

They hurried through the building and out the other side then down the sidewalk to where two men awaited them in front of two black SUVs. The lighting here wasn't as bright and she suspected they'd chosen this spot because it was out of range of any security cameras. Both were big guys, one with military short dark hair, the other's a closely shorn reddish-gold. They wore jeans, boots and black leather jackets. All they were missing were the wraparound shades to complete the imposing appearance. Even standing still their posture and body language screamed former military. If they were friends of Alex's, she was betting former SOF.

"This is Hunter Phillips," Alex said of the dark-haired man when they reached them, "and Gage Wallace. The one-two punch of Titanium Security."

She knew of the company. They'd worked with Alex over in Afghanistan and Pakistan, had a good rep.

Next to her, Dunphy snorted. "And what am I?"

"You're the comic relief," Alex said without missing a beat. "You guys already know DeLuca," he said to

Phillips and Wallace, "but this is Briar."

They nodded to her and she nodded back, glad they didn't seem to expect any social niceties, even though she had a feeling they knew all about her current situation.

"You guys ready to roll?" Phillips asked. When they nodded he stepped aside and opened the back door of one of the SUVs while Wallace did the same to the other.

Zahra and Dunphy climbed into the first with Wallace. Alex, Briar and Matt piled into the back of the second while Phillips slid into the shotgun seat. Behind the wheel sat a woman with dark hair just slightly longer than Briar's. She wore an earpiece and didn't so much as bat an eyelash when they all climbed in. As soon as Matt slammed the back door shut, she pulled away from the curb and followed the lead vehicle out of the airport parking lot.

"This is Jordyn," Phillips said of the driver, leaning around in the front passenger seat to talk to them. "She's quite the expert with a long gun too, Briar."

Briar glanced at the woman, who met her eyes for a brief moment in the rearview mirror before focusing back on the road. Even if these people were here to help and both Matt and Alex trusted them, they were strangers and Briar didn't like them knowing who she was or what she did. Keeping to herself was something she'd learned to do early on and it had been reinforced throughout her training. Opening up to people took monumental effort and she was extremely choosy in who she allowed in.

It said a lot about her feelings for Matt that she'd let him in so deep in the short time they'd known each other.

"Anything said here stays here," Alex said to her, accurately reading her wariness. "These guys all have top security clearances. I brought them in because I've worked with them before and because they're not directly tied to any agency. You two'll be staying at an undisclosed NSA safe house in the area for the time being," he said to her and Matt. "Zahra and I'll be in touch with you about any developments, so rest assured we'll be working on this behind the scenes while you're off grid."

"Thanks," Matt said. Briar didn't reply, still resenting that this was all out of her control. But she knew Alex would never sell her out, so if he thought the safe house was secure, then she would trust his judgment on that. At least for tonight.

There wasn't much talk as they hit the highway and drove south, except for some small talk between Phillips, Alex and Matt. Thankfully no one tried to pull her into the conversation, instead just letting her be.

A few miles up the freeway the lead SUV turned off at a different exit and they continued on. Jordyn drove them to a residential neighborhood and pulled up in front of a two-story stucco-exterior house that looked identical to all the others on the street except for the color. She waited in the vehicle while the rest of them got out and Briar found herself escorted to the front door by three very large, very lethal men.

Even though she was armed and just as capable as them of dealing with a threat, she decided there were worse places to be than in the center of that protective circle.

Alex went in first, he and Phillips doing a quick sweep while she and Matt stayed just inside the door, out of sight of the street. Less than two minutes later they both returned, holstering their pistols. "Everything's secure," Phillips told them.

"There's a scrubbed laptop in the den for you to use, and two encrypted burner phones there as well. I know you know to keep your contact with the outside world to a minimum, but if you need more phones one of us will get them to you. Fridge and pantry have been stocked with the things you asked for," he said to Matt, "and the bedrooms and bathrooms as well. You both know how to reach me."

Briar nodded, taking in the space. The house was clean and cozy and smelled of lemon polish. Someone had been in here to clean recently, maybe even as little as a few hours ago. It wouldn't surprise her if Alex had managed to set this all up during the relatively short time they'd been waiting for their pilot up in Lake Placid.

"Either Zahra or I will be in touch if we hear anything, and of course let us know if you hear something on your end."

"Will do," Matt said.

Alex nodded and started for the door with Phillips but Briar stopped him with a hand on his arm. He looked down at her, his expression unreadable.

"Thank you," she told him. "For everything."

His eyes warmed as he smiled. "Thanks for helping save my vacation house from getting blown up. Grace would've been so pissed."

Briar chuckled and lowered her hand. "How are you gonna clean that whole mess up, by the way?" Their tracks telegraphed every move they'd made on the mountain, and there was a dead body with two bullet wounds lying at the base of that cliff. It was definitely going to attract unwanted attention, almost certainly make the news.

"Don't you worry about that, I have my ways and they're doing damage control right now, along with a cleanup crew I called in. With any luck we'll have the shooter's prints by mid-morning and then we'll run them through our system."

"Fingers crossed that gets us a good lead."

"Sure as hell can't hurt," he said, and left.

Matt shut and locked the door behind them, then turned to face her. Now that they were alone she once again felt that invisible electric vibration in the air between them, almost like faint static electricity on her skin. Much as she wanted him, she was too damn tired to finish what they'd started earlier.

"You hungry?" he asked.

"I could eat." And then she wanted to fall into the nearest bed and crash to get her system back online. All these days and nights without sufficient sleep were catching up to her. She could go for a couple days and stay on the move without sleep if necessary, but with all the emotional turmoil and action lately, she needed a solid eight hours or more of uninterrupted coma time.

She followed him into a clean, white, country-style kitchen and stood next to the counter while he opened the freezer. She assumed he'd pull out a frozen meal or maybe a pizza to heat up, and was surprised when he took out what looked like ice cream. "You seriously want that right now?"

He carried it over to the counter, a smile curving his lips. "No, but I think you do. It's maple walnut."

A squeezing sensation bloomed in her chest. He'd remembered the security challenge she'd answered to Janaia the night of the Ramadi op. The man was just so damn sweet and thoughtful, how the hell was she supposed to resist him?

After scooping a more than generous portion into a bowl, he grabbed a spoon from a drawer and handed it to her. She took it with a murmur of thanks and waited for him to get his own before joining him at the kitchen table. Their spoons clinked against the bowls as they ate, the only sound in the cozy, intimate silence. She hadn't been on that many dates, but to her mind this definitely counted and it was the most enjoyable one she'd ever had.

The familiar, sweet taste of the ice cream brought back a flood of bittersweet memories, starting with her parents and ending with Janaia. Matt was so damn considerate and always taking care of her. She vowed to herself that she was going to do something meaningful and sweet for him when she got the chance.

"So I've been wanting to ask you," he said, dipping his spoon back into his bowl for another bite. "I just assumed you've never been married, but were you ever engaged or anything?"

"Anything meaning…?"

He shrugged. "Living with a guy."

"Well, kind of, once."

He swallowed the bite of ice cream. "Kind of?"

She pushed her spoon through hers. "I met him in my last year of college and we dated for a while. We moved in together about a year after I started doing ops even though he didn't know exactly what I did for a living. For a while I thought he could be *the one*, that I might be able to have what my parents had." She made a face, disgusted even now by her naïveté back then, ridiculous in itself because she'd been a trained assassin. She'd considered herself worldly, jaded and invulnerable to things like deceit. How wrong she'd been.

"He was an analyst working for The Company. I couldn't tell him what I did, but I think he had a pretty good idea. I thought he loved me but it turned out he was using me to help further his career. It took Janaia to show me the truth of what was happening, and it wasn't because she was just trying to protect me as an asset or keep me focused on my job. He'd been hacking into my e-mail and searching through my contacts, hoping to find someone useful I could put him in touch with to help him climb the ladder. As soon as I saw what was really going on, I left. Packed my stuff and left while he was at work, and never talked to him again." He'd called and e-mailed for a couple weeks, then realized it was a lost cause and given up.

Matt was scowling now, looking all kinds of pissed off. "What a fucking douchenozzle."

She laughed at his choice of words. "Yeah. And I

was blind and stupid for not seeing the truth sooner. It could have ended my career if I hadn't woken up. He'd also been snooping around for details about my work in the hopes he could find something of value to add to his analyses and impress his superiors enough to fast track him to a promotion. All my stuff was encrypted and I was always careful to not talk about where I'd been or what I'd been doing, but he was skilled enough to find things out if he'd had long enough to dig. Lying to him all the time was exhausting and I hated feeling guilty about it."

"How long ago was this?"

"Just over five years."

He shook his head, seeming surprised by that. "So that's it? No one since?"

She shrugged and focused her attention on scooping up another mouthful of ice cream, slightly embarrassed. "I went on a couple more dates but I told you I didn't have much experience, and my work just makes getting involved really hard. And messy."

"I know what you told me. But that was before you almost killed me when you went down on me yesterday."

Looking up at him again, she grinned. "If I'd wanted to kill you, we wouldn't be having this conversation right now."

His eyes sparkled with humor. "Is it totally weird that I think that's sexy as hell?"

She grinned wider. "Yes." He was something else.

He sat back, let his gaze roam over her face until it finally settled on her mouth. "I dunno. I'm thinking it wouldn't be a bad way to go."

That focused, absorbed look on his face as he said it wiped the smile from hers as a rush of warmth suffused her body and settled low in her belly. Then he took another bite of ice cream, his eyes smoldering even as he smiled at her.

Definitely time to cash in that rain check.

They finished up and put the dishes in the dishwasher. "We're both beat," Matt said, stepping up behind her to wrap his arms around her middle and set his chin on her shoulder. "Why don't you go grab first shower and then we'll crash?"

She didn't have to ask to know he meant they'd crash together, and she was so on board with that. "Okay."

In the master bathroom upstairs she stripped and checked her stitches before getting into the shower. They were healing up well and weren't that sore anymore, just a little tender in spots and a bit itchy. She stepped under the pounding spray and sighed at the feel of the hot water rushing over her, allowing herself a few moments to savor it before shampooing her hair and scrubbing her body with the bar of soap.

She was rinsing off her face when the shower door clicked open and Matt stepped in behind her. He caught her hips in his big hands, turned her to face him and without hesitation she pressed against his chest, her cheek on his muscled shoulder, a heavy pulse starting between her legs at the feel of his erection sandwiched between them. But he made no move to do anything about it.

Instead he ran his hands through her hair, massaged the back of her neck, her shoulders and the tender muscles on either side of her spine while the water poured over them both. Briar didn't protest because it felt so damn good. By the time he was done kneading her from nape to rear she was both utterly relaxed and aroused as hell, tingling all over and wanting more.

He eased her away long enough to wash himself and she helped, sliding her hands over the beautifully sculpted muscles of his arms, chest and back. When she slid her palms over his stomach and curled her fingers around his erection, he stopped her with a rough sound, pulled her hands away and finished rinsing off.

Turning off the water, he opened the door and

grabbed a towel, wrapping her in it. "Step out," he commanded in a low voice.

She did as he said, quickly toweling off while staring at the way his muscles flexed as he dried himself. Dropping the towel, Matt slid his hands into her hair and kissed her. Briar sighed and opened for him, sliding her tongue along his, eager for him to put out the fire he'd started inside her.

Kissing her slow and deep he backed them out of the bathroom, into the bedroom and reached back with one hand to pull the covers down before lowering her onto the mattress. She wound her arms and legs around him as he lowered his weight onto her, sliding his erection across her belly in the most delicious way that only intensified the growing ache between her legs.

Briar arched into him, loving the feel of him covering her, pressing her into the bed with his greater weight. Her eyes closed as he trailed damp, nipping kisses down her jaw and throat, his big hands coming up to cup her breasts and cradle them for his mouth.

She moaned and grabbed the back of his head when he sucked and tongued her nipples, sending sparks of sensation streaming down to where his hips lay cradled between her thighs. He lavished attention on her breasts for a few minutes, until she was hot all over and squirming, then eased lower and slid his tongue into her navel. Her muscles tensed, her body needing more.

One big hand eased between her legs to cup her intimately, making the throb so much worse. She pressed against it, felt how slick she was as she rubbed against his fingers. Matt made a deep sound of approval and lowered his head to kiss the top of her mound. Briar gasped at the feel of his hot breath washing over her, tensed as he parted his lips and flattened his tongue against her sensitive flesh. A stifled sound caught in her throat, part moan, part whimper.

Staring at her up the length of her body, Matt licked slow and soft, running his tongue in lazy circles around her swollen clit. She gasped again, felt the muscles in her thighs tremble. His hands curled around the tops of her legs and pushed, opening her wider as he stroked and caressed her into mindlessness. Just as she was about to beg for mercy, her breath caught in her throat when she felt his tongue thrust inside her.

Know what else I'm looking forward to? Burying my tongue inside you.

Oh god, he was actually doing it.

Her fingers clutched at his head, her eyes flying open to watch in amazement as he drove his tongue in and out of her. Oh hell, that was so insanely hot. The sensation, the shocking intimacy of it, held her in thrall. She could only tremble and hang on for the ride, pleasure rising in an ever tightening spiral as her hips moved all on their own, shamelessly riding his tongue. Matt groaned low in his throat at her reaction, seeming to love what he was doing, then reached one hand around to circle her clit with a slick fingertip.

Oh my god...

Her head fell back, her mouth parting on a cry of pure ecstasy as that beautiful rush toward orgasm started. Then, suddenly, he stopped and pulled away.

Uttering a sound of protest, she half sat up and reached for him, desperate for the release hovering just out of reach. Matt reached over to the bedside table and grabbed a condom he must have left there, quickly rolling it down the length of his cock.

Her hands curled around his shoulders to haul him atop her, her mouth devouring his, but he didn't plunge into her as she'd expected. Instead he reached up for a pillow and yanked it down the bed, sliding one arm around her hips to lift and place them on it.

"Okay, now," she begged and went back to kissing

him, unembarrassed by the taste of her arousal on his lips, his tongue. It actually turned her on.

Sliding his tongue against hers, Matt settled on his knees and lifted one of her legs over his broad shoulder before wrapping his fingers around the back of her other calf and holding it out from her body slightly. She was panting, frantic to feel him inside her when he finally reached down with his free hand to slide the head of his cock into position. The hand on her calf tightened, brought it up and outward as his hips surged forward, burying him inside her.

Briar whimpered, squeezing her eyes shut at the sudden stretch, the sensation of being filled and having that maddening ache inside her soothed, then made much worse. Now she understood the logic of the pillow because the angle and position made him rub across that suddenly insatiable achy spot inside her. Her hands latched onto his upper arms, fingers digging in to his flexing biceps.

When he didn't move, she opened her eyes to gaze up at him. "Don't stop," she gasped, straining in his grip, trying to move her hips but unable to with him holding her leg.

Matt's face was tight, his eyes burning with arousal as he eased back and thrust forward again, this time bringing her captive leg over his other shoulder. He planted one hand next to her head, his weight braced on it, and stared into her eyes as he surged in and out of her. The last glimpse Briar had of him was like that, expression taut and focused, his gaze devouring her every reaction, his muscles rippling and shifting with each movement.

Then those clever fingers stroked and circled her clit as he took her, and the sudden increase in pleasure obliterated everything. She was nothing but mindless instinct as she writhed in his embrace, incoherent sounds of dizzying ecstasy spilling from her lips. Her hands locked onto his upper arms, her whole body gathering for the coming explosion she needed more than her next breath.

She heard him groan, a raw male sound of need, felt the scrape of his teeth against her neck as he buried his face against her and kept pumping. He was so hard, so thick inside her, his touch between her legs perfect. She whimpered his name, crying out as the orgasm finally hit, rolling through her in endless, powerful waves.

Matt let out a harsh moan against her neck. He gripped her hips in both hands and plunged hard and deep, over and over until he shuddered and groaned with his own release.

Briar lay there, wrecked. As she came back to herself she became aware of the muscles in her lower back protesting at being folded practically in half beneath him, her legs still hooked over his broad shoulders, but she didn't care. She sighed and smoothed her hands over his damp shoulders, his neck, rubbing her fingers against his scalp.

Matt made a low sound of pleasure in his throat and nuzzled the side of her neck, clearly asking for more. Smiling, she kissed the side of his cheek and kept petting him. When the burn in her lower back became flat out uncomfortable she squirmed and he finally lifted off her, gently easing her legs down to the bed.

Briar smiled to herself at the sight of him there, naked and settled on his knees on the bed, awed at the intensity of the pleasure he'd given her. "Now I *really* feel like I've been missing out all these years," she murmured.

He grinned. "Yeah, but it's usually not like *that*."

"I know." She might be inexperienced but even she knew that kind of sex was rare, and that it had everything to do with having the right partner. Still, she was damn happy to know he thought they had amazing chemistry too. She'd never believed in it before.

He left the bed to dispose of the condom in the bathroom then switched off the light there and crawled back in beside her. His warm, heavy arms wound around her, pulling her back to his chest, his thighs tucked behind hers and his breath warm on the back of her shoulder. "Let's get some sleep."

So many things were still outside her control. Briar was worried about what would happen tomorrow and for however long it would take to wrap up the investigation and get a name. For right now there was nothing more she could do and all she wanted was to savor this gift of being with Matt.

She fell asleep wrapped in his arms, part of her wishing the morning would never come.

Chapter Twenty

W ill reviewed the documents spread out on his desk in need of his signature. Not too many now, since he'd already taken care of most of his caseload and had just a handful left before his last full day Thursday. Some were posting orders or intelligence reports, other admin related, and a few were signing off on ops set to begin in the coming days or weeks.

All the ops were aimed at increasing security here in the homeland, though a sizeable portion of them would be carried out overseas to curtail and contain terrorist plots against the United States before they ever became a reality at home.

He'd come in early to get a head start so he could leave early and focus on his retirement speech, and because he was expecting news. Good news, he hoped.

The man he'd sent after Jones and DeLuca had contacted him last night to say he'd tracked them down and would take care of it overnight. Now it was almost six in the morning and still no word. Not unusual if the op hadn't gone off as originally planned, but there should have been an update, especially given what he was paying the man. At least the paperwork in front of him helped take his mind off it for the time being. He only had a few days left here, his big retirement bash was happening Friday night, three days from now.

As always, the TV mounted on the wall opposite the desk was tuned to a cable news network. He had the volume on low but since it was early there was hardly anyone else working on this floor so he could hear the broadcaster clearly as the man reported about the latest developments in the War on Terror. On his desktop, he had a broadcast on from a station in upstate New York, hoping to hear something about the op from last night.

Will set one signed document aside, ready to be sent off for the Deputy Director and Director's signatures. The next had to do with supplying contractors working in northern Iraq, who were fighting various groups of extremists. He perused the file, already familiar with the contents but always made certain he understood all parts of the document before signing.

"And now to some breaking news coming out of New York State this morning," the news anchor on his laptop said.

Will flipped the page of the second document, read the names of the contract agents involved. He recognized several of them, one of whom had unknowingly facilitated the arms deals Will had implemented there. He added his initials at the appropriate places, then turned to the last page where he was to place his signature.

"We have footage taken from Lake Placid early this morning, and conflicting reports about a murder that happened overnight. Police say a man's body was found at the bottom of a cliff, shot twice."

Will stopped and looked up at his computer, his pen poised on the paper. On screen the network showed amateur footage someone had taken with their phone. The quality was bad but it showed a sheet-draped body lying in the snow at the base of a cliff roped off by police tape, the lights of the village twinkling in the background.

"One witness said they saw the man fall from the cliff and others said they heard a gun battle shortly before. Police claim the story is false. It's unclear whether the man fell, or if he jumped to his death while trying to escape at least two gunmen who had been chasing him, according to one witness. Investigators say it's too early to identify the victim but they are saying any claims of armed gunmen chasing him are false."

Fucking hell.

He set his pen down and sat up straight, his stomach knotting. If the assassin had succeeded, he would have contacted Will by now. Which meant that the body beneath that sheet had to be Will's man. Had he killed either Jones or DeLuca? The news hadn't reported anything about other bodies found in the area. Maybe one or both of them had been wounded and were now on the run again.

Dread curled around his spine with icy fingers. If they were on the run now, he had no immediate way of finding, let alone tracking them. Worse still, the assassin might have talked. If Jones or DeLuca had his name…

He shoved his chair back and stood, unable to sit still. Grabbing the remaining files from his desk, he left a note for his personal assistant that he was working from home, then rushed down to his BMW and left headquarters. But he didn't drive home. Not yet.

He had to figure out what to do next. There must be someone in his circle who could help him. Maybe Alan, but…

No. Alan was in deep shit now too. While he didn't know all the details of their financial venture, his name was on the paperwork. If Will went down, Alan went with him, no matter how ignorant he was about the actual operations Will had ordered.

So what now? Hiring another contractor to hunt down Jones and DeLuca now was a high-risk, low-yield gamble, and time was short. And there was no way he could take care of this personally, no matter how much he was tempted to do just that. He had the skill and know-how. Just not the means to do it.

There has to be a way. I can't let up now.

He'd invested his entire life savings in the arms deals. His entire financial and political future depended on the income. He couldn't lose everything he'd worked for over this.

And then there were the people involved overseas. If he was exposed, they would be too, and no amount of money would make them cover his ass by lying. They'd turn on him, one by one. His only other option was his last resort exfil plan: get out of the country and start over.

It would kill him to do it, to leave the homeland he'd risked so much for the chance to make a difference in.

He had enough low-level contacts throughout South America and Europe to make it happen. If it came down to a choice between life in prison or a life outside the U.S, then he would leave the country and reinvent himself elsewhere.

****

Matt woke to the feel of soft fingers trailing over his naked back.

He hummed in his throat and shifted fully onto his stomach to give her more to touch, eyes closed, enjoying the way those sensual fingertips explored his skin.

Briar snuggled closer up against his side, one hand drifting across his shoulders, following the length of his spine. Relaxing and arousing him at the same time. The fingers dipped lower, stroking the very base of his spine and the top of his ass, making his muscles flex and his

eyes pop open. Then her lips touched the back of his neck
and the warmth of her breath washed across his nape as
her tongue trailed softly over his skin. Goose bumps broke
out all over his body, his cock stirring to life against the
mattress.

He had no idea what time it was and didn't care. With
the blinds down and her warm, naked body curled against
him he didn't want to move. Ever.

He loved seeing this affectionate, caring side of her,
couldn't wait for that curious little hand to slip beneath
him and wrap around his straining cock. The way she'd
surrendered herself to him hours ago had been incredibly
hot and gratifying and he recognized it for the gift it was.

"Are you awake?" she whispered against his
shoulder, tongue playing gently as she curled her hand
around his left hip and squeezed his ass.

"I think so. But if I'm dreaming, don't wake me up
until after the good part."

She chuckled softly and nestled tighter against him,
her breasts pressing against his back. "I've been lying
here watching you sleep for a while now and you're just
so damn gorgeous I couldn't keep my hands to myself
anymore. Or my mouth," she added, her teeth nipping
gently at his nape before her tongue soothed the tiny sting.

Matt reached down to catch the hand on his hip and
laced their fingers together as he drew them up to his
mouth. He kissed her knuckles, slid his tongue between
them, feeling her squirm behind him as she began to heat
up.

And then the goddamn phone rang.

Briar sat up immediately and grabbed it from the
nightstand, switching the lamp there to its lowest setting.
As she answered he rolled over and slid an arm beneath
his head, glancing at the clock. Almost ten in the morning,
but they'd both needed the sleep.

Briar stared straight ahead as she listened to whoever

it was, he guessed either Rycroft or Zahra. Matt let his gaze roam over her naked body as she sat there with her knees drawn up, her smooth bronze skin glowing in the lamplight. He stroked a hand down her thigh, pleased when she absently reached down to twine her fingers through his.

"I'm going to put you on speaker," she said, then lowered the phone and hit the button. "Okay."

"It's Zahra. I've got a few updates. Nothing huge yet, but it's a start."

"Let's hear it," he said, curious as to what she'd uncovered.

"First, the situation in Lake Placid is proving harder to clean up than Alex had hoped. He's still working on it but so far at least one person got footage of the body last night. Alex's crew are trying like hell to downplay everything and keep it under wraps, but a local news station has broadcast it."

"Are we in the footage?"

"No, and Alex's sources have been doing more damage control. Your cover's still good. Second, I found out through the grapevine what the CIA has on Briar in terms of evidence at the two murder scenes that started all of this. They've apparently got fingerprints on the second victim's car, in the interior and under the hood."

Briar frowned. "I was never in his car and never touched it."

"Well they've got that plus some of your hair to provide DNA evidence."

She scoffed. "That stuff can be planted easily enough."

"Which is why they did it," Zahra said. "For the guy in Baton Rouge, again, your prints were found at his place. On the doorknobs and on the balcony you supposedly pushed him from."

Now Briar looked insulted. "As if I'm dumb enough

to go in a damn door." She sounded outraged. "So to them I'm not just a rogue agent, I'm a fucking incompetent one too?"

"Well, they've also got witnesses who've given sworn testimony that you were at both murder scenes. Both said they witnessed arguments between you and the victims. One said they saw you doing something underneath the suspect's car before he drove away, and the other said he saw someone go out onto the balcony with the first victim, then push him over. According to them you had both motive and opportunity, so coupled with the forensics located at both scenes…yeah."

Briar shook her head. "So they've paid people off to lie for them," she said, frustration clear in her voice. "What else did you find out?"

"I've been pulling on the strings for those two companies we found dumping money into an account in the Caymans. Turns out there are five companies total, each with different owners and each under a different country's jurisdiction. It's gonna take me a while to uncover everything. The companies are in the Caymans, Gibraltar, Barbados and Bermuda, and one in Baltimore."

Matt pushed up onto one elbow. "Can you send me the info on that one? I can go to the Baltimore field office and check things out."

"Alex said to hold off on that for a bit. I'll have to investigate each one of these individually to see how they're linked and find out if there are any other connections we've been missing."

"How long?"

She sighed. "Could be hours, might take days. I'm working as fast as I can on it—"

"I know you are. Once you have more uncovered, give me the Baltimore details and I'll head over there with some local agents, or even one of the Titanium guys."

"I'll have Alex arrange all that," she answered. "It

also looks like someone else has been running a similar investigation of sorts. Briar's contacts we were looking into have all been flagged in the system, and there's been more research into the Caymans thing. Don't know who's doing it though. That's all I have for now, but do you guys need anything else?"

"No, we're good for now. Thanks," Briar added.

"Okay, I'll be in touch. Hang in there."

"We will." Briar ended the call and set her left forearm on her upraised knees. Resting her cheek on the back of it, she looked at him. "They can't formally charge me with just my prints and some hairs and whatever lies those witnesses were paid to say."

"Sure they can, they're the CIA."

She blew out a breath and sat up, rubbing a hand over her face.

Matt smoothed a hand up and down her back. "Won't matter what evidence they planted once we nail the bastard behind this and get your name cleared."

Glancing over at him, she smiled. "Yeah." She slid off the bed. "I'm gonna go make some coffee. Want some?"

"Love some." And later he intended to take her mind off everything the best way he knew how, get her naked and willing beneath him again. Just remembering the sweet sounds she made when she came were enough to make him hard.

She eyed him from the doorway, letting her gaze wander over his naked body, an appreciative, almost possessive gleam in her eyes that he loved. "You staying here?"

"For now. I'm gonna call Celida, see what's going on at her end."

"Okay. I'll bring you up a cup."

He got a gorgeous eyeful of her naked ass as she walked away, completely uninhibited about her body. She was all sleek, toned grace, her hips swaying in a mesmerizing rhythm as she exited the room.

Smiling to himself, he dialed Celida and filled her in on what Zahra had told them. "Anything on your end?" he asked.

"Alex just got off the phone with a bank contact in the Caymans. Apparently there's only one person with signing authority listed on the account. He's a fifty-three year old local, a laborer with an eighth grade education. The owner of one of the companies Zahra mentioned apparently pays him a salary to issue the checks. I've got police dispatched to question him about the owner. If they pay him well enough, he might not talk, which will force us to get an official warrant to get more."

But the tangle of loose threads was starting to unravel already. Only a matter of time until something materialized from all this. Anticipation curled inside him. "I bet he'll talk. Briar and I'll be holing up here, but if I check out that Baltimore operation, I'll call you."

He'd just set the phone down on the bed when the scent of brewing coffee reached him. He could go downstairs and save Briar the trip up, but decided against it. Stretching out on his back with his hands tucked beneath his head, he lay naked atop the sheets and waited for her to join him, anticipating what he'd do to her this time.

She'd dropped her guard so much already and each time they had sex she let him in even farther. Matt wanted in so damn deep that she'd never be able to get rid of him. Because once this situation was resolved and the danger over, *they* would just be starting.

If he had anything to say about it, after they drank their coffee they weren't leaving this room again for a long while. Things were slowly winding up and the end wasn't far away now. He had only a short time to convince her that he belonged in her life, and she in his.

She might not realize or believe it yet, but with her, Matt was playing for keeps.

Chapter Twenty-One

Briar checked her e-mail on the laptop Alex had left for them, hoping to see some news from Trinity but there was nothing since their last communication two days ago when they'd talked about Janaia and everything that had happened since. Trin had hinted that she was stateside somewhere, had volunteered to come and be Briar's backup until this was all over. A touching offer, though Briar wouldn't disrupt whatever job Trin was pulling right now. Besides, she had Matt.

Three days had come and gone since arriving at the safe house, each with its ups and downs. Zahra and Celida had continued searching for more information on the shell companies dumping money into the Caymans account. They were getting close to the end of the trail and it was frustrating to be trapped here and forced to wait. Briar might like downtime and be a homebody but even she was feeling cagey after being stuck inside this long.

At least the company was good.

"Anything from Trinity?" he asked from behind her.

"No."

"Who is she, anyway?"

Briar glanced over her shoulder to find Matt in the office doorway, a mug of coffee in one hand, shoulder braced against the doorjamb. The light gray T-shirt he wore hugged his muscled torso and he managed to make those cargo pants look sexy. "She's an old friend. And a Valkyrie," she admitted.

Matt straightened slightly, his eyebrows rising. "Do you keep in touch with a lot of them?"

"No, just her. She'd mentioned something about Georgia getting in contact with her, asking if she'd heard anything about us. She knows what happened in Lake Placid."

"Where is she?"

"Don't know. I could try to track her down but it would likely be a waste of my time. She's so paranoid she makes me look trusting by comparison. Something she said makes me think she's here in the States but I can't say for sure."

"You have very colorful friends." He grinned and took a sip of coffee.

Yes, her very tiny inner circle was colorful, and now down to only two people: Trin and Matt. Briar wasn't sure if he even realized how much she'd come to trust him or how much he meant to her. For all his intensity Matt was actually pretty easy going and easy to be around. She was thankful for that because she wasn't used to living with anyone.

He seemed to pick up on her shifting moods as she struggled to adjust to this new reality and let her be when she needed space. She found she was less and less inclined to close herself up in a room away from him, something she absolutely would have done with anyone else. Instead she liked having him in sight, liked being able to bounce ideas off him or discuss things. Although they both had strong opinions and didn't always agree on things like politics or how this investigation should be run, he always had valid points to offer and she valued his opinion.

He was also the most generous and attentive lover a woman could wish for. Just thinking of all the things he'd done to her over the past few days made her toes curl into the carpet beneath the desk. In her wildest dreams she'd never imagined herself as the sensual, erotic woman she became in Matt's arms.

But the best thing of all was the way he treated her even outside of the bedroom. Not as a woman who was smaller and weaker and therefore not as smart or as important as him. He treated her like an equal, with respect.

Against all odds and even though it scared her in some ways, she was falling hard for him and couldn't see herself walking away once this was over. All indications suggested Matt had meant it when he'd said he wanted her to give them a chance. He was the one bright spot in her life right now, and the hope of having more with him, the tantalizing dream of belonging with a man like him, had never seemed so close.

"I think I'd like to meet her one day," Matt said.

Briar half-smiled. "She's pretty curious about you too, so maybe she'll let you."

"Why, what've you told her about me?" he asked, coming toward her. He set his coffee cup on the desk and sat on the corner of it, reaching out to trail his fingers through the hair at her temple.

It was little things like that, unexpected touches or other gestures of affection that did her in because they made her feel important and cherished. She remembered what he'd said about wishing he'd been more affectionate with his wife and he was definitely making a concerted effort to change that now. Briar sensed that he craved it in return and she tried to be demonstrative but it still wasn't second-nature for her, maybe because she'd held herself back from others for so long. So far he'd been patient in allowing her to take forward steps at her own pace.

"Only that you were in the Corps and that you're with an agency now."

His lips quirked in amusement. "Not even telling Trinity the details?"

"I probably will, eventually. I guess I feel…protective of you."

His hand slid around to cup the back of her head, his green eyes heating. "That's sweet, and also pretty damn hot, coming from you."

She could feel herself blushing under that intense stare.

He leaned in until his mouth was poised next to her ear, dropped his voice to a seductive murmur. "I love that you can still blush around me. I wonder what else I could do to make you blush?"

She opened her mouth to say something sharp and witty even though her insides were melting, but stopped when a ringtone went off. Matt immediately straightened and pulled the phone out of his pocket to answer. She watched his face as he listened, wondering who it was.

A subtle tension settled in his shoulders. "Yeah, sure. See you in a few." He set the phone down. "Alex and Zahra are on their way over. They've got something."

Excitement leapt inside her. It had to be something big if they were telling them in person rather than just over the phone. She went to the living room with him and Alex and Zahra arrived a few minutes later. They sat on the couches while Zahra booted up her laptop and turned it to face them.

"We've found the name of the owner listed on the company in Baltimore," Alex announced.

Briar quickly read what was on screen, focusing on the picture of the middle-aged man. Late forties or early fifties with graying, blond hair and brown eyes. Alan Turner. "Who is he?" she asked Zahra.

"A very wealthy lawyer involved in illegal arms smuggling," she said grimly. "There could be others, we're pretty sure he's not working alone and that he has at least one silent partner."

"So we're going to pay him a little visit and find out," Alex added.

"I'll come with you, but I want someone here to watch Briar's back," Matt said. Briar automatically bristled but before she could argue, he looked over at her. "I know you can take care of yourself, but I'm not leaving you here alone without protection."

Briar sighed. He just wanted her safe, and she appreciated that. As much as she wanted to go along for the questioning, she couldn't without risking blowing her cover—being officially declared dead and all. "All right."

"I've already made a call. Jordyn and Ellis are on their way over," Alex said.

"Who's Ellis?" she asked.

"Blake Ellis. Former Scout Sniper, and Jordyn's fiancé. I figured you wouldn't be comfortable having them inside so I've told them to park out front and watch the house. They should be pulling up any minute. If anything happens while we're gone, they're both solid operators you can count on."

Briar nodded. "Okay." She got up and followed the others to the door, careful to stay out of sight in case anyone was watching from outside. Another black SUV had pulled up behind Alex's vehicle.

"That's them," he said.

Matt handed her the burner phone they'd been using then caught her chin in his hand. His green eyes were filled with understanding. He knew she hated being left behind. "I'll be back soon and I'll call you if there's any news. This'll all be over soon." He lowered his head to kiss her and she didn't stiffen even though she knew Alex could clearly see them from the front walkway.

"See you later," she murmured, giving Matt a smile. If she'd needed more proof that she was insanely attached to him, the ache in her chest as she watched him walk away did the job.

She waited until he'd shut the door behind him before stepping over to lock it and arm the security system to stay mode. *Please let this be the break we need.*

****

As they pulled up to the gate of the swanky upscale townhome complex in one of Baltimore's most expensive neighborhoods, Matt surveyed the brick, three-story homes. All of them were done up with strands of holiday lights, wreaths and greenery on the doors and front porches. It looked like something from a Christmas card.

Rycroft gave the guard at the gatehouse his ID and waited for the electronic gate to swing open. He drove up to the second house from the end and parked out front. Matt followed him and Zahra up the walkway, his pistol in the back of his waistband. While he didn't expect to need it, he wasn't taking any chances either.

As it was a Friday morning most people were off to work but Alan Turner answered the front door moments after Rycroft's knock. A slight frown creased his forehead as he studied them, a wary expression on his face. "Can I help you?"

Rycroft held out his ID and introduced himself. "We have a few questions we'd like to ask."

Turner stared at him for a moment, then darted a glance around, as though embarrassed that his neighbors might be seeing this. "Sure, come on in." He stepped back and let them inside a foyer decked out in a Christmas display worthy of a magazine spread.

The scent of cinnamon and baking cookies hung heavy in the air and soft carols floated toward them. Down the hall where Matt could see through another entryway into the kitchen, a middle-aged brunette poked her head out.

Seeing them, she cast an uncertain look at her husband and called out, "Is everything okay?"

"Everything's fine," Turner told her. "I'm just going to talk to them in my study."

They followed him past the wooden staircase wrapped in lighted garland to another door. Turner opened it and headed to a wide wooden desk in a room that easily cost double Matt's annual salary. The entire thing was carved out of what looked to be mahogany. Walls, floors, even the coffered ceiling. It was a room that spoke of money and power and the man seated behind the desk appeared to wear that image very comfortably.

"So, what can I do for you?" he asked, looking at Rycroft.

The NSA agent got right to the point. He laid a document with the company's name and all the charges against him on the desk. "We need to know who your partner is."

Turner paled slightly as he stared at the paper, his expression tensing. "What are you—"

"It's all there in black and white. I wouldn't be here if we didn't have the evidence to back this up." Rycroft leaned back, steepling his fingers together as he regarded the other man. "Your name is on the legal documents. That makes you responsible for the illegal activities the company's been involved in. You're facing tax evasion, corruption, funding terrorists. Treason."

Turner was frantically scanning the document now, unease pouring off him in tangible waves. "Illegal arms deals?" He looked up, met Rycroft's, then Matt's eyes. He shook his head, expression adamant. "You've made a mistake, my company doesn't deal with this kind of shit. Treason? I know *nothing* about any of this."

"Then that either makes you a liar, or just fucking stupid," Matt said.

The man swung his eyes to Matt, looking almost panicked now. Had he really been dumb enough to get involved in this without knowing the details? Guy was a fucking lawyer, for chrissake. There was no way he didn't know his company had been involved in illegal activities.

"Am I under arrest?" Turner asked.

"Not yet, not if you cooperate. We've got warrants to see all your paperwork and trace your calls and e-mails, and enough evidence to put you away for the next twenty years. In Federal prison," Rycroft added, letting that sink in a moment before continuing. "The only way to save yourself now is by telling us who your partner is and agreeing to testify against him when we take him into custody and all this goes to trial."

Turner shook his head and leaned back in his leather chair, clearly shaken. "I'm not saying anything else without my lawyer present."

The guy was scared shitless of his silent partner. That was clear to Matt.

"Great," Zahra said, opening her laptop and setting her fingers on the keys. "And who's that?"

Turner shot her an icy glare and reluctantly told her. Within moments she had the address of the firm.

"We're heading over there right now," Rycroft said, standing, "so we'll follow you."

Turner shook his head and looked like he was going to argue, then thought better of it and rose from behind his desk. He followed them to the front door and called to his wife to tell her he'd be back in a while, then grabbed his coat from the front hall closet.

Matt stayed directly behind him as they walked to the silver Lexus parked in the driveway. The guy was spooked, desperately trying to come up with a way to get himself out of this, and Matt wasn't letting him bolt. Matt drove the SUV over to the lawyer's office, staying directly on Turner's back bumper. He could see the man talking to someone in glimpses given by the Lexus's rearview mirror.

"Must be on the phone with his lawyer," Rycroft said.

Little good that would do him, Matt thought, making a right hand turn off the street to follow Turner behind the office building.

When they stepped into the reception area, Turner confirmed their suspicions by walking unannounced right into the attorney's office.

Without pause, Rycroft slid the warrant for the requested paperwork onto the man's desk. "We need to see all the incorporation documents, as well as any personal agreements Mr. Turner might have pertaining to it." He tossed another envelope onto the wooden surface. "Here's the deal we're willing to offer—immunity, if he reveals his business partner and agrees to testify against him. He can take it or leave it."

The lawyer read the court order Rycroft had given him, the charges laid against Turner, then signaled to his assistant, hovering in the doorway. "Get the files."

They took the files and left Turner to talk with his attorney in private, as the law demanded. Each of them took a binder and began searching through the paperwork, looking for any others involved with the company. Matt flipped through the pages, his heart beating faster. The name they were looking for had to be in here somewhere.

But twenty minutes later when he'd finished looking through his binder, he'd found nothing. Zahra set hers aside and shook her head, then Rycroft exhaled and tossed his on the table before him.

Another dead end.

But they still had their trump card to play.

They waited a few more minutes until the attorney

finally opened his door and asked them to come in. Turner was seated in a chair beside the window, his expression haunted.

"Based on the severity of the charges and the evidence you have against him, my client has agreed to the deal you offered."

"I'd say that's a wise decision," Rycroft said, and pulled out his phone to call in more agents to take him into custody.

Before Turner could move Matt took two steps toward him and stopped, folding his arms across his chest, making himself look as intimidating as possible. He used his commanding officer's voice, the one very few people had ever been dumb enough to ignore, let alone defy. "I want a name. *Now*." He hadn't officially signed the paperwork yet, but Turner was a done deal.

The man swallowed and looked toward the window, fucked either way and choosing the lesser of two evils. A slimy bastard, but not stupid, because he talked. "It's Balducci. Will Balducci."

Chapter Twenty-Two

Briar's heart hammered when Matt hustled her from the front door of the safe house and into the back of the SUV in the driveway. After she climbed in beside Zahra, Matt slammed the door and walked around to slide behind the wheel.

She pushed the hair out of her face, picturing Balducci's face. "I remember him. He was one of Georgia's trainers but I'm not sure about any of the others—"

Matt's jaw tensed. "He was also Janaia's recruiter."

Shock slammed into her. No. She didn't want to believe it. She looked at Alex, who turned slightly in the front passenger seat to look back at her.

"It's true. He recruited her eighteen years ago, was her original handler before being promoted within the agency."

Briar was stunned, the anger she'd shoved deep down rising all over again.

"Alan Turner was his college roommate and fraternity brother," Zahra told her. "They've been in business ventures together since graduation. When

Balducci approached him a few years ago about a new business deal, Turner didn't even blink before forking over money toward it. We think he knew it was outside the realm of legal, but it looks like Balducci went to great lengths to hide it from his investors and the owners of all the other companies involved."

Great lengths such as setting her up and dealing Janaia a torturous death, Briar thought angrily.

She curled her hands into fists and turned her head to stare out the window, fighting back the rage. What she wouldn't give for five minutes alone in a room with him. She knew how to inflict maximum pain with well-placed blows to the most vulnerable places on the human body. With each strike she would make Balducci suffer for what he'd done. No punishment would ever be enough, but at least it would be something.

"So what happens now?" she asked numbly as Matt merged onto the freeway and headed for Virginia. They were going to Quantico where Matt would brief his team and get ready to serve the arrest, search and seizure warrants against Balducci. Assuming the paperwork arrived on time.

"Turner's on his way to the Baltimore field office for questioning," Matt said, shoulder checking to ease into the fast lane. As soon as he was over he hit the gas.

"We're waiting until the last moment to freeze Balducci's accounts, so we don't tip him off," Alex said. "I've already spoken to Celida so she's up to speed. She's getting a team together on her end to carry on the investigation while I handle the warrants. I know certain judges who will pounce all over someone accused of treason."

"Will he face the death penalty?" Briar asked. She wanted him to die for what he'd done. It was the only way she'd ever find any peace.

"He could. All the charges are federal," he answered.

She uncurled her fists, laid her palms flat against her thighs. "When will the arrest happen?"

"Tonight." Matt's tone had a ring of finality to it that she found comforting. "Only a few, select people know about the charges. His retirement dinner is tonight, and there's no way he'd miss it even if he is getting worried. We won't take him down at the party, there'll be too many civilians around, and we can't do it beforehand because we're still waiting on a few last pieces of evidence and we need all the warrants in order first. We want him to think everything's normal, give him a false sense of security, then take him at home. We'll have someone at the party to give us updates, and someone will tail him when he leaves. As soon as he gets home, he's ours."

"I want to be there. I want to see him in cuffs when you guys haul him out of his house." She wanted to see him, for him to look into her eyes before they took him away.

"We'll see," was all Matt said.

"There's a possibility we'd allow you to be a lookout with one of us. But under the circumstances, you can understand why there's concern about you ignoring commands in order to achieve your own agenda," Alex added.

She couldn't even be insulted or argue that point, because it was true. So she nodded. "Fine. As long as I get to be there when it all goes down." Because short of chaining her in place or locking her up, nothing would keep her from going to that house tonight.

No one said anything further to her as they drove toward Quantico, busy talking about the investigation and the remaining timeline. Then they all got quiet when the burner phone in her pocket chimed.

Pulling it out, Briar checked the screen. It was a message from Trinity. *Georgia knows*, it read. She'd added an embedded link below it.

Briar tapped on it, waited for the page to load. Seconds later the opening bars of Wagner's *Ride of the Valkyries* filled the vehicle.

An alarm, and a warning.

Heart tripping, she cast an alarmed glance at Matt, who was watching her in the rearview mirror. "It's Trin. Georgia knows about Balducci. She might be going after him."

And if she reached him before the HRT did, Balducci wouldn't live long enough to be taken into custody tonight.

****

None of his business contacts had returned his calls, and that wasn't a good sign.

Will slid his favorite SIG into the specially designed holster at the small of his back and tugged the bottom of his tux jacket over it. It fit so well no one would be able to tell he was carrying. He had a full magazine in it and a spare in the glove compartment of his BMW, just in case.

Tonight he was taking no chances.

Five minutes until he had to leave for the party and he'd heard nothing from the bank manager in the Caymans, either. The last payment for the final arms sale was supposed to have been transferred to his account this afternoon. When he'd checked just before closing time, the wire transfer still hadn't shown up.

It could just be a technical glitch, something easy that the manager could fix for him over the weekend.

Or it could mean something far worse.

"Will? Are you ready?" Barbara called from downstairs.

"Be down in a minute," he called back, facing his reflection in the mirror. At least his unease didn't show.

He had to show up at the dinner. There was no way

around it. Aside from everything else, the mysterious female supporter he'd been trying to meet with over the past few weeks had indicated she might attend. He'd never met her in person, only spoken to her over the phone and via e-mail. With her financial clout behind him, he could do wonders with his upcoming campaign.

He'd eat, mingle with his guests for a bit, listen to the speeches then give his. After his big announcement, he'd head for a private airstrip outside of town and get out of the country to plan his next move. For a surprise trip, he'd tell Barb.

At the foot of the stairs, his wife awaited him, beautiful as always. She wore a ruby-red gown that made her skin glow, her blond hair twisted into a sleek knot at the back of her head. She looked elegant, refined, the perfect image of a future senator's wife.

Pushing aside his unease he smiled at her and offered his arm. "You look beautiful."

Her eyes lit up at the compliment and he saw the spark of hope there, the hope that he still loved her and that their marriage would mean more than what it had become over the past few years. Will didn't have the heart to extinguish that fragile flame. It seemed ironic, but he needed her more than ever right now.

She smoothed her hands along the shoulders of his tux jacket. "You look pretty gorgeous yourself. Even better than the day I married you."

Giving into the moment, he kissed her gently, felt the tiny ripple of shock that traveled through her before her lips molded to his. When he lifted his head he saw the desire glowing in her eyes and found himself looking forward to later on, when they'd be aboard the private jet he'd hired.

Assuming he made it that far.

****

Nate hustled through headquarters at Quantico and pushed open the door to the briefing room with only two minutes to spare. The rest of his team was already there, along with several other FBI agents he recognized, among them Celida Morales, his team leader's girl. Tuck was standing next to her, listening to whatever her boss, Agent Greg Travers, was saying.

Nate quickly crossed the room to join his other six teammates, all seated in chairs waiting for the briefing to begin.

"Nice of you to join us," Bauer said dryly, slanting him a sidelong look.

"I was busy," Nate said as he slid into a chair beside him. "Didn't hear my phone the first time."

Blackwell leaned over from his seat behind him and arched an eyebrow, staring at his neck. "Dude, is that a hickey?"

"No." He tugged at the collar of his utilities, feeling his face heat up.

Blackwell laughed. "If she gave you that, I can only imagine what other marks you got. No wonder you didn't hear your phone."

"It wasn't like that, I was sleeping." Not alone though.

Jake Evers thumped him on the back in congratulations. "That good, huh?"

"Shut up." His personal life and his reputation with the ladies was an ongoing source of amusement for the guys, especially the taken ones. But Nate didn't kiss and tell so they were getting nothing from him about this latest girl. One date had turned into two very enjoyable days and nights and if things finished up here tonight in time, he was hoping for a third.

"Well, good for you," Cruz said on his other side. "Sow those wild oats while you can, my man."

Nate arched a brow at him, relieved that none of them had seen through the ruse yet and he hoped they never did. The truth was, he wasn't just an easygoing guy as talented with medical skills as he was with a firearm.

No, the real him was a fucked-up mess and the women were merely a form of medication to treat the ever-present darkness inside him. Demons that still haunted him from his childhood and others from his deployments overseas that he battled on a daily basis.

Nate planned to make damn sure no one ever saw that ugly part of him. Especially these guys, whose respect meant more to him than anything. "You make it sound like you speak from experience. You planning on settling down or something? You been holding out on us?"

Cruz just gave him a secretive smile and shrugged. "Nope."

Well, now Nate was dying to know who this mystery girl was who put a smile on Cruz's movie-star face. He turned to Vance, Cruz's best friend on the team. "You know anything about this?"

"'Bout what?" he asked in his deep voice, trying to sound nonchalant.

Nate narrowed his eyes. "You know what."

Vance flicked him a glance, one side of his mouth curving up, the half-grin exposing teeth that were shockingly white against his dark skin. "Nope. Don't know anything. And what about you, my man? This latest girl got you wrapped around her little finger yet?"

"What?" Evers leaned forward once more, looking all kinds of interested. "Schroder's gotten himself lassoed?"

"No, I—"

"Man, I never knew you were into ropes and kinky shit like that. Thought that was Bauer's deal," Blackwell teased, earning a dark, quelling look from the biggest member on the team. Bauer was a former SEAL, the very embodiment of badass, and he had a personality to match. Guy was all business, serious all the time, though he'd lightened up some since hooking up with his live-in girlfriend. Around Zoe, Bauer was a completely different person.

"I'm not getting lassoed, trust me," Nate clarified, straightening in his seat. He was only twenty-eight, way too young to be tied down to a long-term, committed relationship. Way too young to be tied down to only one woman, for that matter, even if he found one willing to take him and his issues on.

"It'll happen," Evers said, sounding convinced as he leaned back in his chair. "One day the right woman's gonna come along and blow your doors off like a breaching charge. Hell, if it can happen to Bauer, you definitely have a chance."

"Gee, thanks," Nate muttered, glancing back at Bauer, who was ignoring Evers's words.

Nate was saved from more ribbing when the rear door to the room opened and his commanding officer, Matt DeLuca walked in. A legend within the HRT, he took up position at the front of the room and waited for Celida to join him. "All right, everybody listen up. We've got a time sensitive situation unfolding that needs to be handled tonight."

Nate noticed two others slip into the room, a man he recognized from the New Orleans conference as Alex Rycroft and—

Holy shit, it was the woman from the night of the Ramadi op. Briar Jones. She looked surprisingly hot for a woman who was supposed to be dead.

Nate couldn't help but gawk at her as DeLuca spoke, filling them in on all the details. They'd been told she'd been assassinated and dumped in a lake.

He darted surreptitious looks at his teammates, noticed them all stealing glances at her as well. Everyone but Tuck, who didn't seem at all surprised that she was standing in this room. Had he known she was alive this whole time? Had DeLuca been covering for her?

He focused his attention back to the briefing and what DeLuca was saying about their target. Will Balducci, a senior CIA officer and former Naval intelligence officer.

Whoa. Nate forgot all about the woman standing against the wall for a moment, totally engrossed with what his CO was saying. This was huge. A plot that had been unfolding for a long time, possibly years, considering the arms deals.

"I think you all know NSA agent Alex Rycroft," DeLuca said, "but you haven't been formally introduced to Briar Jones."

Everyone's attention turned to her. She didn't acknowledge the introduction. Not a smile, not a glimmer of nervousness at being singled out. She scanned the room almost impersonally but something told Nate she'd just memorized each and every one of their faces. Or maybe she'd already known them all before showing up today.

"The FBI has frozen the offshore accounts, so while Balducci's going to be at this party, he might suspect something's up. He's proven very hard to catch at this and he's got plenty of contacts to draw from who could lend assistance. There's one other important piece to this," DeLuca added, pausing to survey the team. "He's former SWCC."

Nate raised his eyebrows and looked around at his teammates. A Special Warfare Combat Crewman, one of the guys who provided backup, infil and exfil for the SEALs. Way more highly trained than their average tango. That was gonna make this op a little more interesting than usual.

"He's also a pilot and he's had lots of practice hiring contract killers so it's not out of the question that he's hired his own personal security team in addition," DeLuca went   on. "We'll assume he's armed and that he's got protection. We've got eyes on him now, we'll have eyes and ears on him at the party, as well as eyes on his vehicle. We'll be taking him at his house once he gets home, then doing the search and seizure right after. His wife will likely be there as well, but she's not a suspect at this time."

Celida took over, showing more pictures of Balducci and schematics of his house. "This intel could be leaked at any time," she warned. "He's got a lot to lose here and he'll likely fight to keep that from happening."

DeLuca took over again. "Agent Rycroft, Miss Jones and I will be your lookouts at the target location. This is a tight timeline but that doesn't mean we go in there without having a rock solid operational plan." He looked at Tuck, nodded once. "It's your show."

Tuck took the spotlight and began going over approaches, infil and exfil strategies, emergency contingencies as he pointed out various spots on the satellite images of Balducci's house and the surrounding neighborhood.

When Nate glanced over at Briar, he was surprised to see his CO standing close beside her. He was resting against the wall, arms folded across his chest, but the way he leaned toward her, the way they looked at each other as they whispered about whatever they were talking about, spoke volumes. They knew each other well and he obviously trusted her, if he'd brought her to the briefing and planned to include her as a lookout before and during the op.

It was clear to Nate that they were more than just acquaintances and it floored him. Everyone knew their CO hadn't gotten over his wife's death. He'd become increasingly withdrawn over the past few years, didn't hang out with the team much anymore, and if he'd dated at all since his wife died, none of them had ever heard about it.

Putting it out of his mind for the time being, he focused back on what Tuck was saying, mentally envisioning the op as he laid it out and finished with, "All right, what do you guys think?"

Tuck always asked for the team's input, always listened to their ideas before they came up with a final plan and passed it by DeLuca for approval. A few of them offered an opinion but Nate kept his mouth shut.

DeLuca joined Tuck at the front of the room again. "We're still waiting on warrants, so even though we anticipate Balducci arriving home between twenty-three hundred and oh-two hundred hours, we don't move until we get the paperwork."

Fuck that. Those court orders had better come through in time. If this bastard was guilty of everything DeLuca had told them, Nate wanted to bring him down, hard, before he had time to prepare.

Chapter Twenty-Three

All night he'd been struggling to shake the feeling of unease that wouldn't leave him alone. Will took a break from visiting with the guests and headed over to the bar. To settle his nerves, he ordered a double and knocked it back.

The party had been a huge success so far, with two notable exceptions. Alan and his wife hadn't shown up. And when he'd slipped into the men's room to check his accounts from his phone, he hadn't been able to access them, instead receiving an automated message that the system was experiencing technical problems.

There was no reason he could think of besides a sudden death in the family that would explain why the Turners hadn't come. And he was suspicious that the message on the bank's site was fake. Those two things together had him extremely worried.

Someone had uncovered all his tracks, then found and apprehended Alan.

His gut said it was Jones.

Maybe his imagination was running away with him, but he had half a mind to leave right now, grab his wife and go, head straight to the airport and hop that plane. But they could be watching for him. If they were he wouldn't make it onto the plane without being caught and leaving now in the middle of his party would raise too much suspicion.

No, he had to finish this, if only for damage control. If he ran now, he'd never be able to hold his head up in the political arena. His competitors would eat him alive and voters would shy away from him.

But if he was caught, he was facing life in prison or death by lethal injection.

Turning back around to face the crowd milling around between the tables and off to the sides of the room, he scanned their faces. Over three hundred people were here on his dime and he knew most of them. The ones he didn't had come as dates for guests on the invitation list and security had been given strict instructions to check I.D. before letting anyone into the exclusive country club reception room.

At one point he'd thought he'd gotten a glimpse of his secret female supporter, a knockout brunette in her early thirties dressed in a body-hugging black gown. She'd smiled at him from the side of the room, winked, then disappeared. Will wanted to meet with her before leaving.

More people approached him as he left the bar. He stopped to chat, pretending nothing was wrong, then took his seat at the head table to listen to the speeches two of his colleagues had prepared. The Director of the CIA spoke last, ending with a joke at his expense. Everyone laughed and Will stood to clasp his superior's hand, thanking him and accepting the same for his years of service.

Then it was his turn at the podium.

Time seemed to slow as he took out his notes and addressed the assembled guests. This speech was critical.

He spoke about his career, his philosophy about work ethic, duty and service to country. Then he began talking about what was wrong with the country and what his vision for it was. He paused between points and he was aware of the hush in the room, every eye on him as they waited for him to continue. He'd always been a gifted public speaker and he used those skills now, injecting all his confidence and passion into his words.

"I believe in the America our forefathers built. I believe in upholding the constitution and defending this great land from all threats, foreign and domestic. This great nation of ours used to be the envy of the world and I believe it can be once again." He paused again, swept his gaze over the crowd, the anticipation a tangible hum in his gut. "That's why I intend to stand up and make the necessary changes. Tonight I'm proud to announce that—"

He stopped when his gaze caught on someone standing at the back of the room, near the door. A brunette dressed in a black evening gown. Not the same woman as before, yet something about her face was vaguely familiar. The intensity of her expression made his heart stutter. She wasn't staring at him in admiration.

She was staring at him with a raw, burning hatred he could feel clear across the room.

Tearing his gaze from her, he composed himself and continued. "With your help, I intend to run for Senate in the upcoming elections next year."

A second of stunned silence met the announcement, then cheers and applause broke out. People all over the room began getting to their feet, giving him a standing ovation. He stood at the podium, flooded with emotion, affected by their reaction, their support. He'd hoped it would be like this. It was everything he'd dreamed it would be.

After a minute or so he held up a hand to dim the

applause, smiling at everyone. When he looked to the back of the room, however, the woman was gone. Where did he know her from? He glanced around the room but didn't see her. Maybe she'd left. He had to stop thinking about where he'd seen her before, finish strong.

Turning to the side, he held out his hand to his wife, who stood waiting in the wings. Barb had tears in her eyes as she stepped up beside him, her ruby-painted lips trembling slightly as she clasped his hand tightly in hers. Once again he was struck anew by how beautiful she was.

He hadn't been the best husband to her, even though she'd tried to please him. Her support was sincere and it meant more to him than he'd realized until this moment. Going forward he would make more of an effort to be a better man and husband, if God would just allow him to get through this a free man.

Will raised their joined hands in the air and the crowd cheered again. They saw in him a strong, capable leader, the kind of man they wanted leading this country.

And he was suddenly terrified that it was all a lie.

****

"He's leaving."

Briar shifted in the front passenger seat of the SUV at Matt's words. "He's early. Think he knows?"

"Maybe."

The country club was less than thirty minutes from his house by car. The remaining evidence needed had come through just over an hour ago, and Alex had called to say that he had all the necessary warrants. They'd briefly discussed changing the timeline, taking Balducci down as he left the country club instead, but they'd decided to stay with the original plan and take him at his home to minimize attention and possible collateral damage.

Once they cornered Balducci, no one was certain how he'd react, or how far he'd go to escape.

With everything in place and all going according to plan thus far, the HRT boys had a green light. All they needed was for Balducci to arrive home and the team would show up in their vehicles, now parked two miles up the road.

After that it would be over in a matter of minutes. No muss, no fuss, no witnesses and no media. With such a high profile case, that was of paramount concern for all the agencies involved. The higher ups at the CIA were still in the dark and would shit themselves when all this came to light within the next hour or so.

The beautiful, brick house was still and quiet, only one security agent patrolling the grounds. He was a new addition, added by Balducci only a couple days ago. Another sign he likely suspected something was up. No one else had come or gone from the house all night, and between her, Matt and Alex, they'd made certain to track everyone entering or leaving the upscale neighborhood.

Briar zipped her jacket all the way up to her chin and tucked her hands into her pockets. It was freezing out and after parking down the block in the shadow of a burned-out streetlight they'd left the engine off to avoid drawing unwanted attention.

"Cold?" Matt asked, reaching across the center console to fish her left hand from her pocket. He took it between both of his and rubbed, raised it to his mouth to blow on it. She smiled at him, wondering if she'd always be surprised by his thoughtfulness. Even here during surveillance with an imminent op about to happen he was concerned about her comfort.

"Better now, thanks."

He kissed her fingers absently, tucked her hand back into her pocket and repeated everything with her right hand. Lowering it from his mouth, he reached up with one hand to tap his earpiece. "Copy that. Got him on screen."

He tapped the handheld tablet on his lap, bringing up a GPS signal from the transmitter an FBI agent at the party had planted on Balducci's vehicle. "Looks like he's still headed home," he said to her.

Briar nodded, watching the beacon on screen. "The agent's still tailing him?"

"Yes." He tapped his earpiece again, changing the frequency. "You got him?" he asked whoever he was speaking to, presumably Alex, who was three blocks south near the entrance to the exclusive subdivision. Two more agents were posted in other locations as a precaution.

Balducci's last minutes as a free man were still passing by far too slowly for her liking.

Together she and Matt watched the beacon in silence. Tuck and the others would be watching the same transmission from their vehicles.

The anger was still there, burning deep and hot. She hated that Balducci might live out the rest of his days in a heated cell being fed three square meals a day at U.S. taxpayers' expense. But at least if he was in jail the world would know what he'd done and he wouldn't get to take the easy way out by eating a bullet.

A few minutes later his vehicle took the expected exit off the I-95. Anticipation swirled through her veins.

Matt spoke again. "Copy." He met her gaze. "Almost over."

Her hands fisted in her pockets. She wanted so badly to be the one to lead the breaching team into the house, be the first one to corner him, take him down. But it wasn't to be.

Less than two minutes later the vehicle on screen made an unexpected turn.

"He's heading east," she said, unable to keep the tension out of her voice.

"Keep him in your sights," Matt warned someone via the earpiece, his body tensing beside her.

Watching the vehicle on screen, Briar already knew what was happening.

He's going to make a run for it.

Chapter Twenty-Four

Will's foot pressed harder on the accelerator. His heart was pounding almost out of control and his palms were slippery with sweat on the steering wheel. The security people at the country club parking lot had assured him no one had been near his car while he was at the party, so there was no chance it had been bugged.

Now Will wasn't so sure. He couldn't see anyone behind them, hadn't noticed anyone following or watching them since leaving the country club, but the closer he got to the airstrip, the more certain he was that he was walking right into a trap.

His wife turned her head to look at him, frowned. "Will, what's wrong?"

Everything. If he was right and if the CIA or NSA managed to unravel everything, he didn't know how to fucking fix it. "Nothing. But we're not going home yet."

"Why not?" she asked, sounding disappointed as he sped down the highway. Christ, he could feel eyes on him. Tracking his every move.

He took the first left, taking a different route than

he'd originally planned. "I've got a surprise planned."

Her frown disappeared and he could all but feel her excitement. "What kind of surprise?"

"A trip."

"A trip? But I haven't packed—"

"I already did. Bags are in the trunk."

"We're flying somewhere?"

He nodded, sped up more. "Southern Spain." From there he could slip across the Strait of Gibraltar into Morocco, get in touch with some of his contacts and find out what the hell was going on.

If he could just make it onto the jet awaiting them.

Barbara gasped. "Really?"

"I know you've always wanted to go there." It sounded like a lame reason even to his own ears but he didn't know what else to say without tipping her off that something was wrong.

"Yeah, I have," she said, sounding as excited as a child who'd just been told they were going to Disneyland.

He kept checking the rearview and side mirrors to see if anyone was following them. Thankfully traffic was light and it didn't seem like anyone was mirroring his movements.

Still, he couldn't shake the building anxiety as he took the next freeway on-ramp and sped off toward the airport.

****

"Shit, where's he going? Something must've spooked him."

Lying on the floorboards in the back of the minivan the FBI agent was driving, Georgia braced as the vehicle did a tight turn and pulled over to the side of the street. She'd slipped her evening gown off, leaving her in her black bodysuit, then broken into the van while the agent had been talking with the security guards. She'd stashed her boots and weapons behind an ivy-covered trellis on the grounds, not far from the entrance.

Security had been a joke. A little flirting and an excuse for not having her I.D. with her and they'd let her walk right into the room without any trouble. She couldn't be sure, but for a moment during his speech she'd been certain Balducci had seen her at the back of the room. She hoped he had. She hoped he'd seen the hatred inside her and that it had sent a bolt of pure terror through his blackened soul.

She'd trusted him once. And now he'd betrayed her and everything she stood for.

Tonight she would make him suffer for everything he'd done to her. For setting her up by lying to her about Briar. For killing Frank and then sending someone out to hunt her. All to hide the evil he'd covered himself in.

And to find out he planned to run for the Senate?

She'd see him in hell first.

Her hand tightened around the grip of her pistol as the agent hit the gas and took off in pursuit. In the rear window she could clearly see the reflection of the GPS display on the tablet he was using to follow the other vehicle. The van was almost a mile behind already. Balducci seemed to be headed east. To an airport?

Suddenly the agent slowed and pulled over to the curb. He spoke to someone via the earpiece he wore. "Roger that. Holding position." He blew out a breath, dragged a hand through his hair in agitation. "How the fucking hell did he *see* me?" he muttered to himself, sounding disgusted.

No more waiting.

Georgia surged up and jammed the Taser against the side of the man's neck. He yelled in surprise then jerked uncontrollably as the voltage coursed through him. Dropping it, she slid between the front seats to grab his arms and secure his hands behind him, took out his earpiece and stripped his phone from his pants pocket. He groaned and shifted slightly but was too out of it to stop her.

Making sure no one was around to see, she opened the driver door and dragged him out, dumping him behind another parked car before jumping behind the wheel and taking off. She checked the position of the GPS beacon and stomped on the gas, speeding through the darkness toward her target.

Once she got Balducci she would use another of her fake IDs to make her way south and get across the border into Mexico. He'd cost her too much.

Even if she had to start over in a foreign country and live the rest of her life without ever setting foot on American soil again, it would be worth it as long as he was dead.

****

Briar gripped the door handle with one hand and the center console with the other as Matt took a hard left, racing after Balducci. Alex and the other two agents were in pursuit in their own vehicles as well. She knew he wasn't getting away, not with this many people after him, and yet her heart was still racing. She wanted him taken down *now*. No more chances for him.

Matt was updating Tuck as he drove, his voice clipped and urgent. He wove the SUV left and right, dodging slower traffic, ignoring the blaring horns, focused on getting to that beacon on screen. The BMW exited about a mile ahead and drove east along a side street. Matt followed but he couldn't drive this fast and navigate via the tablet so she took over with the directions.

"Take your second left," she told him, gaze riveted to the beacon. They were gaining on him.

He followed her instruction, taking the turn hard enough that the back wheels screeched. She jostled in her seat as the vehicle settled back onto its center of gravity and Matt hit the gas, picking up speed. The BMW was slowing, seemed to be stopped at an intersection, was hopefully hemmed in by traffic. She saw a better route to cut him off.

"Next right." The BMW was moving again, gaining speed.

Matt did as she said and followed her next four directions, putting them a block ahead of where the BMW was headed.

"Right again," she ordered.

He turned and up ahead was a red light.

"Hang a left into the oncoming lane. He'll be heading right at us in a few seconds."

Matt blew the light and made the turn, swinging into the wrong lane. The BMW was dead ahead. Even as Briar reached for her door handle, ready to jump out and run, she saw the car slow. Matt hit the gas, the big SUV surging forward.

Ahead of them the BMW swerved. Briar braced herself for when Matt made a countermove but went rigid in her seat as a minivan suddenly burst onto the road from a cross street. It ran the red light and accelerated, T-boning the BMW's driver's side, sending it spinning across the road.

"Shit," Matt muttered. He stomped on the brake to avoid hitting it and before Briar could say anything the driver of the minivan jumped out.

Briar swallowed a cry. "Georgia," she rasped out.

She had blood on her face as she scrambled around the hood of the bashed-in van, a pistol in her grip. Balducci was climbing out the BMW's front passenger side door, shoving his wife out in front of him. The woman fell on her butt on the road, still in her evening gown. She appeared to be unhurt as Balducci scrambled over top of her, yanked her to her feet and shouted at her to run as he shoved her toward the sidewalk. He didn't wait for her but started running, stumbling once as he gained his footing and raced away from the scene.

Georgia raised the pistol, her face a study in determination. Balducci suddenly whirled and whipped his own weapon up, fired twice.

"No!" Briar shouted, stomach grabbing when Georgia ducked out of the way just before the bullets slammed into the van's hood.

Georgia popped up again, using the van's hood as a shooting platform, and took aim.

Before Briar could say anything Matt floored it then stomped on the brake, tires screaming as he stopped them between the two battered vehicles, blocking Georgia's shot.

"I'll stop her—you go after him." She didn't give him time to argue. If she didn't stop Georgia, her fellow Valkyrie would kill Balducci and they'd never get the confession or intel they needed from him to collar everyone else involved.

Briar was out her door with her own weapon drawn before Matt could put the SUV into park, her aim locked on her fellow Valkyrie.

Georgia stood with her own pistol raised at Balducci's retreating figure, jaw set, eyes burning with fury as blood dripped down her face and neck. "Get out of my way, Briar."

Briar shook her head. "Don't do this. Don't throw your life away over him. He's not worth it."

Georgia's hands shook, "He lied to me, set me up. Killed Frank and Janaia. Would have killed you and me."

"But he's going down now. HRT is en route, they'll handle it. Stand *down*." Briar didn't want to shoot her, but she would if Georgia gave her no option.

Georgia met her gaze fully for the first time and some of the wildness in her expression eased. "I want him dead."

She could hear Matt behind her over by the trees now, chasing after Balducci and shouting for him to freeze. Her muscles twitched, wanting to follow and help. "I know. But that's not gonna happen. As much as I wanted him to die for what he's done, a quick death is too easy. Rotting behind bars for the rest of his life is a much crueler fate for him." She paused, praying that sank in. "You do this, you'll go down too." Her index finger was curled around the trigger. If Georgia wouldn't listen, Briar wouldn't hesitate to take her down. She let Georgia see it in her face.

Georgia's jaw flexed once, blood dripping off it from a wound near her hairline. After a long moment she exhaled and lowered the pistol. "Fine. But I—"

Two closely-spaced shots rang out from behind them, followed by two more in rapid succession.

Briar whirled, pulse skyrocketing as she searched for Matt in the trees beyond the buildings across the road. "Matt!"

He didn't answer.

Shit.

Briar took off with her heart in her throat, running as fast as she could toward where those shots had come from. She could hear Georgia charging behind her, didn't slow down or bother ordering her to stay back. All she cared about was reaching Matt and making sure he was okay. If Balducci hurt Matt, she'd kill the fucking asshole herself.

She passed the rear of the closest building, headed for the trees. *Matt!*

Another shot echoed from the trees up ahead, slightly to the right.

God, if he died she didn't know what she'd—

She skidded to a halt when she made out two

shadowed silhouettes a few dozen yards ahead. They were on the ground rolling together, male growls and grunts ripping through the air.

Briar circled around to take them from behind and watched in horror as they took a sudden roll down an embankment. They tumbled one over the other, still locked in a death struggle, finally slamming into a tree with a bone-jarring thud. The figure on top rolled to the side and rested on all fours, breathing hard. The man on the ground groaned and shifted slightly but didn't get up. She couldn't tell which one was Matt as she rushed toward them.

Then the one on his hands and knees pushed to his feet and there was enough light filtering through the trees from the distant streetlamps for Briar to see his face.

Balducci.

Rage like she'd never experienced tore through her, obliterating every thought, every feeling. She charged at him. He whirled, saw her and bent to pick up the pistol on the ground at his feet. Briar fired, hitting him twice in the chest. He grunted and fell to his knees but didn't topple over.

Kevlar.

In reflex she aimed at his leg and fired, hitting him in the thigh. Balducci howled and grabbed his leg with both hands as he toppled over and tried to crawl away.

Briar wasn't done.

She was barely in control, her brain functioning only enough to keep from firing at his head as she sprinted forward and dove at him, a feral snarl tearing from her throat. Her shoulder slammed into his back, knocking him to the ground. Immediately she twisted around to lock her right arm around his throat and wrenched it up and back, squeezing to cut off his air. Her muscles shook with the effort, squeezing as hard as she could. He'd shot Matt.

His hands clawed at her arm, fingers desperately

trying to pry her forearm away.

She didn't let go.

With a terrible wheezing sound he flung a hand up and got her in the face, nails raking across her cheek and jaw. She barely felt the sting, didn't care as she squeezed for all she was worth, focused solely on choking him out, trying to steal a glance at Matt to see how bad his wounds were. He was stirring, trying to sit up.

She turned her full attention back to Balducci and put everything she had into the chokehold. Janaia's face, laughing and smiling with her kids, flashed in her mind. She thought of the explosives that assassin had planted on the house in Lake Placid, and of the murders she'd been framed for.

Someone shouted at her but it sounded so far away it barely penetrated the fog of rage engulfing her. Balducci clawed the side of her neck this time, fingers digging into her windpipe. Briar twisted her body to the side to break the hold, heard the bones in his forearm snap and felt his body arch, his mouth opening in a nearly soundless gurgle of agony as she squeezed the life out of him.

How's it feel? How does it fucking feel to suffocate to death the way Janaia did, you bastard?

She felt him begin to weaken, start to sag in her grip. She wasn't letting go. She—

Strong hands grabbed her shoulders and ripped her backward. She lost her grip. Balducci fell to the ground as her back hit the damp earth, heaving in a desperate breath. She rolled, intending to launch herself back at him but another hand grabbed her upper arm and swung her around.

"*Briar.*"

The urgency, the command in that familiar voice, froze her. She stilled and looked into Matt's strained face. Belatedly she realized she was shaking all over, the sound of approaching sirens growing louder by the second. His expression was tight with pain, blood on the left side of his face. In her peripheral vision she saw Georgia standing before Balducci, her pistol aimed at his head. But she didn't fire.

Briar gulped in a breath of air and put her hand on the blood on Matt's face, unable to stop shaking. "You're hurt. Where are you hurt?" Fear coursed through her when he grimaced and shifted slightly. She could see the blood glistening black against his left shoulder, immediately pressed her hands over it but he jerked back. He swore and shut his eyes, his whole body tensing.

"Matt, how bad?" she asked, voice unsteady as she ripped open his jacket with her free hand and searched beneath it for the wound.

"I'm okay," he rasped out, the strain in his voice alarming her. A lump settled in her throat and a hot blur of tears stung her eyes. Then Matt's hand wrapped around her wrist as she reached for his wounded shoulder once more, his fingers squeezing. "It's okay, baby."

The sound of the approaching sirens grew louder still. Briar straddled Matt's waist and bent over him, trying to see the wound. Moments later men stormed into the trees, seven of them fanning out around them with rifles aimed, shouting commands.

"Everybody freeze! Hands up, now!"

Briar eased into a kneeling position and raised her hands, still shaking all over. They wore NVGs so they could see them all clearly but she knew they were HRT. Three men rushed for Balducci and Georgia, who stood where she was, weapon behind her on the ground, hands in the air.

Briar could vouch for her later. All she was worried about at the moment was Matt. "It's DeLuca," she shouted over the noise. "He's hurt. Schroder, where are you?"

"Right here." He emerged out of the shadows behind another member and rushed toward them. Briar moved off

Matt and eased to the side, keeping pressure on his shoulder wound. She could feel something sharp sticking out of it.

"I don't know if he's been shot and I don't know if there's another wound but his shoulder is bleeding bad—"

"Not shot," Matt managed from behind gritted teeth.

Relief slammed into her, so hard it left her dizzy.

"Let's take a look," Schroder said, totally calm as he switched on the headlamp on his helmet and started looking Matt over. He pulled open Matt's jacket and shirt to expose his shoulder and Briar saw why he was bleeding.

The wicked end of a KA-BAR knife had pierced through the muscles at the side of his left shoulder, going clean through it beside the strap of his Kevlar vest. Another few inches to the left and it could have hit his lung, maybe nicked his heart.

Nausea hit her, her stomach contracting into a sickening ball.

"Anywhere else?" the former PJ asked, grabbing her hand and pressing on it in a silent command to keep pressure there.

"Just...ribs," he said, trying to shift onto his side. "It's all right."

"Stay put for me, okay big guy?" Schroder said.

And it *wasn't* fucking okay, because there was a big dent in the side of the vest where a bullet had punched into it.

Briar swallowed the bile rising in her throat, aware that if he hadn't been wearing the vest, he'd be bleeding out right now in front of her. She pressed her lips together and sucked in a steadying breath through her nose. She wanted to wrap around Matt and hold him, make him stop hurting and just feel him warm and alive in her arms.

Schroder finished checking him over, put a dressing

on his shoulder and closed the cut on the side of his head with some steri strips. "Can you stand?" he asked him.

Matt nodded. "Yeah." He grabbed Schroder's hand, allowed him and Briar to pull him up, then leaned against her as he got his footing. She tucked her body into his, lending him her support.

He shot her a terrifying glare and yelled at her. "God*dammit*, woman, you fucking scared me to death, tackling him like that! You're not even wearing a vest for Christ—"

"Too fucking bad!" she shouted back, still shaky as hell and not regretting her actions one iota. She'd do the same all over again to protect him. "You were lying there bleeding to death for all I knew and I wasn't letting him get away with it!"

They glared at each other, both breathing hard, until strangled laughs from nearby broke the taut standoff. She whipped her head around to see three HRT guys standing there, watching the show. The lighting wasn't great but from the glimpse she got, she thought she saw Evers, Bauer and Tuck, all grinning at them.

"Come on, boss, that's actually kinda hot," Schroder said on a laugh. "All one-hundred-and-thirty pounds of her took him down to protect you. It's sweet."

"Sweet my ass," Matt fired back, his eyes now shooting daggers at the medic. "God-*dammit*."

Schroder didn't seem to take his CO's wrath to heart. "I know you're not gonna want to hear it, but you need that looked at some more," he added, nodding at Matt's shoulder. "They'll wait to pull the knife out at the hospital. Let's hope you don't need surgery."

"Fuck," he snarled, and this time she felt some of the anger drain out of him, his body sagging against her.

"Is there an ambulance coming?" she asked.

"Yeah, should be here any minute," Schroder answered. "Come on. I'll help you get this wounded bear out to the street."

"I can fucking walk on my own," Matt growled, but his arm tightened around her shoulders in a possessive grip, clearly not wanting to let her go.

"Okay," Schroder said cheerfully. "I'll just walk a step behind, ready to catch you if you keel over."

They started walking through the trees toward the road. Up ahead she could see the other four members of the team standing around Georgia and Balducci, both lying facedown on the ground with their hands cuffed behind them. With a broken arm and a bullet wound in the leg, Balducci had to be in a shitload of pain. The thought made Briar smile.

She moved slowly with Matt, trying to hide how weak her legs felt. The adrenaline crash had left her cold all over and slightly queasy. All because of her terror for Matt.

When the ambulances arrived medics loaded Balducci onto one and Alex was there to assign someone to ride with him to the hospital. She explained to him about Georgia but he insisted she be brought in for questioning. Mostly to do with an FBI agent she'd assaulted and dumped on the side of the road, the government-owned van she'd totaled and the pesky matter of interfering with a federal investigation.

Matt grumbled and protested the paramedics' attention but he finally sat on the edge of the ambulance's deck and allowed them to check him over, his mouth pressed into a thin line of displeasure while Schroder stood by to discuss everything with them.

Briar left him to walk over to Georgia, who was about to be put into the back of another SUV, Alex standing next to her. The other Valkyrie glanced over as she approached, pale blue gaze piercing. She still had blood on her face and neck but the paramedics had bandaged the cut near her hairline.

Briar stopped when she reached her, offered a smile. "I'm glad you didn't kill him."

Georgia studied her eyes for a moment, clearly not as happy about the night's outcome. "He'd better either get a life sentence or the death penalty."

"He will," Alex said from beside the vehicle's back door. He set a hand between Georgia's shoulder blades. "Shall we?" It wasn't a question, even though it was posed as one.

Georgia obediently turned and allowed him to help her slide into the backseat. She met Briar's gaze just before he shut the door. "You'll be around?"

Briar nodded. "Got a few things to take care of here." She glanced over to Matt before looking back at her.

Georgia's mouth twitched in the semblance of a smile and her frigid eyes warmed slightly. "Yeah, guess you do."

Alex shut the door then rounded the back of the vehicle and slid into the back with her. Briar raised her hand in farewell as it drove away. When she looked back at Matt, he was watching her with his arm secured in a sling, the hilt of the knife still protruding from the back of his shoulder.

But he wasn't merely looking at her, she realized. He was staring at her with such respect and longing in his eyes it turned her heart over.

She crossed to him, stuffing her hands into her pockets. He was gonna be damn sore for a while and pulling that blade through his shoulder wasn't the most fun way to spend an evening. The bandaged cut on his head had stopped bleeding, leaving only dried blood on his face and neck.

He reached out his free hand, caught her forearm and tugged her to him. She set one hand on his uninjured shoulder and the other on the side of his face, her thumb stroking gently over his whisker-roughened cheek. "That looks pretty damn nasty."

He grunted. "Speared by a fucking KA-BAR." He sounded utterly disgusted by that.

In the expanding silence they stared at each other for a few seconds. "I'm still not sorry," she admitted.

His lips curved, his eyes twinkling with humor. "I know. But I'm sorry for yelling." He groaned and bent his head, leaning his forehead against her chest. Briar bent over him, pressing a kiss to the top of his head. "You would go right for my bald spot," he grumbled, sounding mildly annoyed.

The idea that he was self-conscious about such a silly thing even while wounded and in pain made her laugh. "It's not bald, it's only thinning a little and it's not very big anyway. And you're so damn sexy I'd want to do you even if you were totally bald."

He grunted but didn't lift his head, as though he was content right where he was and didn't want her to let go. "You're going with me to the hospital, right?"

"Yes." No one was going to stop her, though she didn't think anyone would protest her going along.

"Good. Because I can't goddamn stand needles. And I have a feeling I'm gonna be getting a few of those."

Really? Big, tough guy like him, afraid of needles? "I think you're right," she murmured, smiling again as she kissed that same spot on his head. She'd kiss it over and over again until he understood how perfect she thought every part of him was. "But don't worry, I won't tell anyone, and I'll be right there to hold your hand."

Chapter Twenty-Five

Matt covered a wince as he turned to wave goodbye to Tuck, who'd been kind enough to give him and Briar a ride home from the hospital. The local anesthetic they'd injected him with before removing the knife and stitching him back up had worn off a long time ago and he was looking forward to curling up in his bed with Briar for the rest of the night.

The expected paperwork and debriefings would be handled tomorrow, in deference to his injury. He'd insisted that he could take care of it tonight, but under the circumstances the higher-ups had given him the night to himself and he knew enough to keep his mouth shut except to say thank you.

"So this is it," he said to Briar, leading her up the front walkway to the two-story house he'd bought a little over a year ago. Once inside the door he disarmed the security system and stepped aside to let her enter. She looked around as he flipped on the foyer light, the livid scratches on her face and neck reminding him of when she'd taken Balducci down while he'd been powerless to help or protect her.

Bastard was gonna get what was coming to him. It was a huge relief to know he was no longer a threat to Briar or anyone else.

Matt shut and locked the door behind them, a bit startled to realize it was the first time he'd looked forward to being here since he'd bought the place. It had always depressed him to come home but with Briar here he found himself anxious to settle in with her.

She took off her boots and followed him through the kitchen into the living room. He paused when she stopped, looked back to find her staring at the framed picture of him and Lisa he'd set on the mantelpiece above the fireplace. She was good at hiding her emotions but he could see the uncertainty flitting across her face now, as if she wasn't certain whether or not she was intruding on his privacy.

Matt crossed back to her and stepped behind her, wrapping his good arm around her waist to bring her back against his body. "I've never brought a woman here before."

She twisted her neck to look up at him in surprise.

"This wasn't our place. I sold that house a few months after she died. Couldn't take the constant memories every time I walked in the door and saw the pool in the backyard. I rented an apartment for a few years after that before buying this." He gazed up at the picture, at Lisa's gorgeous smile. "She'd want this for me, for me to be happy. You'd have intimidated the living hell out of her with your background, but if you two had met, I know she would have liked you." He was quiet a moment. "I can take it down if it bothers you."

"No," she said, her tone adamant. "I don't want you to take it down." She relaxed in his hold, her tension easing. Her hand folded over his where he cupped the side of her ribcage, her fingers rubbing over his wedding band. "I think I'd have liked her too."

He smiled against her temple. "Yeah, I think so too." There was such sweetness in her, a side of her she didn't let many people see. And he planned to move that picture anyway, minimize the reminders of Lisa around his place. He wanted Briar to know she was the number one woman in his life now and didn't want her to feel like she had to compete with his former wife's ghost.

"Come upstairs." He took her hand and led her up the wooden staircase to the master bedroom. As she looked around he was glad he'd bothered to make his king size bed before he'd left for Colorado. Seemed like a helluva lot longer than nine days ago though.

She ran her gaze over him, lingering on the blood staining his skin and shirt. "You need to be cleaned up before you crawl in there. Come on." She started for the master bathroom, which he was also grateful he'd cleaned recently. While the shower ran she helped him out of his shirt, an awkward procedure with his arm bound to his chest. She found some medical tape and a plastic bag under the sink to cover his bandage with, then stripped and got into the shower with him.

"Just stand still," she told him, then proceeded to gently wash the blood off his face, chest and arm. Her touch felt like heaven.

Next she poured some shampoo into her hand and began washing his hair, careful to stay away from the bandages holding the cut on the side of his head together. Matt groaned at the feel of her fingers rubbing over his scalp and she increased the pressure, massaging in circles until shivers of pleasure cascaded through him. When she got to the back of his neck and began kneading the stiff muscles there, he couldn't hold back a moan. Smiling, she rinsed the rest of him off then he felt her gentle kiss at the top of his spine before she shut off the water.

Once they were dried off they both climbed into his bed. She pulled the covers up and snuggled against his side, her head resting on his uninjured shoulder, one leg draped across his waist. Matt wrapped his right arm around her and closed his eyes on a sigh, grateful to have her next to him in the darkness. He was half hard from having her naked and sprawled over him but there was no way he was up to anything more than a cuddle at the moment.

"Tomorrow we'll start getting your life back," he murmured against the top of her head.

"Can't wait." She smothered a yawn and nuzzled the side of his chest with her nose. Her fingers trailed gently across his left pec, just below the edge of the bandage. "I was terrified that I'd lost you when I heard those shots," she said quietly after a while.

He stroked her hair, understanding what that felt like because he'd experienced the same thing when she'd tackled Balducci. "You know the real reason why I yelled at you after, right?"

"You were worried about me."

"Yeah, but that's not the only reason." He sighed. "I've already lost one woman who meant the world to me and I didn't want it to happen again."

Briar stopped stroking his chest and tilted her head back to look at him, even though she probably couldn't see much of his face in the near darkness.

"So if I tend to be overprotective of you sometimes, that's why. I can't control it. I'm sure as hell not going to apologize for it."

"I feel the same way about you."

He grinned, remembering Schroder's comment about her protecting him being sweet. It was, and he was a lucky bastard to have earned that kind of protectiveness from her. "Then let's hope we'll never have to deal with anything like this again."

Briar sighed in agreement and nestled her cheek against him once more. She was quiet a long time before speaking again. "I don't know what I'm going to do now. Where I'll live, what I'm going to do about my job, or with us." She let out a hard breath. "Matt, I seriously don't know what the hell I'm doing here. I'm a project. A big one."

She was trying to warn him off but he wouldn't listen. He tightened his arm around her, squeezing, savoring the feel of her warm, sleek body pressed close to his. "Everyone's a project, honey. But I'm still willing to take you on," he teased.

He felt her smile form against his skin and then she fully relaxed into him. "Don't know what I did to deserve a man like you, but I'm not complaining."

"You mean, besides being insanely sexy and amazing?"

She laughed softly. "Yeah. I'm just warning you you'll need to be patient with me. I'm way out of my element with this. I don't want to mess things up between us."

"We're gonna have moments where we stumble, that's just life. There's no secret, no magic words to making a relationship work. It takes effort from both people, and a conscious decision to keep working at it. If we both commit to doing that and never quitting, we've got it made."

She made a murmuring sound, kissed his chest. "Sounds deceptively simple and scary as hell at the same time, but I'll try." He heard her swallow hard. "I—I've never felt like this before and I'm afraid to trust it because everything's happened so fast. I'm afraid of doing something wrong and losing you—"

"You won't lose me." And the truth was, Matt had never felt this way before either. "Not unless you want to," he added.

"I *don't* want to." She tightened her hold on him, clearly battling her inner demons and it touched him deeply that she was willing to make this leap into the unknown for him.

He lowered his voice to a murmur. "So stop worrying. We'll find our way, one day at a time." He'd never thought he'd fall in love again after Lisa died, but he knew without a doubt that he loved Briar. What he felt for her was different than he had for his wife. It burned hotter, fiercer than anything he'd experienced before. Though he wanted to say it, he'd wait. She was struggling to adjust to everything and he didn't want to push her too hard too fast. As a sniper he'd learned to be patient.

Keeping Briar in his life was worth every bit of patience he had.

"You'll show me the ropes?" she whispered.

Matt buried his lips in her hair. "Every single one I know, honey. And the rest we'll learn together."

Chapter Twenty-Six

T he peal of the doorbell woke Matt the next morning from a deep, dreamless sleep.

"I'll get it," Briar mumbled, already sitting up.

He struggled up on his right elbow as Briar rolled out of the bed, dragged on the clothes she'd worn last night and rushed from the room, tucking her pistol into the back of her waistband. He sat up and blinked to clear his vision. The clock on the nightstand read a few minutes after nine.

Groaning, his wounded shoulder sore as fuck, he managed to yank his shirt and pants on before hurrying after her. Familiar voices reached him from near the front door. He started down the stairs. Rycroft, Celida, Tuck and Bauer were all in the foyer, talking to Briar. They all looked up at him as he descended.

"You look like shit," Bauer told him.

"Morning to you too," he muttered.

Tuck lifted a tray full of coffee cups. "We come bearing gifts."

"And good news," Rycroft added.

Matt dragged a hand down his face, still trying to

296

clear the last of the fog from his brain. "Go ahead and sit down," he said, waving them toward the kitchen/family room. He sat on the couch next to Briar, wrapped an arm around her shoulders. "So, what's the news?" he asked, nodding his thanks as Tuck passed both of them a coffee. The moment the first sip hit his tongue his brain perked up.

"Bauer and I wanted to check on you," Tuck said.

Celida snorted at her fiancé. "He means they're both nosy as hell and wanted to hear this before anyone else does."

Rycroft lowered his cup, looking at Briar. "You've got some meetings and debriefings scheduled at Langley in a couple hours, but to save you the suspense, the CIA is dropping the charges against you. You're name's being cleared."

She sighed in relief and relaxed against Matt with a smile. "That is good news."

Rycroft nodded. "The Director and Deputy Director are both going to meet with you personally this morning. You'll likely be asked to sign a non-disclosure agreement to keep this from going public."

"I'm fine with that. I'm the last person to want publicity, let alone for all this."

His gray eyes studied her shrewdly. "Think you'll stay on there?"

"No. I'm done with The Company. I'll make that clear today."

Now Rycroft grinned. A pleased, shrewd grin. "Thought you might say that. I'd love to have you work for me. Let's set up a meeting to talk things over."

Briar sat up straighter, seeming intrigued. "Work for you in what capacity?" She'd told Matt she was burned out on doing hits, but he didn't think the NSA did that sort of thing anyhow.

Rycroft shrugged. "We'll work something out. And

you could work from the Fort Meade office. If you were thinking about moving into the area," he added, glancing between her and Matt.

Matt set his coffee aside and hugged her close. They hadn't talked about the details yet but he absolutely wanted her to move down here. Hopefully into his place when she was ready. He wanted to learn all her habits, good and bad. Find out more of her quirks, her interests, likes and dislikes. Fall asleep beside her and wake up to her face every single morning they were both home together.

"I appreciate the offer. I'll think about it," was all she said, though Matt could tell she was secretly excited about the idea. It was getting easier to read her.

"And now for the good stuff," Celida said, placing her coffee cup on the table. "Balducci's still in the hospital. They operated on his leg and arm last night. Your shot busted his femur and he needed plenty of plates and screws to put his bones back together," she told Briar, dark eyes gleaming with satisfaction. "So far he's been denying everything but we've got more than enough evidence to show he's lying and of course everything he says is being recorded.

"He and his lawyers know he's in deep shit, so it's just a matter of time before he confesses to avoid the death penalty. All his accounts and assets have been frozen and half of Washington already knows what he's done, even though it hasn't hit mainstream media yet. There won't be any deal to reduce his sentence. He's done and will be put away for the rest of his life."

"Good." A wealth of emotion filled Briar's voice, her eyes blazing when Matt looked down at her. "What about his wife?"

"He says he shoved her toward the street after the crash to send her to safety. She's got some whiplash and minor abrasions but that's about it. And as far as we can tell, she was totally in the dark about what he'd been up to behind the scenes. Not surprising, given how good he was at covering his tracks. Oh, and the guy you tangled with in Lake Placid? Former Mob hit man." She sat back and folded her arms across her chest, her expression fierce. "The asshole who killed Janaia and Frank was also caught last night, trying to get across the border into Mexico. I can't find out anything more about him, but at least you can feel good that he's being put away."

Briar let out a relieved sigh. "Thanks for telling me that. I needed to hear it."

"I can imagine."

They talked a while longer, mostly rehashing last night's op, then Bauer stood and picked up the empty coffee cups. "Too bad we can't recruit her for one of our sniper teams," he said to Matt, grinning as he shot a look at Briar on his way to the kitchen. "I think she'd be one hell of an addition."

"She would," Matt agreed, smiling into her upturned face. He'd trust her to have his or his guys' backs on an op any day. Just one more reason why he'd fallen so hard for her.

"If you want me to wait while you get ready, I can take you over to Langley," Rycroft said to her.

"Oh." She glanced up at Matt. "You'll be at Quantico for most of the day, right?"

"Probably, yeah. But if you're not done by the time I finish, I'll head over to Langley and meet you." Even though he knew she was strong, he didn't want her to have to do this alone, go through the grueling debriefing process where she'd have to relive everything that had happened over the past few months, including Janaia's death.

She turned to Rycroft. "Sure, thanks." Standing, she offered Matt her hand and helped pull him to his feet. "Be down in a few minutes," she said to the others, and led him to the stairs.

Up in his room Matt shut the door. She looked back at him, paused in the act of undressing to jump in the shower. Her eyes flared with unmistakable arousal as he held her gaze and began stripping off his own clothes, still awkward because of his sore shoulder.

A sexy smile curved her lips as she took in his swelling erection. "If you're thinking what I think you're thinking, we don't have time."

"Showering with a friend is the environmentally responsible thing to do," he argued. "It saves water. We'll be helping save the planet."

Her dark eyes sparkled up at him, filled with hope and happiness. "I'm getting my life back today."

He grinned and cupped the side of her face, stroking the scratches there. "Yeah you are." Kissing her smiling lips, Matt wrapped his good arm around her waist and backed her toward the shower.

****

At CIA headquarters in Langley five hours later, Briar walked to the conference room door with Alex and paused when he stepped aside.

"I'll be right outside waiting for you," he said with a smile, as though he knew how tired she was and that she was nervous about this last meeting. She was mentally exhausted and had a feeling this final meeting would be the most draining of all.

Nodding, she knocked on the door and turned the handle when a male voice called out for her to enter. A fifty-ish man with glasses and graying light brown hair sat at the far end of the long rectangular table. He stood and rounded the end to shake her hand. "Miss Jones. Glad to see you're well."

"Thank you." He gestured to the seat beside his and

she sat, looking at the papers he'd set out.

The Director eased back into his own chair and regarded her with shrewd blue eyes. "I realize there's nothing I can say that will make up for what you've been through, but you have my sincerest and most heartfelt apology for everything that's happened."

Briar blinked, a bit taken aback by his directness. She hadn't expected him to offer a personal apology. "Thank you." She sounded like an idiot, repeating the same thing, but she didn't know how else to respond.

"I know you've been briefed about all this paperwork already," he added. "There's the standard non-disclosure agreement and a statement guaranteeing that you won't sue the agency." His expression turned hard. "Though if anyone had a right to do just that, it's you." While she mentally raised her eyebrows, he cleared his throat. "I'll personally be overseeing how Mrs. Miller's case is handled. Her family will be given a sizeable compensation package, though we won't be disclosing the details of her death. You'll need to sign a non-disclosure statement for that as well."

Having already expected that, Briar simply nodded. She'd missed the funeral yesterday, for obvious reasons, but it still upset her greatly. At first she'd wanted to tell Barry everything so he'd know the truth, but after thinking it through and talking with Matt, she realized it would be far crueler to tell him how Janaia had been murdered, and if she did there'd always be the additional risk that someone within Balducci's contacts might target them to maintain their silence.

Briar was done with the people she loved being at risk because of her ties to the CIA. Barry would go on believing that his wife had died of an asthma attack and Briar would have to live with that.

But before she signed the documents guaranteeing her cooperation and silence, she had a question of her own. She studied the Director intently. "Did you suspect he was involved in anything like this?" She'd sign another non-disclosure agreement about this too if it would get her the truth.

The Director stared at her for a long moment, so long she thought he wouldn't answer. But then he did. "Yes."

Below the table her hands fisted tight. "How long have you suspected?"

"Three weeks."

Briar absorbed the news in silence. Three weeks. Well before the Ramadi op and yet The Company had left her out in the cold without any warning or protection from what was going on. She found her voice. "And how did you find out?"

"After speaking to you about it Janaia alerted us to the possibility that something illegal was going on," he said, dropping the formality. "When the asset in Baton Rouge died I got more directly involved. When Jerry died I assigned someone to look into everything about your situation and she alerted me a few days ago that all signs pointed to Balducci."

"She?"

The Director looked past her to the end of the room. Briar followed his gaze, startled to find a woman standing there, watching. Briar had been so focused on the meeting she hadn't been fully aware of her surroundings as she'd entered the room.

The woman stepped out of the shadows into the light and Briar gasped. "Trin?" she asked, half afraid she was seeing things.

Trinity smiled and came forward, elegant and sophisticated in a navy skirt suit and heels, her thick black hair cascading down her back. The warmth in her deep blue eyes did nothing to dull the razor sharp edge to her. She was only four years older than Briar, but had always seemed far older than that to her, an old soul in a young

302

body. Of all the Valkyries Briar had known, Trin was the best. And the deadliest.

"Hi, sweetie."

Briar's throat closed up. It had been well over a year since she'd last seen her. She shoved to her feet and reached for her friend without thinking.

Trin wrapped her arms around her and held her close, whispering to her. "I'm so sorry I couldn't tell you what I was working on when we talked last, and that I didn't figure it out in time to save Janaia."

But she had sent that warning about Georgia. Always looking out for her fellow Valkyries.

Briar shook her head and squeezed her eyes shut, holding on tight. "How?" she gasped, struggling to make sense of it all. "When?"

"I began with digging in your old stomping grounds in the Middle East and went from there. When I found the Caymans account I narrowed the holder down to four possible suspects, but a hunch told me it was likely Balducci so I started investigating him. I pretended I was interested in funding him if he ever ran for office, and had contact with him a few times though I never saw him in person until last night at his retirement dinner."

Briar pulled back to look at her. "Did you see Georgia there?"

"No, or I would have stopped her." Trin smiled and wiped beneath Briar's eyes. "It's good to see you."

"Good to see you too." She hugged her friend again, unashamed that she was showing so much emotion in front of the Director. She was done with the CIA anyhow and would be out of here shortly. Pulling back, Briar smiled. "Guess I should sign the papers now."

Trin nodded. "You get a fresh start as soon as you do. And I hear you have a good man to start over with."

Given everything else, she wasn't surprised that Trin knew more about Matt than she'd told her. "Yeah, I'm a lucky girl. He wants to meet you, by the way."

Trin arched a perfectly groomed black eyebrow. "Does he? I'd kind of like to meet him as well. Put the fear of God into him about what will happen if he doesn't treat you right."

Briar grinned. "No worries there, he will. He's amazing." Feeling lighter inside at the prospect of closing this dark and lonely chapter of her life and beginning a new one filled with love and possibilities, she sat at the table and picked up the pen, giving the Director a nod. "Let's do this."

With Trinity standing at her side, she signed the documents that liberated her from the heavy yolk the CIA had placed around her neck, and took back her freedom.

Epilogue

Three weeks later

T he smell of something burning reached her mere seconds before the smoke alarm went off.

Briar cursed and tossed the mascara wand onto the vanity counter in the master bathroom then raced down the stairs in her stocking feet. The lower floor already had a thin layer of smoke hugging the ceiling and the air in the kitchen was hazy. She'd only been officially living at Matt's for nine days and she'd already managed to start a freaking fire.

Grabbing the potholders from the stovetop, she turned off the oven, ripped open the door and coughed as a wave of smoke hit her in the face. Squinting, her eyes stinging and probably making her stupid makeup run, she grabbed the smoking casserole dish and dumped it onto the granite counter.

Her shoulders slumped. The appetizer she was supposed to bring to the party was ruined beyond salvation.

Scowling, she snagged the towel hanging on the

oven door handle and stalked over to where the smoke alarm was still shrieking overhead. She dragged a chair over to stand on it and reset the thing but it didn't stop. She flapped the towel around in an effort to clear the air, and when that didn't work, ran over to open the windows above the sink. Within a few minutes the ear-splitting noise stopped.

Just great, she thought in disgust, turning back to the counter and the sad remains of her dish. She didn't have anything else in the fridge she could just throw together— maybe some people could make a dish out of what was left in there, but she wasn't exactly domestic—and there was no time to go to the store and buy more ingredients.

"Briar?"

The back door closed. She whipped around to see Matt in the entryway, frozen, taking in the scene before him, alert but calm. His shoulder was almost healed up and he had full range of motion back already so he'd been back at work since the day after Christmas. It had been the best Christmas of her life since her parents had died, ending with him making love to her on the floor in front of the tree they'd decorated together.

His gaze finally landed on her and he raised his eyebrows. "Everything okay?"

She resisted the urge to wad up the towel and huck it at him, wipe that half-amused, half-wary look off his handsome face. "No, everything's *not* okay," she snapped, all the stress she'd been withholding for the past three weeks suddenly overwhelming her and bursting free. "I cremated the fucking meatballs."

For a moment he stared at her, then he made a strangled sound and she saw his mouth twitch as though he was fighting like hell not to smile. She narrowed her eyes in warning, fisted her hands at her sides. "Don't you dare laugh." She was righteously pissed all of a sudden, mad enough to take it out on him even though he didn't deserve it.

He shook his head and held up both hands in self-defense, but lost the battle with the smile. A laugh burst out of him before he could smother it. Briar's chin snapped up. She threw the towel onto the counter, whirled and stalked from the room.

"Hey, come on, it was funny," he called out, laughter in his voice.

She heard him coming after her up the stairs but ignored him and stomped up to the second floor, a haze of smoke still clinging to the ceiling. In the master bathroom she closed the door and braced her hands on the sink. Closing her eyes, she took a deep breath. Dammit, she was on the verge of tears because of some stupid burned meatballs.

It's not the meatballs, you idiot.

No, it wasn't. It was everything all at once.

Taking the plunge and clearing her things from her place in New York State, moving in here with Matt until she found something else, even though she knew he was hoping she'd stay and she didn't really want to go anywhere else. It was not being employed for the first time in her adult life, not having a plan other than giving serious consideration to Alex's offer to join the NSA.

It was feeling like a fraud by bumbling through this relationship with Matt when he deserved way better, someone more experienced in matters of the heart than she was. It was freaking out at the thought of the party tonight and being surrounded by his team, worried they were all wondering what the hell Matt saw in her.

Well, she didn't know, because she wondered that same thing every freaking day.

God, she was acting like a deranged maniac. She had to get hold of herself. Briar forced in several slow, deep breaths.

Once she was back in control she put the mascara

wand back into its tube and confronted her image in the mirror. It was strange to see herself this way, hair and makeup all done up, wearing a cocktail dress that ten minutes ago she'd thought sexy but now just made it seem like she was trying too hard. This polished, sophisticated woman in the mirror wasn't her. Sure, she could pull it off and had multiple times in the past for a job, or for events like the security conference in New Orleans where she'd met Matt. But it was only an illusion.

A soft knock sounded on the other side of the door. "Hey. You okay?"

She sighed, embarrassed by her outburst. "Yeah, fine. You can come in, I promise not to rip your head off."

He pushed the door open and stood there, meeting her eyes in the mirror for a moment before his gaze raked over the length of her body and back up again. "Look at you." The frank male heat in his expression helped ease the worst of the nerves in her stomach.

She shrugged, her muscles strangely stiff. "I wasn't going to your team's New Year's Eve party looking like a homeless person." But this was just a costume, an act. She far preferred wearing jeans or cargo pants and T-shirts that didn't impede her ability to move, to throw a kick or a punch if she needed to. She didn't know how Trinity did it.

Matt entered the bathroom and eased the door shut, coming to stand directly behind her. His big hands curled possessively around her hips, his gaze stuck on the cleavage revealed in the V-neck of her little black dress. She'd chosen her outfit carefully, had even gone shopping earlier for the black lace pushup bra and matching panties and thigh highs she had underneath. All because she'd wanted to see this very same intense, hungry expression on Matt's face when he saw them.

Her unease began to subside as his touch and nearness grounded her. His fingers flexed on her hips as he met her eyes in the mirror. "You're so beautiful." The wealth of pride and appreciation in his voice made her lips curve into a reluctant smile, made all this stupid stress worthwhile.

"Well, I can fake it when I need to."

He released her hips to slide his arms fully around her waist and pulled her into the curve of his body. "It's not fake, it's just another side of you."

She sighed at the feel of him against her back, tall and strong and warm. Dropping her gaze to his hands, she did a double take when she noticed he wasn't wearing his wedding band. Without thinking she grabbed his left hand and lifted it.

"I took it off this morning," he murmured. "After I woke up with you curled naked against me in my bed and knew I wanted to see you there every morning."

She met his gaze in the mirror once more, concerned he'd taken it off because he'd sensed her insecurity. That ring meant a lot to him and she absolutely didn't want him to do it because she was acting stupid. "Why?"

"Because it's time. In a few hours it'll be a brand new year and I want to start it fresh with you, without the past weighing us down. I know she'd want me to let her go."

Briar softened. From all the wonderful things he'd told her, she really wished she'd had the privilege of meeting Lisa.

She turned in his arms, putting her hands on his wide shoulders. His expression was serious, his eyes full of a warmth she could feel inside. "I wouldn't have asked that of you." But she was so damn relieved he'd felt ready to take it off on his own.

"I know, and that's half the reason I wanted to do it." Lifting his hand, he stroked it over the back of her hair she'd carefully styled with a straightening iron.

"What's the other half?"

He gave an almost imperceptible shake of his head,

his stare unwavering. "Because I love you."

Her breath hitched and her fingers tightened on his shoulders as her eyes began to sting. She'd known it deep inside, felt it even though he'd never said the words before. Instead he'd shown her by the way he treated her, the way he'd looked at her and touched her. She got the impression he'd been waiting to tell her because he hadn't wanted to scare her.

She pressed her lips together, blinked as emotion swamped her. All those songs and poems about how much love could hurt? They were true. She'd never known feeling so much for another person could twist her heart until it ached. "Dammit, you're gonna ruin my eye makeup."

He laughed softly and leaned his forehead against hers. "So don't cry."

"I'm not." God, she'd made an absolute idiot of herself in the past few minutes. Briar closed her eyes and took a deep breath, digging her fingers into his shoulders. He was so strong, so solid and dependable she could never express how glad she was to have him in her life, at her side. She'd asked him to show her the ropes and he had, every day they'd been together.

Now she owed him the words to express what was in her heart.

Easing away slightly, she slid her palms up to cradle his face and looked him dead in the eye. "I love you back. More than I ever knew I could love anyone." There. The delivery was clumsy and it still didn't tell him the depth of her feelings for him, but it would have to do.

A slow, hot smile spread across his face, that little dimple appearing in his lean cheek, now sporting a sexy five-o'clock shadow. "Then that makes me the luckiest guy in the world."

Briar thought he was crazy for thinking such a ridiculous thing, but she wasn't going to argue. "Sorry for the freak out earlier. I haven't been handling the stress very well, I guess. I just wanted tonight to be perfect and make a good impression on everyone." The people coming to the party were important to Matt; they were his extended family. She didn't want to let him down.

"Tonight's already perfect, so don't stress about the party. We'll go for an hour or two and if you're still uncomfortable, give me the signal after we've stayed long enough to be polite and we'll leave." They'd decided on a slow wink, which she had every intention of using at some point. She would go and be social for a while, but parties and forced small talk were never going to be things she was comfortable with. Thankfully, he seemed to understand and respected that.

"And make a good impression? Seriously? After everything that's gone down my guys are already half in love with you, especially since you can hold your own with the best of them on the range. When I walk in there with you looking like this on top of all that? They're all gonna be insanely jealous. Well, all the single guys, anyway. And to be honest I'd rather be back here early anyway, so we'll be alone when I kiss you at midnight." He lowered his head to murmur against her ear, sending a shiver through her. "In case I get carried away."

"Hmmm, or in case I do," she whispered back, rubbing against him slightly, loving the way his gaze heated. His hands locked on her ass, pulling her tighter to his growing erection. She bit her lip, looked up at him through her lashes. "I bought you a present today. I'm wearing it underneath this."

He eyed the dress with renewed interest. "What is it?" he murmured, sounding intrigued.

He leaned to the side as he hooked his fingers beneath the hem of the dress, halfway up her thighs. His fingertips stroked gently over the silky fabric of the stockings, smiling at the little hum of pleasure she made.

He slowly eased the dress upward, exposing the lace tops of the thigh highs and black thong panties. A low growl rumbled up from his chest as he jerked the dress up to expose the curve of her ass, his hands cupping her flesh, squeezing in that possessive way she loved.

Heat ignited low in her belly just as it always did when he touched her, need for him making her heart pound. Before she could stop him he straightened and peeled the dress up over her head and dropped it onto the counter behind her, leaving her in just her underwear. His eyes were absolutely molten as he stared at the curves of her breasts, pushed up by the bra, down her abs to the tiny scrap of black lace covering her mound.

"And now we're gonna be late," he muttered, his voice heavy with feigned regret as he dropped to his knees and buried his face in her cleavage.

Tingling all over, Briar smiled and cupped the back of his head with one hand. She leaned back against the counter, letting out a soft moan at the feel of his lips and tongue sliding across her exposed cleavage. Her nipples tightened even more against the lace cups, an insistent throb pulsing between her thighs.

The man knew every one of her hot buttons and used that knowledge to his advantage every chance he got. He was as lethal with his hands and mouth as he was with a rifle, all things she found unbearably sexy.

And for some reason she would be eternally thankful for, as unbelievable as it seemed, he was all hers.

Before she completely lost the ability to think, let alone talk, she slipped a hand into his hair and tipped his head back enough to look into his face. "What about the meatballs?"

"We'll scatter their ashes in the morning," he answered, and pulled her down into a searing kiss.

—The End—

Complete Booklist

Erotic Romance (writing as *Callie Croix*)

Deacon's Touch
Dillon's Claim
No Holds Barred
Touch Me
Let Me In
Covert Seduction

Acknowledgements

A big thank you to the team who helped me get this book ready for publication! Katie, Kim, Joan, couldn't do this without you.

To my hubby and kids, thank you for being patient when I'm working under deadline. Love you all to infinity.

About the Author

NY Times and USA Today Bestselling author Kaylea Cross writes edge-of-your-seat military romantic suspense. Her work has won many awards and has been nominated for both the Daphne du Maurier and the National Readers' Choice Awards. A former Registered Massage Therapist, Kaylea is also an avid gardener, artist, Civil War buff, Special Ops aficionado, belly dance enthusiast and former nationally-carded softball pitcher. She lives in Vancouver, BC with her husband and family.

You can visit Kaylea at **www.kayleacross.com.** If you would like to be notified of future releases, please join her newsletter. **http://kayleacross.com/v2/contact/**

37418148R00197

Made in the USA
Lexington, KY
25 April 2019